JONATHAN SHELTON.

NO WORD OF A LIE: AN AUTOBIOGRAPHY

jonathantortoise.com

ISBN 9798502697965

First printed edition: 2022.

Does anybody even read this page anyway?
On the off chance, here are the credits.
Written by: Jonathan Shelton & Ryan Lawson
Based on an idea by: Ryan Lawson & Steve Morgan
Cover design and illustration: Kevin Russell
Animal trainer: Terry Nutkins

Printed in Great Britain.

"Age appears to be best in four things; old wood best to burn, old wine to drink, old friends to trust, and old authors to read."
- Francis Bacon.

"It's not easy being green."
-Kermit The Frog.

It is over a lettuce lunch with a familiar acquaintance that the idea of jotting down a few of the fascinating tales I'd shared with him is first mooted.

"A hundred and eighty-five years on earth is a long time," my associate says to me as the waiter pours the water. "More than most of us get anyway, a lot more. Perhaps Jonathan, it would be a timely idea to compile these riveting anecdotes into some sort of collection before you pop your...before they are lost forever".

"But surely nobody is interested in what a silly old tortoise like me has to say?" I reply quite modestly, for I am indeed a very humble creature.

"Yes, you're probably right,"

The salubrious restaurant we sit in is on London's South Bank. All exposed a la mode brickwork and goldfish bowl windows with bad Wi-Fi, high ceilings and higher prices. I wait patiently for the waiter to leave before speaking again.

"So you mean an autobiography?"

"Maybe." he replies, scanning the wine list for the most expensive bottle.

"A grand sweep of names and places perhaps?"

"Perhaps."

"Or do you suggest more of a memoir focused on a particular time and place?"

He shrugs, so I decide to push him for more clarity. "So essentially a document of living history that could inform and enlighten future generations, yes?"

"Jeez, I don't know. I'm not a literary guy," he snaps. "I'm just trying to make conversation whilst I look at the menu."

Nonetheless, the idea had been firmly planted, and as you grow to know me better, you'll discover that despite my slowness I'm all about spontaneity.

"Ok, I'll do it."

"Well I'm glad you're in the mood to share," he replies with a sneer as he looks at me over his dark glasses. "And who knows? Perhaps a few of your stories might even be true."

His snarky remark bounces off my shell. Over the years I've learnt to live with this kind of ignorance and scepticism. After all, I have seen everything from the invention of flight and the abolition of slavery, to the grisly assassination of Martin Luther King Jr. But try telling that to the kids of today and they barely believe you.

And by the way – when I say kids? I mean anyone under the age of 130.

The waiter approaches our table and I ask him to give us another five minutes. I've lost all interest in the menu now. Instead, the flame of nostalgia replaces the hunger in my reptilian belly as I begin to explore the annals of my long memory, hoping to stumble upon friends and foes of the last one hundred and eighty-five years as I peel back time for a tentative peek. It's been a long journey and it's one I'm now ready to share, so I invite you to take my claw and meander with me through the history of the last few centuries.

What you are about to hear is no word of a lie.

"So what do you fancy for starters?" my companion asks, as he peruses the menu and ignores the buzzing of a nearby fly that has been pestering fellow diners ever since we'd arrived.

I gaze out of the window at the pensive skies above with a faraway expression upon my worn face. It looks like rain.

"I know exactly where to start." I say, as I take a sip of overpriced water before I look to the heavens once more in painful reminiscence of a distant memory plucked fresh from the far-flung past.

CHAPTER ONE

Laika was a bitch. And by that I mean of course, she was a lady dog. But as I watched her sitting smugly in the cockpit of Sputnik II, all dressed up in her space clothes with her tail wagging that morning of November 3rd 1957 I couldn't help feeling a sense of betrayal, deeper even than space. There is a common misconception amongst nature lovers that tortoises are slow and lazy creatures, but you'd be wrong. We just prefer to spend the majority of our time enjoying the sunshine, topping up our tans, and unwinding in energy saving mode. Nevertheless, with the benefit of wisdom I should have been a lot quicker off the mark in spotting the double-crossing methods of certain canines.

I've always been an inquisitive creature by nature. My common curiosity governed by wild instinct, animal desires, and an herbivorous appetite for adventure. Space was no exception. Even as a hatchling barely out of the egg, I'd harboured a bottomless fascination with the outer limits that hover teasingly above our inconsequential heads at night. Whilst the rest of the planet plumped up its pillows and took out its teeth before bedtime, you would find me hiding from the world and perched high up on a rock, stargazing endlessly into the beguiling blackness above. Tortoises, by design, are diurnal creatures (active during the day) but it was when the stars awoke and blinked into life that my senses were truly stirred. My eyes would be glued continually to the halcyon skies that shimmered with ethereal promise of far-flung places, and during those twilight hours in the very dead of night I've never felt more alive as I was sucked into space.

In 1835, I was your typical adolescent growing up on an atoll of tedious sameness, a place where nothing much happened and even the trees glanced at their watches in silent abandon. You could say that time crawled at tortoise speed on the Galapagos archipelago I called home, and sitting many miles off of the Ecuadorian coast there were no such minutiae as television, mobile network coverage, or even cheap cider to fill the daily humdrum. Instead, Ursa Major, with its stellar cast of stars in the celestial sphere became both my escape and primetime binge-watch after the watershed. That vast, unchartered darkness with its own juicy secrets to tell has always held boundless possibilities for me, and I'd trace the stars in the sky each night with the familiarity of an old friend.

"What do you think is up there?" I'd asked my cousin Wincey one evening long ago, as we'd rested our plump plastron bellies on the still warm rocks, kicked back, and gazed up in wonderment at the blanket of sparkles above.

"Bats?" she replied.

"No. I mean high up there, amongst the stars."

"Dunno," she'd shrugged. "Alien bats?"

I shook my head, unconvinced. "There must be more than extra-terrestrial pipistrelles flying around up there, surely?"

"Well if you must know, my Mum says that's where we all go to once we fall of our perches and croak it."

"Really?" I'd replied, keeping my focus firmly fixed upon the dead sea of space. "Like a huge graveyard in the sky, you mean?"

Her eyes scanned the firmament once more. "Yeah… kinda."

I pulled a typically teenaged face. "That's totally gross!"

"See that bright star over there?" Wincey had whispered, pointing to a far off twinkle in the clear night with her little claw. "That's Grandpa Erwin, way up there."

"Flapdoodle!" I'd teased. "Have you been licking cane toads again? Or nibbled too much fermented fruit perhaps?"

"No. I'm telling you Jonathan. The twinkly star, that's Gramps,"

"Well if it is, then he's lost weight since last I saw him," I'd joked in my usual gut-busting manner, and soon our emphatic laughter was echoing off the un-amused rocks and threatened to wake the whole island. Of course, I didn't have the heart to tell her it was in fact the *'Polaris Star'* she'd pointed out to me that evening as we sat together passing the time, but I did find it noticeably naive that she'd mistook our late grandfather for a fiery ball of hydrogen and helium gas that dangled in the black-blue sky.

Deceased relatives floating in space didn't particularly interest me then, and I don't suppose they do now. Instead, I was more infatuated with the potential that lay in that ocean of emptiness upstairs, and to borrow an old analogy from a once famous father of rocketry: *The Earth is a cradle for humanity, but mankind cannot stay in the cradle forever.* I guess I was hoping this astrological metaphor didn't apply exclusively to humans, because I was convinced a black heaven of infinite constellations and a solar system chocked full of far-away planets, awaited me. It had always been a childhood dream of mine to visit them one day, to reach those distant stars and explore unearthly worlds wearing my space boots, bubble helmet, and a grin spread wider than a galaxy. I might have made it up there too, were it not for a scruffy stray mutt plucked from the hungry streets of Moscow one dreary afternoon.

Fast-forwards to 1957, and equipped with debonair looks and a well-honed Bolshevik accent picked up in spy school, I'd relocated to Moscow at a time when relations between east and west were frosty if not sub-zero. It was the height of the Cold War and already an iron curtain had been drawn across the continent to deter nosey neighbours and western spy-rings, but so far I'd slipped unnoticed behind this steely drape of secrecy. I'd heard whispers on the soviet grapevine that the imperialists were conspiring to launch a clandestine mission to send the first animal into orbit before their American counterparts. With my plucky persona and blatant love of space, of course I'd wanted in.

Amongst the crumbling slums of a capital still living in the shadows of war, high-ranking members of the Soviet Space Programme were in town and on the lookout for fresh candidates. Loitering around a snow-capped Kremlin that morning, it wasn't long before I was talent spotted (KGB style) and bundled into an unmarked van, my feet and beak bound with heavy duct tape, as I was earmarked as a potential top seed in a far-reaching mission they'd been plotting for years. My intrepid spirit and hard-knock traits had made me the perfect applicant to become the first ever creature to orbit the earth, but I had competition.

Laika had also been clutched from the streets en route that day too, and because she'd fought for scraps and slept in shop doorways most of her life, they thought she also displayed qualities a cosmonaut would require for the tough realities of space. Granted, she didn't have the life experiences that I'd amassed due to my vintage, but life as a stray can be challenging at best, and so it was, we would both be put through our paces at boot camp together as the space race between reptile and canine began.

Much to her credit, Laika was tougher than her eleven-pound frame would suggest, but that counts for very little when you're being spun around in pressurized hyperbaric chambers at 450 GHz per second and you have to hold in your wee for a really, *really* long time. It's true that she excelled far beyond me in the physical agility tests and there is no doubt I was left to dine on her dust as I crawled the hateful assault courses that snaked sinuously through bear filled forests, but when it came to mental aptitude and alertness she was left chasing her tail. Physical prowess counts for little without the brains to back it up and besides, what use is jumping through tyres and picking up sticks when you're off to space in an eight by six foot metal pinecone?

After weeks of flight simulators, intensive training and acclimatization in pretend micro-gravity (far less fun than it sounds) we both knew that when the day finally came, there would only be room for one successful passenger on this historic mission into space. My focus was set like a flint, my eyes on the prize. As a naturally competitive reptilian I've never lacked the required confidence for a challenge, but although I had one olive-hued buttock nestled in the hot seat heading to beyond, I definitely underestimated her artfulness and cunning. Little did I know this clamber to the stars also included canines hell-bent on fame, fortune, and getting their furry face plastered across every magazine cover from Red Square to Gorky Park. Of course, at the time nobody even knew for sure whether anything could survive up in space long enough for the radiation not to soften their brains in zero gravity, but we did know that whoever made it up there first was sure to be lauded a hero upon their return. The smart money was on the guy in green (that's me) just so long as I didn't take my eye off the ball and could retain a full bladder.

On the eve of the scheduled mission, myself, Laika and two other lucky finalists were uncivilly shaken from our beds in the early hours and transported under cover of darkness across the land border to the Baikonor Cosmodrome in Kazhakastan. Once there and with eyes still gooey from sleep, we were shepherded towards a large draughty hangar (essentially a giant fridge) on the fringes of the airfield and summoned before a panel of fur clad adjudicators, each wearing blank expressions on their humourless faces and unsightly ushanka-hats upon their heads. Lined up before them for billet inspection, stood firm to attention in our matching CCCP nightgowns and carpet slippers, we ultimately faced the sausage machine of fame.

"Well, I guess this is it?" I'd said, perhaps a dash over confidently to my fellow cosmonauts who shivered in the cold regardless of their furry coats. "May the best animal win!"

"Woof, woof!" Laika had barked restlessly, but despite my speaking many languages I don't speak dog, so I've no idea what she was

trying to communicate. Besides, I needed to focus my full attention on the race for the rocket in that moment, because beneath those lambent studio lights with our nerves stretched tighter than Orion's belt, we were about to be told which one of us lucky souls had made it through to the final and had bagged the coveted seat into orbit.

The head judge for the mission, a man called Vladimir Yazdovsky, had risen from his swivel chair with an air of self-importance, stale alcohol and Polo mints, his eager fingers burrowing through well-thumbed notes before he stopped with a pregnant pause that felt weeks overdue. An imposing and serious looking biped, his eyes seemed permanently bruised, crimson capillaries crawled up the sides of his nose like fairy-tale vines and a severe buzz cut framed his cube shaped face as he stroked his chin in deliberation. This despotic man was the kingmaker of the entire programme, the fixer of dreams if you will, and as he paced back and forth in military boots that clicked like castanets on the concourse, he sized us up and down with an owlish eye before finally, his commanding gaze fell upon me.

"Cosmonaut Shelton, isn't it?"

"Yes sir!" I barked (although I'm not a dog), as I saluted with a primordial claw and looked towards the Russian flag with what I hoped was rabid patriotism in my eyes. I'm ashamed to say any loyalties to the west had been usurped by my eagerness for the outer reaches and the fame it would elicit.

"So you think you have what it takes for space, do you boy?" he asked with interrogating eyes.

"Sir, yes sir!"

"And you know your elbow from Uranus?" He began to laugh a lot more than was necessary in appreciation of his own wit, and of course I joined in so as to flatter him, but he was certainly no Mike Yarwood.

"Sir, yes sir!"

"Very well then," he said, as he looked me up and down, then up again. " If a potato can become a vodka, then I guess it's within the realms of possibility that a tortoise has a chance of becoming the first creature to conquer space, wouldn't you agree?"

"Sir, yes sir!" I repeated, rather predictably.

"And you can hold your wee-wee in for a really, *really,* long time?"

"Sir, yes sir!"

"Well, I'm afraid I don't like what I've seen," Yazdovsky had spat with military ugliness, only inches from my green beak. The pungent fumes of bathtub vodka had stung my eyes, making my ancient knees buckle as I squinted up at the vast gulf that now lay between myself, and the toenail moon that hung appealingly in the sky. Failure has never been a facet woven in to the fabric of my long-winded life so although I wasn't immune to feelings of incompetence I was disappointed that the weeks spent training in the neutral buoyancy lab, the toilet abstinence, and the late nights of unbroken study in Siberian temperatures had been in vain. My thwarted space hopes now hung by an anorexic safety rope tethered to the mother ship of ambition, and as the realisation sunk in and I dragged a claw down my handsome green face in grief, my lower beak began to tremble on the precipice of tears. I was crestfallen, or as the Russians might indeed say: удрученный.

"No, I don't like it at all…I Love it!" he concluded, a huge smile playing across his oblong face. "Congratulations. You are to become the first creature to orbit earth."

It was a cruel rouse, often adopted by abysmal Saturday night talent show judges for dramatic effect, but I soon forgave him if it meant I was booked onto the next available rocket into space. In that euphoric moment I half expected golden ticker tape to rain down on me from above, my fellow finalist congratulating me with giddy smiles, mini-fist bumps and warm hugs, but instead there was only a light smattering of applause and paperwork to fill in as they measured me up for my suit. The decision had been unanimous however, and the next day I was to be placed inside the chamber of the satellite Sputnik II as it launched off into space to make history.

Laika was to serve as my reserve whilst the other two (Mushka and Albina), were to remain on the ground as control dogs to test instrumentation. I'm convinced those two mutts had known in their canine hearts they were always destined to be also-rans, but I could see Laika had the right royal hump on. That aside, I happily shook her paw as she held it out in gracious defeat though I must say, I was less impressed when she began sniffing around my back-end with too much over familiarity. Regardless of this intrusion upon my tailpiece, after a lifetime of wishing and wanting for outer space, the enormity of what I'd achieved hit me like a bucket of ice water. I was going up there. I was really going where no animal had been before.

That evening, the four of us had gathered around the dinner table for supper in our quarters, the ladies enjoying a meal of marrowbone and biscuits whilst I slurped a boil-in-the-bag, beetroot borsch that I spat out in disgust. The Russian cuisine has never been to my taste and as you might expect, vegetarian options were as rare as hen's teeth in a place famed for such delicacies as eyeball soup, jellied meats and herrings under a fur coat (please don't ask). In all honesty, I think a serving of hen's teeth would have been more appetising than the slop that stared back apologetically from my plate that evening. The fare really was unspeakable, so I won't speak about it. Only to say that even the dogs wouldn't touch it and I was very much looking forward to vacuum-packed space food for the next few months, let me assure you.

Laika, upon seeing my disappointment at the bubble-gum pink meal, disappeared and minutes later returned with the most delectable and verdant looking Batavia lettuce clamped between her jaws. My shrunken stomach sighed with relief (and reprise) as she dropped the leaf vegetable into my lap with a friendly wag of her tail and instantly I felt moved by her canine kindness. This little pick-me-up gesture from my space school chum was just the thing I needed, and made me realise the importance of good friends and a well-balanced diet. I gave her belly-fur an enthusiastic rub before getting to work on the yummy green with relish. It was the first decent thing I'd had to eat in months.

"This is deeeeeelicious," I'd lamented through muffled mouthfuls as I attempted to lighten the mood and make them giggle, but I've often found that much like Americans, dogs don't get my avant-garde sense of humour. But that's not to say I didn't enjoy their company. Despite the lack of banter and table manners that dogs possess, what with their constant begging for titbits and chewing the furniture, it was still a splendid evening spent with fellow noble cosmonauts as we celebrated my last supper on earth. Even Laika seemed to have gotten over her initial disappointment as she whined at all my jokes (in a good way) and lapped up some smuggled-in vodka, though sensibly I decided not to partake before the momentous day.

"I'm doing this for my family." I'd said to them after pudding, being careful not to let the accent slip. "Before I left the Galapagos under a cloud in 1835, I'd promised my mum I'd go far in life and make her proud. You don't get much further than space, right?"

Laika had regarded me with her slanted whiskey brown eyes full of understanding and I'm sure in that poignant moment she knew just how significant this trip was to me. Yes, she knew all too well, I'm convinced of that to this day. Once Mushka and Albina had gone to walk off supper and squat in the grass as lady dogs do, Laika padded over on little paws and placed her fleecy head in my lap. "I'm sorry there isn't enough room for two up their girl," I'd whispered affectionately, giving her hairy ears a playful stroke as we looked out together at the starry night. "Maybe one day you'll see the splendour of it, just like me."

Laika had nuzzled at my shell with her wet nose as she let out a sentimental whine at my departure and in retrospect all I can say is she was a terrific actress. When the others returned, I bid the pack goodnight with a smugness I regret, retired to my bunk, and dreamt of galaxies far, far away.

At 4am I awoke to thunderous, excruciating stomach cramps and rushed myself to the bathroom where the bottom abruptly fell out of my world and the world fell out of my bottom…straight into the waiting toilet bowl. As I sat welded onto the pot with my backend spitting liquid fire, I peeked out of the small window at the stars that shone seductively in the night sky and metaphorically at least, it was a window that was slowly closing. I knew I wasn't going to be visiting them any time soon and as another hot jet of vivid green horribleness fell out of me with a sickly splash, I began to weep. I usually have the constitution of a warthog and I'm sorry to chronicle this episode in such animated detail, but the conniving, malicious mutt had spiked me. Of that I was sure.

At 5am I was still there, my poor tail twitching nervously as my bowels violently evacuated more liquiform lettuce that burned hotter than Galapagos lava. I dared not move. It was truly horrendous and just when I believed there couldn't possibly be anything left inside of my hollow insides, more nastiness exited my splayed rear-end like bullets from a Nerf gun on automatic. I was dreading what Yazdovsky was going to say…and the wipe.

At 7am Moscow time, I finally summoned the effort to get off the toilet and crawled shakily out of my room, already knowing it was too late. Laika was in the cockpit by now, getting wired up into her harness whilst a small hose connected to a heater kept her warm against the cold and an army of ground staff punched buttons and flicked switches at the command of Yazdovsky. He had squeezed himself into full military uniform now, his chest decorated with a sea of medals that twinkled like stars in the morning light, serving only to remind me further of my failings. He looked at me with a contempt he barely bothered to conceal and a quick glance at the clock told me it was only 120 seconds to lift off. Unless disaster struck in the next two minutes I was going nowhere, even if my tummy had allowed it.

"Prepare the engines for take off," ordered Yazdovsky, wiping sweat from his meaty palms as he took a hefty snifter from the canteen flask of potato vodka he held with trembling fingers. I imagine the nerves were getting to him after all the years of meticulous planning and Soviet millions spent, and now, as anticipation filled the morning air and the final safety checks were completed, he was mere seconds away from his greatest achievement.

Before the hatch was closed on Sputnik II, a few of the technicians kissed Laika on the nose as if to say goodbye, and it was at that point, as the doors closed shut on the Russian street dog and tears welled in their eyes, that I realised something was wrong. They had no intention of bringing Laika back down, at least not alive. This was a one-way ticket. A suicide-mission. She was to make the ultimate sacrifice.

"Laika, wait!" I'd shouted as I started towards her, but Yazdovsky held me back with an unshakeable grip just as the mammoth engines of the rocket spluttered into life and the countdown clock continued to shed its seconds. "You need to stop this!" I hollered to the operator at the control desk, but he just looked at me hopelessly and I knew by then it was already too late. "Please! You need to stop!"

Mushka and Albina must have sensed the foreboding too, both letting out a sad howl in unison, swiftly drowned out by the deafening thrusts of Sputnik II (or Muttnik II as the press later dubbed it) whilst the engines fired up fully for lift-off. As we all stood back from the ferocious heat and watched the tin rocket take off on its momentous journey, I realised then, quite selfishly, what a lucky escape I'd had. Before the little space bucket became just another speck in the early morning sky, I felt anguish deep within and quickly ran for the toilet once more.

Laika did make it into orbit. As we gathered around the communications deck that gelid afternoon, we kept our paws and claws crossed and prayed for good news. She survived up in that hostile atmosphere for around six hours (almost two days in dog years, I suppose) until, on her fourth time travelling around the earth, no further life signals were recorded on-board. It turned out the cooling systems had failed and I guess the temperature had become too much for the girl as she finally succumbed from overheating.

I spent the rest of that evening perched on the toilet lid contemplating my missed opportunity, but when I weighed up the alternative, meh, it was clear who came out on top. You won't be surprised to learn I was discharged from the space academy, the following morning by Yazdovsky. Apparently, highly trained cosmonauts aren't allowed to be floored by weapons-grade food poisoning or to be outwitted by dogs. So, with bags packed and my aspirations of space travel now swallowed up by an infinite black hole, I decided it best to head back to London with my shell still intact and my tail firmly between my legs. At least the climate was more preferable and I could finally get something decent to eat at Magic China, just off of the Holborn High Road.

 Today, all these years later when I look up at the great beyond through much wiser eyes, I'm not entirely convinced it's our place to be up there anyway. Millionaire entrepreneurs promoting space tourism and oligarch money seeking out new planets all seem marginally perilous nowadays. For me, space has never lost its sparkle but just suppose for a second we did find extra-terrestrial life out there? Or these nonhuman visitors found us first? How do we explain to them the thousands of movies, books and video games we've already created all based around obliterating their race into teensy pieces? Lettuce leaves for thought is all I'm saying, but I imagine even the very slipperiest of politicians (so most of them) couldn't talk their way out of that predicament, especially with a laser gun aimed at their most delicate parts.

You could say Laika jumped the queue that day, but on my part there are no hard feelings, even considering her poor showing of old school subterfuge. She returned to the earth's atmosphere five months after she'd left and her metal coffin had circled our orbit 2,500 times. Sputnik II broke up on impact and her remains were never recovered, but she did get the fame and recognition she craved with column inches in all the world's media, her furry face placed on stamps, and a bronze statue was even erected in honour of her achievement in Star City. Not gold, but bronze is pretty impressive nonetheless. Today, she's one of the most famous canines in the world and so far as I'm concerned, although her life was cut brutally short, her star will forever burn bright. I hope this sentiment of forgiveness can set the tone for much of what shall follow in these pages you hold, but still, nobody likes a pusher-inner. Although I don't want to demean her efforts, there is something to be said about waiting your turn.

CHAPTER TWO

Some events that happen to us as we ride along life's rocky road can change our outlook forever, and what you are about to encounter is perhaps one of the biggest pot-holes in mine. It's high time I made peace with my own fragile conscience, but that being said, even in my dotage I still blame myself for what happened one disastrous day in 1835. I've often heard it bandied around by certain morons that time is a great healer, but take it from someone as ancient and bone-tired as me, it's unquestionably not. Even after years spent roaming this repetitious earth I still feel ruined with guilt as the fires were lit, the sails were unfurled, and the boat slipped anchor that cloudless afternoon long ago. It turned out to be the worst day of my life and believe me I've had some absolute stinkers over the past few centuries.

It was the first day of the warm season and that morning had began much like any other for the Shelton family as we awoke from our interminable gluey slumber to a dewy newness, our bellies nagging with hunger after a long winter of self-enforced hibernation. I'd sat at the breakfast table beneath the dappled shade of a large Scalesia tree, elbowing for position with my much larger cousins as I scrimmaged for food and the sun brought its usual glow to breakfast festivities. I was indulging in my second helping of prickled pear cactus when all at once the finches, loitering like panhandlers in hope of crumbs, had scattered in a chorus of feathers and flutters as an unfriendly shadow fell across the cheery tablecloth. Though far from commonplace, this is how the worst days of your life tend to begin in my experience.

"What on earth is that?" my dad had squinted nervously, popping another clump of saltbush into his herbivorous beak as he leaned over the shaded table and fumbled unsuccessfully for his glasses. Rearing up on trunk-like legs and shielding his eyes against the Galapagos sunshine, he looked out to sea with concern. "Marilyn, where's my readers? I can't make it out."

The portentous shadow that crawled across black sands and bare rock seemed to be growing larger now, my table manners quickly forgotten as I crammed more food into my covetous beak. At that point my main concern was that a hungry marine iguana might have caught scent of breakfast on the southeast trade winds and was prepared to fight for his quarry. In reality, that would become the least of my worries.

"It's a tidal wave, innit?" remarked my middle cousin Merle, whose first port of call was always to expect unconditional disaster. "Or a rogue wave though even, innit bruh?" he'd added, with his strange turn of phrase that could become rather grating and annoying in any dose. Standing on tippy-claws he followed my fathers gaze out across the blue expanse with a confident shake of his head. "Yep, thought so bruh. Definitely a sea monsta with huge buzzin' teeth innit, come to gobble up the whole fam, innit."

"Well, that's a comfort to know," I'd acknowledged, not quite understanding what he meant, but accelerating my eating just in case he was right. And in a roundabout way, I guess he was. Turns out it was definitely some kind of monster.

"It looks more like a shark to me," my cousin Wincey had squealed in delight, "I love sharks."

As previous experience had taught me, Wincey wasn't the sharpest tortoise in the reptile house, but soon my entire family (with the exception of my fat and lazy uncle Brian) were bouncing up and down on the black volcanic sands like red coats at a holiday camp, just on the off-chance a hungry predator with massive teeth hadn't already been aware of their presence. We didn't get many visitors on our little island you understand.

"Are you sure it's a shark Wincey?" asked my cousin Fig, who'd stopped his hopping around and was now scratching his head in doubt. He was three years my senior, something he'd remind me of on a daily basis, but he did have a persuasive point. "I can't see many teeth in its face, or any face in fact?"

"Oh, right, yes," blushed Wince, her scales hot with embarrassment. "Well I've never actually seen a shark, like up close…you know…but it might be one?" The others rolled their disappointed eyes, but to be impartial she was only trying to be helpful and this was a time way before Shark Week on Discovery, or indeed any television had been invented. However, that still meant we had no idea if it really was a huge carnivorous fish or some other unfeeling predator heading our way to join (or eat) us for breakfast.

"Well, whatever it might be, it's enormous," agreed Marilyn (aka: Mum), as she turned her attention back to the cocktail blue ocean with a glowing grin and dimples that shone as deep as the water beside which we lived. "Isn't this exciting, Jonathan?" she cooed, instinctively wiping cactus juice from my juvenile chin with a maternal claw.

"Totally," I lied.

Unlike the rest of my creep, I wasn't so giddy about the prospect of an apex predator within our midst. As creatures that inhabited an island that straddled the equator and was surrounded by water, we'd always been brought up to fear sharks (just as humans are wary of these killing machines, that stand second only to wasps on their terror chart) but to me, this didn't look like any shark I'd seen before. This looked like much bigger trouble and it was heading our way.

"I think perhaps we should hide," my father had decided, his skittish eyes now searching for the quickest escape route as a fierce and sulphurous smell escaped him. It wouldn't be unfair to assume that he could be a pathetic and timorous imbecile at times. Most times actually. But then I guess you can't choose family now, can you?

"It's getting closer," hollered cousin Josh, who'd taken up watch on a nearby rock and with neck at full stretch, provided a running commentary of unfolding events. The wind had already picked up without warning, shaking the graceful branches of the trees above and I began to develop a queasy sensation in my innards. It's an unsettling symptom I've experienced many times since, but one I haven't ever wholly gotten used to. I call it raw fear.

"Well, I don't care what it is," grumbled fat uncle Brian, unconcerned as he inhaled breakfast from behind the fluttering of his morning paper. "It's just ruined the most important meal of the day."

"Seriously Brian?" sniped my much put upon Aunt Wilhelmina, not unreasonably. "Can't you think of anything other than feeding your face with food?"

"Meh," he'd gestured with a dismissive claw, returning to the task of filling his considerable belly despite potential danger. If my overweight uncle had cared to look up at that precise moment he would have noted the cursory glint of menace in my auntie's eyes as she prepared to release her salvo, but he didn't. Instead, he took a sneaky scratch of his nether regions as she launched a cactus husk at his head. Then another. Third time she struck lucky and he wisely put down the paper to join the rest of us, all now congregated on the shore and trying to work out the best way to approach whatever was approaching us at bruising speed on the Humboldt Current.

On closer inspection, my dad (whose eyesight at a 133 year old was never the best) thought perhaps it was an off-course sea cow or manatee, but as the speck grew closer and the salt rusted chime-bell rang out ominously across the whisper still water, I knew exactly what it was.

"Dad. It's a boat."

The blood drained from his cowardly face as his eyes locked onto the peculiar vessel, it's mammoth white sails now visible on the horizon. The murmur of unfamiliar voices carried across the water and this was his prompt to visit the toilet, whilst mum, brimming with nervous energy, went about clearing the plates from the table and brushing the sand from the chairs in preparation of these eleventh hour guests. She was a creature obsessed with tidiness my mother, and if we were about to be invaded by a tribe of pillaging troglodytes, then god forbid things weren't spick and span upon their arrival. I think she'd rather have died than have someone accuse her of being untidy, a scenario that was now looking highly likely. As we peered out towards shore, an epic sense of despair began to fill my thoughts and I noticed for the first time that the boat had already reached the shallows. Screwing up my eyes, I could faintly make out the name written upon its painted hull.

"What does it say Jonathan?" asked my aunty with her usual bluntness, busily knitting another woolly patterned tail warmer with a nervous hum.

"HMS Beagle." I'd squeaked.

The clickety-click of the needles accelerated as if somehow, deep in her essential nature she sensed her time was growing short. In contrast, my uncle Brian merely shrugged his shoulders and rubbed his still stinging head in circles as if trying to polish away the pain. "Ok, so we know it's a boat with a weird name," he chimed in. "Can we get back to finishing breakfast now?"

"It's a proper lame name for a boat though bruh, innit," chirped up cousin Merle, and it's fair to assume I agreed. But as much as I would have loved to stand around chatting street slang all morning, I had more pressing matters tugging at my conscience right then. Like, why were they here? Why hadn't they rung ahead? And more importantly, what on earth might they want?

"Do you think they'll be any girls on board?" asked my cousin Elias hopefully, checking out his reflection in a nearby rock pool.

"Maybe?" I'd shrugged with pretend indifference, but looking back now it was obvious neither of us had taken seriously the peril we faced as we preened our shells and sucked in our tummies, just on the off chance there might soon be females to impress upon.

With dad off hiding somewhere in the thicket, the rest of us had slouched cautiously towards shore for a closer look at these odd specimens who now assembled by the waters edge, each of them standing on upright legs with elongated front feet I later discovered to be called arms. As we made our tardy approach across the shingle I noticed that one of this strange cast looked particularly freakish with more nose than was necessary, tangled hair that sat upon a narrow chin, and a pair of forlorn eyes that poked out from beneath thick, unruly eyebrows. I couldn't take my eyes off this ruddy-faced anomaly as it shuffled on balled feet across the sand, and though I'd been brought up better than not to stare, I couldn't help but do just that as it began to speak from the dark hole I could only presume was its mouth.

"Hello. My name is Charles Darwin," announced the peculiar creation with a flourish as he offered up his dainty hand for my uncle Brian to receive. "Is it ok if we take a look around your beautiful island for a few days? We'll be no trouble, I promise."

"You're not on one of those booze cruise holidays are you?" my uncle had asked with growing suspicion as he folded two flabby arms across his toneless paunch. "This isn't one of those party islands with blue drinks, happy hours and nightclub touts."

Mr Darwin shook his head with a compliant smile and it seemed obvious to me right then, that he wasn't really the partying kind. "Of course not," he grinned. "You have my full, undissembled word on that"

"Right…well that's good then," my uncle had mumbled, slowly nodding his head in accordance. I knew all too well he didn't have the foggiest idea what *undissembled* meant.

As we sized up these out-of-towners from the sea, I have to say their manner seemed a little cagey and aloof at first. They looked like a band of misfits and dissenters, all skin and bone, with more than a resemblance of the unwashed about them. I'd grown up on ancient campfire stories of maritime savages who'd travelled from faraway lands on similar wooden frigates, marauders hell-bent on pillage and plunder, and as my mind strayed to darker places I could already feel a kaleidoscope of butterflies begin to flutter inside my stomach, which was odd as I'm strictly vegetarian. Nevertheless, after a few awkward moments spent together without thievery, dustups or bloodshed occurring, my wimpish father emerged from the Bracken Ferns and had feigned 'actor-level' delight at our visitor's unscheduled arrival.

"Helllooooo," he'd announced emphatically in the voice he kept for best, much to Aunt Wilhelmina's disdain. "What an honour, I must say. Please, I insist you use the amenities on our island for as long as is needed."

"That's very kind of you," spoke the creature Darwin.

"No problem," my father had said, as if taking one for the team. "No problem, at all." For a second I thought he was going to go the whole hog and curtsy before them, but he soon thought better of it when he noticed (or perhaps even felt) my Aunties cold, unflinching stare upon him. Instead he shuffled anxiously on the sand as her eyes judged him with such an intensity, I wouldn't have been at all surprised to see them wearing horsehair wigs and black robes. Her gaze shifted momentarily towards a nearby cactus husk, and swiftly my dad went about shaking claws with each of this strange crew fervidly, blatantly using them as artillery cover. Myself, and Mr Darwin exchanged a conspiratorial smirk at my father's temerity and already I was warming to this unusual mammal called man, much to my misgiving.

Later, as we'd gathered with our guests around the Halloween orange glow of the campfire with our faces toasted warm by the flames, Mr Darwin went on to describe how an old naval acquaintance of his (Vice-Governor Nicholas Oliver Lawson) had passed by our home a few years previous and had noted with interest, how the tortoises that inhabited each of our far flung islands looked decidedly different from one another. Apparently some of us had sloped shells, others more protruding neck plates, and a few unfortunates were cursed with teeny tails (I have a substantial tail for the record).

'Big deal,' I'd thought to myself, as I teased the fire with a stick and my belly gurgled its disapproval at having to wait for our guests to be served first. My mother had always brought us up to be individuals and to think on our own four feet. So what if we all seemed different? And how could this guy talk anyway? He was the most unique looking thing I'd ever seen in my life.

Mr Darwin slurped from one of mum's best teacups as he went on to describe how he'd hoped to collect research and samples to support a ledger he was writing called *On The Origin Of Species*, a composition explaining how animals could adapt and evolve depending upon their surroundings and circumstance. The survival of the fittest is what he'd termed it -if my memory serves me proper- and he'd chosen our island specifically because of its rich flora and varied fauna...or so we were led to believe.

"Whilst Man, however well behaved, at best is but a monkey shaved," the naturalist had declared with a peal as he lifted a cup to his hairy lip and drank a toast along with his expedition, all of them drying their socks out on sticks as they passed about a rum bottle with good cheer.

"Well, they'd better bleeding behave," uttered my uncle Brian with a low growl as he lifted his cup with the rest of the party, whom he'd watched with a wary eye and a twitch of his tail.

Carelessly, I'd let Darwin's beguiling nature get the better of me and his endearing idiosyncrasies had snared my infamous curiosity, so with permission from my parents I offered to be his guide during their short stay on shore. The west side of the island could be especially dangerous if you didn't know where you were treading as the rocks still bled with fire and the cormorants could get very narky if taken by surprise. He'd gladly accepted my suggestion with another raise of his (mum's) fancy cup before he'd gulped down the hot tea laced with sailors rum and burped his contentment for all to hear. "I think you and I will be great friends Jonathan," professed a cheery Darwin, heartily slapping his hand on my nodular back as he began swaying back and forth despite the lack of any breeze. "I can't wait for you to show me around the place."

"And I can't wait to show you," I'd babbled, with cringing compliance at the time. I felt honoured to been given such an esteemed task so flowing with enthusiasm, I immediately began drawing up an itinerary in the sand under the jealous green watch of my older cousins. You have to understand, the cyclic days dragged at funeral pace upon our little island and this wanton melodrama was everything I'd been hoping for to break the unvarying monotony of my jerkwater home. However, in retrospect it appears that in my eagerness to please, I'd become something of a fulsome boot-licker. I've since learned you should always be careful what you wish for, especially when naturalists are involved.

"I almost trained to be a doctor like my father, you know," confessed a drunken Darwin to me later that evening as he watched the dying flames flicker with a rum bottle clutched close to his chest, the rest of his merry band having already stumbled to their makeshift hammocks for the night.

"So, why the sudden career change Mr Darwin?" I'd asked, not in the least bit interested in heading bedward after the day's remarkable events.

"I guess I must find you animals far too fascinating," he'd smirked. "Plus the sight of blood makes me squeamish." He'd burst into a fit of giggles at this acknowledgement, but gradually his giddiness subsided as he looked purposefully into the fire that threw dark shadows across a face that sagged with sadness. "Instead I trained to become a man of the cloth, a clergyman for want of a better word, but after some soul searching as I've ventured the globe, I believe I have grown to no longer see Christianity as a divine intervention."

"You mean to say you no longer believe in God?"

"The mystery of the beginning of all things is insoluble by us Jonathan; and I for one must be content to remain an agnostic."

"So that's a no then?" I'd whispered, just in case the man upstairs was listening, but Darwin didn't answer. Instead we sat there for a few moments, comfortable in each other's silence as we watched the flames perform their final dance amongst the embers and the hour grew late. Finally he spoke up once more.

"Do you have a girlfriend Jonathan?"

"What's it to you?"

"Dear, sweet Jonathan. The power to charm the female has sometimes been more important than the power to conquer other males in battle," he paused to shake the last remaining drops from the bottle into his waiting mouth. "When I return to London I intend to find myself a wife. An object to be beloved and played with- better than a dog anyhow."

I was barely the size of a dinner plate and knew nothing about the intricacies of lady humans, but I was certain this wasn't the best compliment to extend to a potential mate. Still, despite the verbiage, I wished him well in his pursuit for romance as I watched his eyes grow heavy like anvils and he drifted off into peaceful slumber, thanks in part, to the drink. I covered him with a blanket and left the fire to tamper out as I continued to observe this curiosity that dribbled and mumbled as it slept. Years later, he would indeed find the love he so desired when he married Emma Wedgewood (his first cousin), which I find surprising given the fact he was the first to emphasise the importance of superior genetics in natural selection.

*

"This is my distant cousin," Darwin had explained to me the next morning as he washed his feet in the rock pools and fished a crimpled illustration of a chimpanzee from his pocket. Despite the hangover, he was unable to contain himself as I stared intently at the hairy creature that looked back at me from the postcard with wistful eyes. "Amazing isn't it?"

"Well he's got your ears." I remarked, quite taken aback by the uncanny resemblance. Humans did indeed look like an ugly version of their simian ancestors, disproving the fact that things always bettered with age as I'd been led to believe. I guess, as a tortoise, you've got to believe that.

"We stopped looking for monsters under our bed when we realized they were inside us," Darwin had said to me rather cryptically as I'd set up the chequered battlefield for a game of chess after breakfast. I wish now that I'd paid more attention to his black-hearted motives, because it appears that tortoises make for ideal snacks on a long and treacherous sea voyage home.

Although hardy walkers, we don't move very fast and can store water in our neck sacks for months at a time. A helpful fact I was unfamiliar with when they'd bundled us aboard the Beagle that very afternoon, together with an odd assortment of barometers, chronometers and the promise of observing our island from a whole new perspective.

"You're going to love the view," Captain Fitzroy had snickered, his lip curling into a smirk as he'd lowered the gangplank with a slippery wink and bulging arms coloured with tattoos. The hollow assurance of cactus husks and cold beer on-board was all the encouragement my father and uncle had needed as they clambered aboard the Beagles creaking decks without a seconds hesitation. Without minds of our own, the rest of the family soon followed suit like a line of obedient cars boarding a ferry, or perhaps cattle being led to the slaughterhouse might be a more appropriate term for what would unfold.

This was to be the final time I ever stepped foot on the powder black sands of my home, or took delight in the sweet soundtrack of its native finches chirping at my ear. Ever since that ghastly day, I've often wondered if perhaps I have too soft a heart for such a hard world, but it seems some two-leggers just make for horrible human beings. I find no joy in this assumption, but you must admit that as a race, you humans are quite aggressive and unsound of mind. With your constant stream of wars, genocide, and reality television shows, it's easy to understand why. We'd foolishly placed our trust into the hands of men and as is often the case, it would be a mistake most of us wouldn't live to regret.

"Anyone hungry?" Captain Fitzroy had leered at us through narrowing eyes as the ship set sail, the fire was lit and the sky grew overcast for the first time in months.

"I could murder a pear cactus panini, if there's one going?" declared an oblivious uncle Brian, his eyes searching the adumbral decks for elusive cold beer.

"And I…could murder a tortoise," tittered Darwin with gallows humour from behind his knotted beard, as right on cue, my father evacuated his bowels on the newly polished decks and my uncle's claws shifted uncomfortably. As the seagulls began to circle above, our little island became no more than a smeared dot on the horizon and the unvarnished truth of our fate became as clear as the glassy ocean upon which we sailed. Summer was over. We'd been hoodwinked.

Now, I will assume you've never been advertised as a *'dish of the day'* on a restaurant menu or had a special sauce prepared to compliment your tenders, but witnessing your family members being dragged off to the galley to be boiled with vinegar until the flesh slips like butter from their bones; well that's something that stays with you. And I'm not talking about indigestion or acid reflux. Before Darwin had decided to show up, the only real danger I'd encountered was severe sunburn so this jeopardy had come as quite a shock. Those we once considered friends now began setting out the table, pouring the rum and licking their lips like cartoon cats as the mood grew as dark as the sin they were about to commit.

"I think these hombres are gonna make us into kebabs, though innit," cried a distressed cousin Merle, and despite his usual pessimistic outlook, this time he was bang on the money as our primordial instincts kicked in, albeit a week or so too late. I had to agree though, we were most definitely *innit*.

Uncle Brian was the first to be yanked below deck to Chef Phillips Galley, most likely because of his considerable girth and constant blaspheming. It had taken three of the strongest men to wrestle him through to the kitchen, one of the boatswains almost losing an eye in the process, but in the end his efforts were futile. After the screams had subsided and the raw flames had finished their malefic work, his meat and bone fed the crew for six whole days before they came back for more. They always came back for more.

"I hope I give you bleedin' food poisoning," growled my recently widowed Aunt Wilhelmina, her unfinished knitting torn from her elderly claws as she was manhandled towards the pot by tow of the burly crew. I'd never seen my older cousins cry before, but as the cold wind howled out across the endless black sea, so too did they. And I'd joined them, our faces a sombre canvas of tears and pain that mourned the loss of another Shelton elder. I imagine you didn't expect this book to be such a hoot.

On day nine they came for my father who, as you might suspect, didn't put up much of a fight. "I can't see a thing," he'd whimpered as the sous chef stood sharpening his knife with a gormless simper and as they grabbed him by the legs and carried him away, piteous pleas tumbled from his mouth at the speed of a seasoned horseracing commentator. "Where are you taking me? I don't want to die! I'll do anything. I don't want to die! You want money? I've got money. Where are you taking me? I've got a child. I've got money! Please! I don't want to *die*!" Mum held me tight towards her plastron to drown out his squeals and screams, but die he did. And just like the others, his demise was signalled with a ringing of the dinner bell and the clattering of crockery as the crew pulled up their chairs and tucked into supper beneath a blood-red moon.

The loss of a parent hit me hard and will be forever impaled upon my memory, but I didn't have much time to repine his passing, because on the twelfth day at sea they came for my darling mum too. I still remember with searing clarity how, with a silent grace, she'd kissed the top of my head with a dipped chin, holding me tight against her plastron plate one last time as the hungry sailors closed in around us like a curtain of sour, common flesh. "Be brave Jonathan and promise me you'll always keep yourself nice and tidy," she'd whispered typically, a solitary tear running down her leathery cheek as she gently stroked the infant shell of her only-born.

"I will mum, I promise," I'd sniffled hopelessly, as I caught sight of Darwin lifting his clenched fists up to his eyes and making an exaggerated play of rubbing them in a cruel, mocking *'boohoo'* manner. My juvenile claws were no contest for the sailors strapping arms and as they prised son and mother apart in the middle of the Atlantic Ocean, I had to crush my eyes tight shut like prison doors to stop the tears escaping like wayward convicts. I wasn't going to let Darwin see me cry, but I was broken inside, the indelible image of my mother being led away forever festering upon my conscience like a weeping wound that no passage of time can heal. I swore vengeance upon the crew for the atrocities committed towards my dearest that day, but the hinterland primitives were far too busy stuffing their unshaven faces and playing drinking games to hear my diminutive threats. In that moment I hated this creature called mankind, and I still believe I had very good reason.

Over the following weeks Kurt, Wincey, Elias, Josh, Fig and finally Merle, all went into the sailors greedy bellies in that same order and I was left to grieve their premature passing alone, but for the morbid squawking of gulls who fought for scraps of family flesh in the sky. It's impossible to comprehend, as you read these words in mere seconds, just how long I've laboured in my attempts to compose them. I'm acutely aware how this book (or audio book if it's a glowing success) has been sold to you as a cheery romp through my long and packed life, but although I've since experienced the soreness of grief a hundred times over I still find the demise of my family at the hands of Charles Darwin and his entourage far too painful to convey, even after a hundred and eighty years past. It's not something you can sum up in a soundbite. They were simply murdered, cooked and washed down with flat ale. Their empty shells tossed overboard like takeaway chicken boxes en-route to new land, leaving me an orphan, but for how long was anybody's guess.

"I'm loving it," Darwin had said to me with a smile one evening as he knelt beside my cage on bony knees, hungrily biting into the roasted breastplate of one of my relatives that was held between two ship biscuits.

"Go to hell," I'd growled, a fresh swell of rage rising inside me.

"Hell?" he'd smirked before licking clean his fingers. "What a book a devil's chaplain might write on the clumsy, wasteful, blundering, low and horribly cruel work of nature!"

"You are your father's wasteful blunder," was my curt response, before I suggested a few inventive places he could shove his biscuits. I'd been the youngest and smallest of the family, the runt of the litter, a truncated specimen likely left to be served up as a light nibble once closer to shore. But though I felt equally seasick and homesick at my predicament and bereft of any morsel of faith in any God, I still hoped for some form of miracle.

That miracle finally came one evening as I looked to the night stars for salvation and instantly they were swallowed up by foreboding clouds that begun to twist and thicken above. All at once I could taste change in the dense salty air as the stale breeze picked up and its haunting whistle skipped through the Beagle's sails. As the windjammer crew eyed the skies nervously and the sea became restless, they scrambled to bring the boom under control and to save their beer from going overboard, their collective mood growing ominous as the darkening sky sucked the colour from their faces. For a few termless seconds there was an eerie still, the only sound a gentle creaking from the lanyard that strained to hold the Beagle's mainsail.

Then came the downpour.

"The Karma before the storm!" I'd yelled at the top of my little lungs from behind the bars that held me, the rain beating down like meaty fists from heaven against my infant shell as the storm pounced without warning.

"Christ on a bike," moaned one of the boatswains, stumbling back against the rails with a slack jaw and eyes as wide as a tarsier. He pointed out to sea with a shaking finger and a scream lodged firm in his throat. I followed his eye-line and watched in astonishment as a monolithic wave, easily the height of a mill chimney, rose unerringly from the black depths like Goliaths hand and loured over us with menace. I blindly grabbed onto whatever I could as seconds later the unstoppable sea smashed into the side of the baroque with a crashing din and potent force. The angry water tore at the flesh of the ship with its saline fingers, knocking me clean off my claws, whilst the petrified crew rocked back and forth on the perilous deck like actors in a low budget B-movie.

"Batten down the hatchways," commanded Captain Fitzroy, wrestling with the wheel that spun violently in his hands as if trying to escape his grip. As the storm continued its sudden rage and barbed bolts of electricity lit up the gruesome skies above, I caught sight of my sworn enemy as he fought to keep his balance on the slippery deck, his nonsense writings and badly drawn finches wedged tight beneath his arm as the wind threatened to steal them away. Our eyes met across the Beagle's bow right then. Mine locked firm onto his as shards of debris, torn from the rigging above, fell like missiles all around. Like an eel down a hole, I watched as Darwin and his sun bleached beard scrambled for shelter before another wave hit and the boat threatened to succumb. Finally I'd seen him for the coward he was.

The fearful screams of the sailors filled the night sky as they tried in vain to bail out burbling seawater in bucket loads before we sank. And, as more waves came crashing down upon us like granite, splintering the cedar and shredding the rope holds, I knew this wasn't going to end well for anyone. Captain Fitzroy, his drenched clothes now clinging to him like a second skin, pointed the bow towards the waves and attempted to steer the Beagle through the swirling seas before our lungs filled with brine and we all met a watery end, but I felt no fear.

Shielding my eyes from the stinging saltwater, I could only imagine this was the wrath of my Shelton ancestors bestowing vengeful rage upon those who had dared to wrong their brethren. Past generations rising in unison to fulfil their paternal duty of protecting the last of their bloodline that was in very real danger of being rotisserie on a spit, gobbled up, and lost for an eternity. Or, perhaps it was just really bad weather.

Darwin and the other ship rats cowered below deck, the famous naturalist uttering a mumbled prayer on trembling lips despite his claims of being agnostic. If, indeed survival was all about being the fittest, then now was my time to shine. I clambered out of my mangled prison cell on unsteady claws and staggered towards the side of the boat as it was tossed back and forth like chip paper in a hurricane. We heeled violently to one side, the scattered cages that had once incarcerated my family now buoyant in the flotsam as my hot tears were quickly beaten back by the arctic rain.

"When I get back, I'm going to kill you," I hollered into the whipping wind, before holding tight my beak and jumping into the dark hellscape below with a less than elegant splosh. I hit the frigid sea at speed, my defiant scream quickly transmuting into a drowning gurgle as I took on water. One of the few upsides of being an ectothermic (cold-blooded) animal is that we don't suffer from hypothermia, but unlike our testudine turtle cousins, tortoises are land dwellers and certainly aren't the strongest of swimmers. When you're carrying the weight equivalent of a small child on your back and are born bereft of flippers, you can see why we find it a challenge. In fact I'm often mistaken for a turtle, which I find incredibly racist seeing as we look nothing like one another.

As I'd flailed hopelessly in the irk of the sea, the Beagle, with its torn white sails flapping the colour of cowards, had whimpered off into the nether like the conquered canine it was, whilst I prepared for a slow and painful death. My life on earth had been short and uneventful, but at that point I was glad it was coming to an end after a litany of terrible things. Mother Nature (or pure adrenaline) had a serious commitment to keeping me on earth however, because in that ultimate moment, just as speedily as the storm had arrived unannounced, it suddenly passed through into shallower depths and a passive calm returned to the seas once more.

Thankfully the Beagle did not. Obeying the five-second rule, it had dropped its food source (me) and had decided not to return and pick it up, much to my relief. A passing merchant ship had plucked me from the water a few hours later, half drowned and fully delirious but alive. I'd been given a second chance, more than the rest of my creep had been afforded, and I didn't want death to be the most important thing I ever did in life. I intended to grab any future opportunity with both shivering claws and vowed never again to waste my misspent youth lazing in the sunshine, comparing tan lines and gorging on roots. And of course, I promised to keep myself tidy and respectable, just like mum had wished.

"Where are we headed?" I'd managed to croak once safely aboard and swathed in blankets for warmth, very much hoping this new crew had already eaten.

"To a land where it rains even more than here," replied one of my wizened sea dog saviours as he filled up his meerschaum pipe, stuck it into his face and steered the ship into the sun as its crest rose over a new day.

I outlived Charles Darwin, of course. He died of suspected Chagas disease in 1882. To be honest, I haven't lost much sleep over it.

CHAPTER THREE

I was hatched Jonathan Jennifer Shelton on the island of San
Cristobel in the Galapagos, in 1829. The same year that Robert
Peel first established the Metropolitan Police Force, rickets
seemed all the rage and a quick-tempered Andrew Jackson was
sworn in as the 7th President of the United States. I imagine my
parents had been hoping for a girl and had either forgotten, or
were simply too lazy, to think up another middle name for me
once I'd entered into the race, but I guess that's family for you.

Or was.

Now I was an orphan, torn away from my loved ones by the
gluttonous hands of humankind and left to fend for myself
somewhere unfamiliar and far away from home. In fairness, my
rescuers had been kind to me (by that, I mean they'd had the
good grace not to eat me) but although my faith in humanity had
been slightly replenished, they still possessed teeth and I still
remained wary. I was glad to reach land that dreary October
morning in 1843, although the biting wind and lashing rain that
welcomed us into harbour told me this wasn't a t-shirt and shorts
type of town.

I'd glanced my sea-worn saviours bid me farewell with little more
than a weak wave, before I was swallowed up (metaphorically) by

a clamorous mess of silk merchants and spice traders who unloaded consignments of exotic cargo that dripped with opulence and seductive aromas from faraway lands. As I'd weaved between a welter of heavy Dockers boots and foul language that morning, I quickly found myself growing quite at home in this place of constant rain, whose inhabitants seemed adverse to preening and were still untouched by modern dentistry. I had arrived in England.

I was penniless, and although I carried a mobile home upon my back, I knew I'd need more adequate lodgings as I shed the sobriquet of juvenility and undertook this new chapter into the unchartered. As a dear friend once told me: empty pockets never held anybody back, only empty hearts and empty heads can do that. Still, I needed a job. The question now, was doing what?

Back on the island when I'd been little more than a hatchling, I remember one day fooling around down by the rocks and dancing to the waves that provided my own brand of breakfast radio, when all at once my father had called me from the south beach to come quick. There was urgency in his voice and I almost fainted on the spot when I witnessed his disembodied head lying still on the sands before my eyes. My first concern was that I'd been too late and he'd suffered the fate of a swift tail's lunch. As it turned out, he hadn't been gruesomely decapitated by a predator from the skies, but instead had been buried up to his neck by a few of my more mischievous cousins whilst enjoying his mid-afternoon nap. His expression that day had been one frozen in fear as a cast of red rock crabs dangled from his twerpish face and he'd begged for help. Being a tortoise, I'm far too slow for competitive sports, but that afternoon, as I excavated dad from the warm sands I discovered something I was good at. Digging.

This being the case, now in Victorian London I began work as a mud-lark, digging the feculent banks of the Thames with an old fig drum slung across my shell as I joined freckled orphans at low tide to scour the wet mud for anything that could be bartered for money or exchanged for food. I'll always remember the riverbank harboured an unsettling smell in those days. A cloying casserole of emptied bowel interlaced with bin juice (and just a hint of late stage leprosy in the base notes), but thankfully my able claws made light work of the super black river ooze. Amongst the raw sewage, detritus and dead cats that the river gave up, I'd often hit pay dirt when stumbling across a lump of coal, rivets from an old ship, or on a particularly good day, a lost coin. It was a tedious, unforgiving job, but a tortoise has to eat…and of course, drink.

When I wasn't up to my beak in river sludge, I'd often find myself enjoying the more illustrious benefits the capital had to offer. One of which was exploring the multitude of drinking dens that lined the narrow streets and snickets of the shambolic city, with it's buildings built so closely together that the locals dubbed them kissing lanes, though from my experience they seemed more prone to attracting serious acts of violence than romance. Teetotalism held little weight in the capital amongst the lower classes in those sour times too, and you were far more likely to meet your death by drinking the unsanitary water pumped from the Thames than you ever were from misadventure or liver failure.

In those days, there were no government guidelines on the average weekly amount of units you should drink, and any mention of 'Dry January' would have gotten you lynched, feathered and flogged by the parched natives I suspect. With this in mind, I must confess I didn't exactly hold back in knocking back whatever I could. I seldom drink nowadays (havoc for my gout-ridden claws), but in more care-free times I'd escort the fumes of cheap booze that clung in the air as I staggered from hole to hole, freely guzzling down the straw coloured brew from tarnished tankards until my eyes became cloudy, my legs no longer worked, and I found oblivion.

I was a regular green face amongst the unruly pack of the east end. A boisterous lot who enjoyed nothing more than long boozy lunches and late night sessions in those stale and gloomy pothouses of the eighteen hundreds. Dangerous drinking dens they were too, that mostly reeked of pipe tobacco and unchecked armpits, at least until the smoking ban came into effect in 2007. I'm quite ashamed to say I had turned to a life of debauchery in those toilsome times, and the taverns and alehouses that had already witnessed centuries of intemperance and intoxication going on beneath their worn oak beams became my new home. One invariably stuffed full of character, which regularly spilled out onto the soily streets for a brutal mafficking come closing time. It was inside one of these more colourful haunts, barely illuminated by candles and with floors made sticky by years of spilt sin, that I first met the acquaintance of a man who would change my life forever.

He was short and drunk (as were most people of the time) and looked much like a drama teacher were it not for the blackened eye he wore on his lined face and the gin glass that shook in his hand as he rocked on fluctuant feet. I'd seen men move like this before, usually as they attempted the slippery decks of a ship during high seas, and I feared this fellow might take a tumble not overboard into icy depths, but into the taverns open fire that snapped angrily like a dog with distemper.

"Steady how you go there, friend," I'd cautioned as I waited to catch the barkeeps one good eye amongst a sea of thirsty heads. Erstwhile, the wobbly man before me went sideways in a valiant attempt to stay on his feet, before staggering into a wine cask and -without spilling a single drop from his glass- landed heavily on his backside with a fleshy thud. A loud cheer went up from the drinking crowd at this extraordinary feat of skill and I should have known then that I was in the company of genius.

"Giles Swithins," slurred the soak as way of introduction, as he got to his feet with a gladiatorial wave at the reprobate crowd before eyeing me with suspicion. "And who might you be, I ask?"

"I'm Jonathan Shelton," I'd answered with a courteous nod as I turned my shell back to the crammed bar and feigned interest in the selection of brown nappy (slang for beer) that was on offer. All I'd wanted was a quiet drink and to warm myself by the fire after a tough day larking, but I suspected I was about to become embroiled in conversation with the local pub nut. I've always had a knack for attracting trouble of some kind or the like. I just have one of those faces.

"Chuzzlewit," the man blurted out suddenly.

"Pardon me?" I'd said, imagining this was some kind of obscenity thrown in my direction. Most things ending in 'wit' tended to be.

"Chuzzlewit," he repeated.

"You'd just better watch your mouth." I warned with clenched claws. He reached for a small wooden comb in his pocket and ran it through thick wavy curls -his own of course- as he looked at me with eyes that bulged like expectant hernias.

"Well? What do you think of it?" he probed, but before I could garner a response he'd slapped a folded booklet down on the bar with a flourish as my heart sank inwards, the hopes of a quiet night evaporated. At first, I'd assumed it was some form of nonsense religious literature, or perhaps an invitation to a spiritualist church that this carouser had offered me, but it seems I was mistaken. That being said, the words contained within its worn pages would be scriptures that I'd follow religiously for the rest of my tiresomely long life.

"Oh!" I'd mumbled with genuine surprise, realising it was one of those monthly written serials of fiction held between printed wrappers that two-leggers liked to read for entertainment in the day. In between badger baiting, cock fighting and kicking dogs, of course.

"Well?" said the eager Swithins, placing the comb back into his breast pocket after several attempts.

"I can't say I've read it," I'd responded in my ignorance, picking it up tentatively for closer inspection.

"Neither, it seems, has anyone else," chuckled this curious fellow as he leant on the bar top for stability, though I detected something more behind the laugh as he drained the last of his glass and wiped down his impressively manicured moustache. I was intrigued, not with his facial topiary you understand, but with the tatty literature I now held in my claw.

These illustrated instalments of fictitious suspense were very popular in the 1800s and would be eagerly awaited by people anxious to discover the next twist or turn that lay ahead. In those meaty tales held between thin pages were stories of romance, heroism and villainy that gripped a nation and had people deliberating over pint pots and garden fences about what could possibly happen next. Those literate enough to read would often share these stories aloud with their friends and family who would gather around meagre tables on cold nights, listening with fervour as they conjured up exciting new worlds which allowed them to escape their own sorry existence, if only for the evening. Much the same I suppose, as lumpy, middle-aged women engross themselves in copies of: *Fifty Shades of Grey*, nowadays.

"I think it's my best work yet, you know," remarked Swithins with a sigh, as he unbuttoned his trousers and grabbed a nearby chamber pot from the shelf. I was puzzled by this admission. I'd never heard of a writer who went by the name of Giles Swithins before, but as I turned the dog-eared programme in my claw it didn't take me long to realise my error. I must have misheard his gin-drenched introduction to me in the noisy saloon and immediately the penny dropped, almost as quickly as this drunken man's trousers, as he relieved himself into a brass pot by the bar with a grunt.

Charles John Huffman Dickens had an even sillier middle name than I, but (spoiler alert) he was also one of the greatest writers and social critics of his generation. Although a celebrity of his day, he seldom posted selfies and so far as I'm aware, never had a twitter account. Instead, he used only his imagination and quill pen to show off his multi-layered talents that would shine a light on the injustices of civil rights, child cruelty and poverty. Nowadays, I find it a rarity to see a celebrity with even the thinnest sliver of talent as I'm sure you'll agree, but this fine man would spark social reform for the helpless and downtrodden almost single-handedly, creating a ground-swell of support for their predicament through the use of his captivating characters and sublimely crafted tales. Tales packed full of grotesque caricatures with preposterous names that offered a glimmer of hope to the masses in such bleak times and believe me they were bleak. He was a true portraitist of his era and the stories he conjured up are regarded today as some of the most important works of fiction in history. Nowadays, almost everyone has read one of his books or has at least pretended too.

Nonetheless, when I first met him in 1843 as he'd squeezed the last droplets from his diseased bladder, he was having his difficult 'third album' moment. Just like his previous novels, the new one he'd recently embarked on had been serialised and fed to the public in regular monthly instalments, no doubt so his agents could monitor response through marketing research and encourage him to tinker and change to suit their sales forecasts.

Unfortunately, his latest yarn entitled: *The Adventures of Martin Chuzzlewit,* was bombing quite badly amongst its audience, and in only its third month of release had shifted barely half of his last written hit. The figures had been so disappointing that his publisher Chapman & Hall had made the hasty decision to drop him from their roster and it seemed he was now very much drinking to forget.

"Let me buy you a drink," he'd offered kindly, zipping himself up before pulling out bare pockets and realising he had no money left over.

"Don't worry, I'll get these," I sympathised now I knew I was in the company of such greatness. "Hard Times?"

"What a great title for a book. Would you mind if I used that in future?" he asked with a glint.

"If it helps on your journey through this bleak house of existence then please, be my guest,"

"And could I get some peanuts too perhaps?" he ventured rather cheekily.

Our drinks finally arrived, and we retreated to a corner snug by the fire for warming. Although it was summer, the London nights could be bitter cold, much like the 'bow wow' mutton pudding the customers always complained about to the lazy, one-eyed barkeep at the *George & Vulture*. I'd always stick to the pre-packed sandwiches that were almost edible, but the place would be obliterated on Trip Advisor nowadays.

"So Mr Dickens. What do you intend to do about these lagging sales?" I'd asked the national treasure sitting opposite me as he took out his comb once more for some personal grooming. It did seem the man was quite particular about his appearance and it wouldn't have at all surprised me if the fellow had Obsessive Compulsive Disorder, I'd contemplated, before rearranging the peanuts into a neat line on the table, and setting up our pint pots so they were symmetrical and proper.

"Please, just call me Boz," Dickens had insisted as he leaned forward, our knees almost touching together in the cosy booth as he brought his voice down to a murmur. "Simply put Jonathan, here's the secret sauce. I think I'm spent. Call it a textbook case of writers block if you must,"

"Surely not?" I argued.

"I feel a wrong kind of fire burning within me Jonathan, the spice of the Devil. Perhaps I need to shake things up in the next instalment?" he'd spoke to himself more than anyone else as he shook his head in frustration, which rather ruined his hair.

"How do you mean?" I queried between sips of my drink. It seemed to me that the beer had been brewed for a less seasoned palate than my own.

"Well…they always say an author should write about what they know best, so maybe I should go back to writing about debauchery, poverty and drink…or move the plot to America. Something crazy like that?"

"I beg your pardon. Did you say America?" I asked as my ears pricked up, despite me not actually having any ears.

He nodded wordlessly and took a healthy swig of his booze through gritted teeth before he spoke once more. "Kate and I travelled there last year for the summer. We were thinking of going again this year, but holidays get expensive with ten kids so we'll probably do Spain instead."

At this point I could barely contain my excitement. I'd been made aware, through general rawgabbit, of this far-flung utopia called America, but I'd never heard of anyone who'd actually been there. Rumours floating around the bars and boathouses at the time held promise of a place rich with industry and enterprise, where you could make real money with the gift of free land. I'd never met anyone who'd gone any further than Poplar since arriving in London and my enthusiasm escalated at the prospect of learning more about this spellbinding country where the grass grew greener, the accents thicker and the food portions larger.

"You aren't pulling my tail? You've really been to America?" I'd urged him once more, just to be sure. He took a sip of his drink and nodded. I was in desperate need of some distraction, and even if I couldn't actually afford to get to America myself, perhaps I could visit there in my imagination if only Charles would write about it. I was fond of England, but I'd grown tired of all the mud-larking around and living life to the knuckle. The river had been frugal of late, and the urchins always beat me to the best spots along the banks in the mornings due to my slowness.

"I think that's a splendid idea Charles. You must write all about America," I'd exclaimed enthusiastically. "I for one, would love to read about the place and I'm sure others would too. Please write something about America. Please?"

I didn't realise it at the time, but I'd had grip on the lapels of his sober suit and suddenly, it was I that looked like the pub nut as conversations halted and necks craned to see why the most famous writer of the times was being manhandled by a Galapagos tortoise, if indeed they even knew what I was. I've often found that despite their being an estimated 8.7 million other species that live with them on the planet, humans are quite blinkered when it comes to recognising breeds other than themselves. I mean honestly, without wanting to repeat myself, do I really look like a turtle?

"You really think that people would be interested in reading of a place rife with slavery and tobacco tinctured spittle wherever one walks?" Dickens pondered, as he straightened up his waistcoat with a squint of suspicion in his glazed eye.

"Like, totally dude!" I'd whooped.

"A place where if I turn on the street, I'm followed by a multitude?"

"Well hell-yeah!"

"You don't suppose people will think I've sold out?"

"No way, man," I'd reassured him, more in hope than expectation. "They'll think you're awesome!"

Dickens combed his hair (again) as thirsty mouths returned to their drinks and I returned to mine. He seemed deep in thought for a moment or so, before his face broke into a flammable smile that set his eyes alight. "Very well my wrinkled green friend, for you I shall," he announced with a newly found vigour as he chinked my glass. "For you, I will write about the forsaken place called America, so all can know it's darkest secrets. Crooked politicians, slavery and public tobacco spitting…and didn't I say you should call me Boz?"

He'd chosen this nickname for himself after a character from his favourite novel entitled 'The Vicar Of Wakefield' by Oliver Goldsmith (1728-1774), and already he was quick becoming my favourite Charles, although at that point he had little in the way of competition other than the descendant digesting Darwin, it's fair to assume.

"Splendid. Another drink then, Boz?" I suggested, already feeling the effects of the booze, which, in truth had become the main staple of my daily diet.

"Why the Dickens not!" he'd agreed, rising unsteadily to his feet. "Bring in the bottled lightning, a clean tumbler and a corkscrew," hollered the self proclaimed 'Sparkler Of Albion' as he replaced his hair comb once more and hooked his drunken arm into mine as he yelled for the elusive barman. Dickens was such a joy to spend time with, unquestionably dependable, and my type of guy.

The drink arrived (finally) and performed its job of loosening both mind and tongue as we sucked from the bottle late into the night. He was magnificent company and carried no heirs or graces, though much like the queen- both Elizabeth and Victoria- he seemed not to carry money either.

"I luuurvveeeve you man," Dickens had slurred affectionately after we'd polished off the third bottle between us with a glug.

"I love you too Boz." I'd said, because I did.

We were spirits bonded together by circumstance and a shared love of hard drink and hard times. The last few years had been trying for us both and it felt good to meet someone with whom I held so much in common. We'd both been abandoned by our parents (albeit for different reasons), had both been lumbered with stupid middle names, and we'd each been forced into hard labour at an early age. Myself, as a mud-lark, and Dickens; sticking labels onto bottles in an ink factory run by a callous boss who rode roughshod over his workers. Thankfully, this hadn't stymied his ambition as a novelist and had instead provided him with plenty of first hand material for his many books.

"Fan the sinking flame of hilarity with the wing of friendship; and pass the rosy wine," he'd gushed and of course, I obliged.

The hour grew late as we burned through bottle after bottle of the spiky elixir, the wreckage of a drunken evening strewn out across the table before us. I confided in Charles about the murder of my dear family and my time spent at sea, he, in turn confessed of his recent marital problems with his wife Kate, whom he said had grown rather fat and boring.

"We forge the chains we wear in life," he'd reasoned sullenly with dark eyes, as I filled his glass to the top with more gin.

"If I ever find out where Darwin lives, he's toast," I'd seethed, curling my claw into a cathartic ball and thinking my own bad thoughts. At the time, I'd already made attempts to track down the back stabbing naturalist, but he was proving elusive. I'd done some digging around (of a different variety) on the natural historian and as it turns out, it wasn't just tortoise flesh he was partial to. When it came to eating animals nothing was off menu it seemed. He'd consumed everything from plates of puma and broiled armadillo to rodents and owls, whilst on his travels. He'd even meet with likeminded connoisseurs every Tuesday to feast on these unfortunates, in a macabre group called the *Glutton Club*.

Dickens was horrified by my account. "There never were greed and cunning in the world yet, that did not do too much and overreach themselves. It is as certain as death,"

"Let's hope so," I'd said at the time, and I'd certainly meant it.

That evening, as if often the case with gin, we fell ungraciously from jovial revelry into a melancholic mist. I mourned the demise of my family, whilst Charles reflected on the recent death of his pet raven 'Grip,' who had sadly perished after eating lead paint chips. He became quite tearful about the passing of the crow, now stuffed with straw and perched in his office, but I guess that's the gin bubble for you.

"Heaven knows we need never be ashamed of our tears, for they are rain upon the blinding dust of earth, overlying our hard hearts. I was better after I had cried, than before-more sorry, more aware of my own ingratitude, more gentle."

Thankfully a scuffle broke out in a nearby booth, and the sight of a man hitting another man over the head with a thick wooden chair never fails to lighten the mood and raise spirits, wouldn't you agree?

"You've inspired me Jonathan," Dickens garbled with dampened cheeks as he slammed his glass down hard on the table and rose shakily to his feet. "I shall indeed write the book my public desherves to read, the book you desherve to read my friend. I shall write about Ashmerica,"

"Hurrah!" I cheered, now quite squiffy. "One for the road?"

"No thank you, my dearest chuckaboo, I must leave. Best sellers don't write themselves now do they?"

"I suppose not," I'd agreed, quite taken aback. Had he just referred to me as his dearest chuckaboo? Which if you aren't aware, in Victorian terms meant best friend. I felt a cosy warmth come over me in that moment, then realised to my surprise, that Dickens had missed the chamber pot again as he emptied his bladder one last time before the short walk home.

My new best friend combed his fine locks a final time, before bidding me a fond farewell as he tumbled out of the pub and towards his sluttery writing desk. He'd also been absentminded about the bar tab too, but because tortoises aren't best equipped at doing runners (especially drunken ones), I squared the account on his behalf. As I stumbled out onto the cobbles and the lazy barman had snapped the bolts closed behind me, I thought it a fair price to pay in order to discover more about an America that I dreamed one day to visit.

Over the forthcoming weeks, the days by the river grew shorter and the mud harder, as winter began to show its teeth and the first frosts settled. My claws were cold but my heart aglow as my new companion remained true to his written word and the next episodic chapter of Chuzzlewit hit the shelves. My soul sang with hope as I'd skip the customary after work drink, and instead, rushed back to the cow-house where I slept to read by candlelight the story of a young Martin and his fictitious friend Mark Tapley, as they relocated overseas to begin new exploits in a strange, wondrous city called New York. I would revel for hours in the delicious writings as the sights and sounds of a Dickensian New York leapt from the page and took form on the blank canvas of my imagination like paintings come to life. I could taste the air, smell the dirt and experience in vivid colour, the place that I ached to visit and explore for myself. For me, Charles had lifted a large pebble from the pond of my mind, and as the waters cleared, I could see exactly where I hoped my future lay.

With its despicable characters, hucksters and anti-heroes, *The Adventures of Martin Chuzzlewit* still remains my most cherished of Dickens' literature today, but at the time not everybody agreed. On release, this selfish novel about love, murder and insurance scams, was heavily panned by the critics and the Americans especially despised the way in which they'd been portrayed by this stuck up Englishman who should, and I quote; really keep his nose out of their affairs and learn to tie his laces. The reviews were scathing at best, slanderous at worse, and some even believed this unfathomable American twist to be career suicide.

'We are all described as a filthy, gormandizing race,' harked the New York Courier and Enquirer, who seemed particularly hurt by his words.

"Total and utter pants," remarked the Gloucestershire Herald (probably).

"Those buffoons haven't a clue about literature," Charles would retort on the several occasions we'd meet for a tipple and he'd mislay his wallet. In truth he hadn't held any punches when showing his disdain for slavery and public tobacco spitting, but the backlash he received seemed unfairly brutal. American politician George L. Rives even later wrote:

"It is perhaps not too much to say that the publication of Martin Chuzzlewit did more than almost any other one thing to drive the United States and England in the direction of war."

These bad reviews deeply troubled Charles. They warred within and bothered him almost as much as the inequality and poverty inflicted upon the downtrodden working classes. But, if you're the type who considers old books to be boring, then I urge you to pick up a copy of this fantastic novel and decide for yourself. Not right this minute of course, because you're reading my page-turner, but perhaps pop it in your amazon basket for later. I assure you it's full of Dickensian wit (obviously), and acerbic social commentary. Admittedly, it can be a little heavy handed and sentimental in places, but for me it was his funniest and most satirically scathing work produced. Though as I swiftly learnt, Americans don't do satire too well.

"I think that *Chuzzlewit* is in a hundred points immeasurably the best of my stories," Charles would say to me, and I would often agree as we sat in the Grapes on slowpoke afternoons, drinking Jerez sherry under the watchful eyes of stuffed beasts. "There are other books of which the backs and covers are by far the best part," he'd always add.

"Isn't it your round?" I would find myself saying meekly.

Mercifully, war over the Oregon boundary dispute was avoided, but much like my friends The Kinks who would come many years afterwards, Dickens' career in the States would take a major downturn as the rabid American press tore him apart like timber wolves, the relationship soured beyond saving. During this 'Quarrel with America' the public revolted against him too. They defaced a bust of him that hung in the park theatre gallery and burned locks of his hair bought as mementos, along with his books that now rested on smoldering pyres instead of library shelves. I expect you may be wondering at this point whether I felt in some way, a pang of guilt or responsibility for his predicament? Well, in truth, not really. It wasn't I that wrote the thing, although I wish I had.

But Dickens was far from spent. The 'inimitable' still had plenty of ink left in the pot and despite the resentment he quickly went about penning his next novella, a warming tale of forgiveness and redemption that would win over the fickle American public once more with its sparkling good humour and childlike humanity. It would also spurn his first Christmas number one, cementing forever his place in the annals of yuletide tradition alongside excessive drinking, roasted turkey and Jona Lewie. '*A Christmas Tale*' would serve to restore his reputation as the peoples champion and guarantee enduring popularity and applause for the rest of his life. Nowadays, quite rightly, he is held up as one of the greatest writers to ever grace our times, but to me he was also one of the greatest human friends a tortoise could ever wish to have. And you know I'm not the biggest fan of your variety.

Charles John Huffman Dickens was a fine man with fine hair, and even if he did dodge his round from time to time, his heart was always in the right place even if his wallet wasn't. The wonderful novel he had gifted to me would serve as a sizzler reel for the mind-tingling possibilities that lay in wait, all thanks to his craftsmanship, friendship and kindness. Even today after all these years passed, when I blow away the dust from that cherished first cloth bound edition that sits upon my shelf, I find it comforting to know that he, Martin and the America he envisaged are never far away.

"The pain of parting is nothing to the joy of meeting again," Dickens had mused as he waved me off at Southampton docks, having scraped together what meager savings I could muster for the voyage to New York.

"Take good care Boz," I'd said, as the ship sounded its horn for departure.

"Jonathan, life is made of so ever many partings welded together,"

"Ok well I'd better go. I'm going to miss my…"

"No space of regret can make amends for one life's opportunities misused,"

"Erm…I really must dash."

"Every traveller has a home of his own, and he learns to appreciate it the more from his wandering,"

I made it onto the boat with only seconds to spare. With the familiar fire flickering in my belly I was ready to begin my new life, and as you are about to discover, it was one filled with many twists and turns that would span the centuries that followed. My only quandary now is choosing which route to take you on as we continue forwards into the past.

CHAPTER FOUR

The first splotches of rain mottle the American sidewalk (or pavement if you prefer) that is lined with tricksters begging for change, archetypal chancers hawking stolen goods, and rag-picker scamps urinating in doorways. But this wasn't New York City, and it isn't 1845. Instead it's over a century later, December 1955 in fact, and you can almost smell Christmas in the gritty air of this giant atoll of undesirability. I'm a much older version of myself now, a version getting slowly soaked and already panting like a short-faced dog as I rush with all I have, to close the distance between 'me' and the oncoming bus one grey and drizzly afternoon in the Yellowhammer state of Alabama.

Do forgive me if I've blind-sided you (this book is as messed up as my life) but the tides of my memory are forever shifting, and the ability to visit any given event in life without a chronological agenda is the beauty of compiling a memoir and of course, time travel. Because I do believe recalling special times in the recesses of ones mind is, in a profound way, a form of purgative transportation. It beats public transport anyhow, especially the Montgomery City Bus Line.

My average walking speed clocks in at around 0.16 miles per hour, but that's not to say I can't find another gear when I really have to. If you've ever seen a tortoise travelling at maximum pelt, you'll no doubt know it's a rare sight to behold. Especially a tortoise chasing down a bus. With few natural predators we aren't really designed for velocity and whenever the anomaly of a tortoise moving at speed is witnessed in the wild (or in this case, the high street) you'll always get some joker pipe up and ask; *'Where's the hare?'* as if we haven't heard it a thousand times already. Very scarcely, if ever, will anybody ask if you're ok.

"Are you ok?" a pretty black lady asks from beneath the shade of her round brimless hat as I narrowly managed to jump aboard the sunny coloured bus that dismal afternoon. Bent double with exertion and no longer in the early flushes of youth, I'd plonked myself into the lumpy seat beside her, very out of puff and very close to death. "You certainly don't look very ok."

'I'm fine," I'd gasped asthmatically, sucking in cold air through wheezing lung pipes as the doors close and we begin our way down Cleveland Avenue with a similarly discordant splutter. "Just legged it for the bus, that's all,"

"Well ain't you the lucky one," she complains with a mouthful of teeth and a bothersome frown hardening on her face. She unclasps her clutch purse and kindly offers me a cough sweet that I hope will ease the tightness in my timeworn chest, and as the bus rattled on in a blur of winter-brown trees, she leans in close and lowers her voice to a whisper. "*Psssst!* Did you know, the last time I paid my fare and went to get on at the back, the darn idiot driver sped off without me?"

"He drove away?" I enquire rather naively, still struggling to fully catch my breath. "Didn't he see you?"

Her seething eyes shoot discerningly towards the front of the bus then back to me. "Dang right he saw me!"

"Oh, I see," I replied meekly, and I begin to feel pretty stupid as the *'plink'* of a penny drops.

I'm a reptile not usually partial to vague metaphors, but I've often thought that the human race works a lot like Sudoku. Things have to be put in boxes, it's yawningly boring, and at the end of the day, is it really worth the bother of trying to work out anyway? Despite having lived amongst your kind for almost two centuries, I still struggle to determine what constitutes a pure human being from a cretin (if you do, email me). It seems, for every Florence Nightingale or Gandhi that comes strolling along the annals of your history to illuminate the way, there's always a Vladimir Putin, Amelia Dyer, or Shia LaBeouf ready to darken humanities doorstep. You're an inconsistent race. At best a lucky dip, and I fear every new parent must lay awake at night in swathes of worry, deliberating as to whether they've just sprung a saviour or serial killer upon the world. Humans, are indeed a divided and knotty creature to fathom so although I was horrified at this bizarre bus behaviour I must admit I wasn't in the least surprised.

In 1955, Montgomery Alabama, along with the rest of America, harboured some rather hoary and blinkered opinions regarding where those of colour should eat their meals, watch their movies, or indeed sit on a bus. Today, this behaviour is traditionally known as racism, and though I'm rarely one to adhere to convention (I am a talking tortoise after all), having green skin myself, I'd always made sure to sit in the rear section of the carriage with the rest of the *'coloured'* folk, as was customary in those times of commonplace partiality. Nonetheless, although I was new around the place and didn't like to cause a scene, being told where I could and couldn't sit on a bus because of my skin colour certainly didn't sit well with me. It was only going to be a matter of time before, to phrase it politely, the excrement impacted on the rotating blades.

As the Montgomery City Line passed Dexter Avenue Baptist church and crawled in at the next stop, I could already see a line of people shaking rain-beaten umbrellas and wiping down sodden raincoats as they waited to jump on-board the 2857 to escape the weather. "Here we go again," sang the lady beside me with a trundling roll of her eyes, and I was soon to discover why. Once the doors had opened with a swoosh, I caught sight of the portly driver who rose slowly from his seat, leaving the engine running so the bus threw out plumes of blue smoke that spoiled the Christmas air. As he made his way towards us, scuttling down the aisle like a scabrous lizard approaching its prey, I knew trouble was about to pay a visit. And this particular variety of trouble wore a standard issue peaked cap, toe capped boots and a face you'd happily hold underwater for a long time.

"You'll have to stand up now," he croaked with a smug condescension and a flick of his lacelike tongue. Smiling through citric lips, he pointed a grubby finger in my direction as though I belonged in a pet shop window. "That means you too, pal."

Regardless of being born with a thick reptilian skin, I knew immediately that we were never going to become pals. "Stand up? But why?" I'd asked, just about recovered from my exertion.

"So the white people can sit down, of course," he scoffed.

Already, a queue of milky white people began forming behind him impatiently, but I've always ferociously refused to play by the rules that others choose to live by. "But we were here first," I'd argued with an air of defiance. "I've paid my fare, don't you understand?" He didn't.

"I don't care wrinkles, shift," he growled with impatience. It was obvious this man, with his sulky negatives, had taken a dislike to me and in the interests of transparency and fairness, the feeling was reciprocated. His eyebrows began to leap around his forehead, as if he were grasping for something intelligent to say in the empty locker of his mind. You can tell a lot from someone's eyebrows, actually. "C'mon turtle, I haven't got all day."

"What is your problem?" I retorted with a sculpted glower, one perfected over several years of lingering in the mirror. "Is it because I is green?"

"Yes it is. And because I say so."

"This is ridiculous," I reasoned, growing tiresome of his banal windbaggery. "Surely white people have legs too? Why can't they stand up?"

"Because they don't have to," he barked with impatience. "Now just shift before I throw you off the goddamn bus."

I could see he wasn't taking my complaint at all seriously, and already a handful of black people had arisen from their seats in relinquished compliance, but not I. Because of my bantam height and poor vertical reach I couldn't hold onto to the handrails safely, but perhaps more importantly, it was wrong that I should even have to. This bus driver, with his ignorant mouth frozen in an eternal downwards curve, seemed no different to me than the Nazi officers I'd encountered during the war and I'd rather hoped things had moved on since then. "Well, I refuse to move,"

I continued, with a steadiness in my voice despite my anger. "I'm pregnant!"

"Nonsense," the angry driver had snapped, though he'd phrased this reply in a much more industrial manner that my publisher insisted I change. "Now skidaddle!" he'd grunted, gesturing with his thumb that I should vacate my rightful seat and comply. I stared into his callous eyes as my annoyance grew, but still he stood there as if soldered to the spot. We were like two outlaws in a Mexican standoff, or stand-up-off, if that's even a thing? Neither of us prepared to back down.

Believe me when I say Montgomery bus drivers really were a law unto themselves in those backwards times. They would strut the lengths of their rusty carriages like officers on a prison wing, regarding hard working people as unruly inmates rather than honest paying customers. They'd growl orders with wilful ignorance, demanding in viperish tones that black passengers must stand whenever there weren't enough seats free for the white folks to sit down. And if there was no more standing room available? Well, then those of colour (including green) were plainly ordered to leave the bus and walk to wherever they needed to get to. This seemed notably unfair to me, as I'm sure it does to you, but I was prepared to discuss this issue of racial inequality like any grown adult reptilian, given the chance.

"I have an idea how this can be resolved," I'd said, in an attempt to appeal to his better nature, though I doubted he owned one.

"Oh, you do, do you?" he'd sneered, adjusting his cap so I got a better view of his serpentine eyes and the warts that clung to his chin like stubborn barnacles on the side of a boat. "And what might that idea be?"

"I'll stand up, so long as you sit down," I'd beamed, raising my middle claw-tip with a grin as a collective intake of breath carried around the carriage. I've always found maturity to be overrated, but the driver hadn't succumbed to my wit. Instead, I could see the angry veins pop in his forehead as his temper went into high gear and my mood began to lift.

 "Y'all better make it light on yourselves, and let me have those seats," he threatened with a nose full of hair and a portending whisper. "So, are you going to move or what, you green waste of space?"

"Nope. I'm going nowhere, and neither does it seem, is anyone else," I remarked with unblinking conviction. I refused to be flustered by this moron and was happy to step above the parapet as we reached a stalemate, even if nobody else was willing to make a similar standpoint.

"I don't think we should have to stand," objected the lady besides me in the decorous hat, finally swooping to my aid whilst other passengers scoffed and complained of missed appointments and shallow engagements. Her name was Rosa Parks (1913-2005), and I know this because of the Montgomery department store badge she wore on her oatmeal duffle coat. She let out a long suffering sigh before gazing out of the window at the miserable weather and tenement slums that stuck out like broken teeth along the high street. "I'm tired," she said with a resigned look etched upon her obviously tired face.

"Aren't we all? I've done a six day shift this week." The driver replied vaguely, completely missing the point.

"No. I mean I'm tired of the way we are being treated." Rosa protested, with a disapproving glower. By this stage the other passengers looked pretty fed up and ready to lynch us.

"My heart bleeds for you lady," the bus driver ridiculed, obviously running out of repartee and patience. "But if you don't stand up right this minute, I'm going to call the police and have you both arrested. What we're dealing with here is a complete lack of respect for the law."

I swallowed my anger, then decided I didn't much like the taste, so spat it out again. "What we are dealing with here is an idiot who wears a white hood and lights fires at the weekend." I roared with verbal rebuke.

A lucent smile crept across Rosa's face right then. It was if somewhere a light bulb had switched on in her head and her purpose became as clear as a Galapagos morning. Of course, if this public display of defiance had occurred today, I'm in no doubt someone would have recorded the whole episode on their pocket phones before uploading it to social media, harvesting millions of 'likes' and stirring a viral uprising. Instead, this was a time long before everyone was devoted to their screens like slaves, so you'll just have to accept my accurate account of events.

"That was very silly…" Rosa had giggled coyly with a squeeze of my forearm as the driver returned to the wheel, suggesting beneath his breath that I'd had an unhealthy relationship with my mother. "But it was also incredibly brave what you did, Sir."

"All in a days work," I'd explained with a recusant smile and a biggety wave of my claw. I felt a strong sense of triumph right then as I looked around the packed bus carriage at strangers who congratulated me on my gallantry. They didn't actually say as much, but they didn't need to, the look of thanks in their eyes told me everything I needed to know. "I doubt we'll have anymore trouble from that blatherskite with his hollow threats."

The police arrived shortly afterwards and arrested us for a violation of Chapter 6, section 11, segregation law of the Montgomery City code. I'd been read my Miranda rights on occasion in the past, and sitting on a bus certainly wasn't tantamount to fraud, racketeering, or drug trafficking. Being incarcerated for not standing up on a bus? At my distinguished age I was a pensioner twice over for goodness sake, what on earth was the world coming to?

"Why do you push us around?" Rosa had asked the police officer a little while later as we were bundled into the back of the meat wagon and a chattering crowd gathered to speculate on why an innocent lady and a strikingly attractive tortoise were being treated in such an unjust way.

"I don't know, but the law's the law, and you're under arrest," the officer had snarled with a stock reply, before slamming shut the doors and off we went to the jailhouse.

I never imagined then, as we both sat in a cold cell awaiting our lawyer, that our actions that afternoon would spark a seminal civil rights movement that would echo throughout history. I guess it goes to show, you just never know what the day might throw at you once you get out of bed in the morning...unless you're my uncle Brian, in which case it's most likely cactus husks and empty beer bottles.

"So, now what?" Rosa had asked, whispering between the bars that separated us in the local jail as we sat amongst the usual drunks, car thieves and corrupt politicians.

"I don't know," I'd said. "But I imagine we might miss supper."

"Well, don't we get a phone call or something?"

"Yes. Don't worry," I'd responded with a kind smile. "The pizza won't be long,"

Rosa had ignored my attempts at humour and began circling the airless cell like a caged animal, a look of distraction held on her face. "However did we end up here? Thrown in the state pen for refusing to give up a bus seat? A goddamn bus seat!" she shook her head, throwing a look my way. "I mean, really, who would do such a thing?"

"Humans." I said.

On hearing of our public arrest, the local community had gathered in the church hall later that evening with a tumult of anger, deciding amongst themselves that they were no longer going to accept their place in the social pecking order. Fed up of being under the jackboot of a prejudiced legal (and transport) system, they vowed to fight back in the best way they could. When the baseball bats, Molotov cocktails and rioting didn't have the desired effect, a boycott of the buses was hastily organised instead. The proud commonality of Montgomery had decided to vote with their feet, refusing to ride the bus to work even in the foulest of weather. Our unshakeable noncompliance to stand up on public transport had meant we'd finally stood up to the authorities and their out-dated convictions. The question now, was would the world listen?

In the face of controversy and with growing political pressure, we were granted bail later that evening. As we strode out of the county jail, blinking into the dying sunlight with our heads held high, we were hailed as heroes of a new era by a sea of paparazzi flash-pops and the wriggling mass of deafening demonstrators who'd been awaiting our release with placards and homemade handbills plastered with citations. A gleeful tear came to my eye right then, because without wanting to bang my own bongo, I had sparked a revolution that would in time, inspire millions.

Once the Montgomery Advertiser had picked up on our story the news began to go 1950s viral. In no time, our courageous actions were making national headlines as far away as the east coast, and similar protests soon began to spring up across the whole of America as our ideals gathered momentum. Things kind of started to snowball thereafter, and like most things, I wasn't sure where it was heading.

People of every colour and creed began to march in unison; from the mountains of Montana to the swamplands of Louisiana, even out across the Bible Belts and beyond for our cause against the intolerants. All of this colossal achievement managed without a single tweet posted or social campaign seeded. Just because our skin was of a different colour to theirs, it didn't mean we shouldn't eat at the same restaurants, drink from the same water fountains, or sit on the same bus seats as everyone else. Amen.

"All I was doing, was trying to get home from work," Rosa had told the gaggle of paparazzi congregated on the steps of the courtroom that day. "Our mistreatment was just not right, and I was tired of it,"

Never one for limelight, I still felt it my duty to elaborate on our plight so I grabbed a directional microphone with reluctant claws. "This kind of inertia is unacceptable," I'd proclaimed to the hard-bitten pressgang with impassioned words. "Nobody else was going to do anything about it, so I did."

Disappointingly, the shutterbugs seemed more interesting in getting a shot of Rosa for their front page than of hearing the assumptions of an old reptilian pioneer like myself wading into the debate. Evidently, wrinkles don't shift newspapers and my words would never make it to print, but on the upside, without the custom of black people and green reptiles travelling on their buses the transport system remained virtually deserted, the economic distress alone making it impossible for the authorities not to sit up and listen to our demands for equality. It took a good while and at times it felt as fruitless as throwing rocks at the moon, but after 381 days of demonstrations and empty seats, President Eisenhower (1890-1961) could no longer ignore the events that had gone down in Montgomery, Alabama.

"Stand for something, or you will fall for anything," I explained to Rosa one afternoon over milkshake at Kress' Lunch Counter. It was my treat. "Todays mighty oak is yesterdays nut that held its ground."

"I'll remember that," she'd said with a courteous smile and a slurp, but of course she did more than that. She later stole my line and passed it off as her own.

Begrudgingly, the then-President had pushed through legislation that created a civil rights decree meaning an end to all apartheid on buses across America. We'd managed to ignite a revolution that day, and it's something I wish I'd done more often in life, even if the history books have a tendency to scratch certain names from the credits list. I guess that's one of the reasons I've written my own history book, just to put the record straight. At the risk of sounding repetitious, in these new egalitarian times that I'd helped shape through lobbying for non-segregation, the world was now free to sit wherever it liked on a bus, regardless of their colour. Not bad for an old tortoise with an inflamed prostate, flatulence issues and failing eyesight. Wouldn't you agree?

Rosa Parks star would rise too of course. She went on to become a willing poster girl and role model for racial equality and change universally. Her (though heavily censored) story would forever be used to highlight oppression and wrongful asperity across the globe, her account of that day retold in classrooms near and far to educate one generation to the next. Despite the sour-sweet matter of not mentioning me once in the years that have followed, I must stress this message of human acceptance can only be a good thing for society against the ugly spectre of racism.

"We did it Jonathan," Rosa had announced to me that day, before she'd buttoned up her duffle coat and sped off in a flurry of black curls and camera clicks to attend another photo shoot for Housekeeping Weekly. "We only went and bloody did it."

"I certainly did, didn't I," I smiled at this mother of modern freedom as she headed out of the door in a squall and a scramble. "I certainly did."

The fight for racial equality across the world still rages on as I write, and I guess waiting for change can sometimes feel a bit like waiting for a bus. Maybe one day, we'll all live in a pellucid world of peace and perfect harmony. One in which skin colour is no longer seen as a stigma or social barrier and where fellow humans can treat one another with nobleness and respect. I shan't hold my breath though, especially when you look at your track record. Speaking of which…

CHAPTER FIVE

I knew Adolf Hitler was trouble the moment I'd laid eyes on him in 1892. Not for the first time in my life I was doing time behind bars when one late August afternoon, the dictatorial overlord decided to pay me a visit at the local zoo. Granted, he was still a toddler at the time and didn't sport his trademark moustache or signature side parting, but even then his curious manner and shuffling blue eyes left me on edge. That being said, unless you count pulling faces at the monkeys as an act of pure evil, he seemed just like any normal kid. There wasn't the slightest hint of the cataclysm to come.

That time-faded summer still shines bright in my memory, because although I've always been implacably against the idea of animal prison in principle, curiously I'd found myself serving as an inmate at Schonbrunn zoo, a sprawling menagerie that sat predominantly on the outskirts of the capital; Vienna. This came about after I'd foolishly agreed to a prearranged blind date of sorts. It was a rendezvous that would involve me partaking in a first-stage breeding programme with one of the zoo's more promiscuous tortoises called Georgina, who'd described herself as an attractive and outgoing reptile with a passion for the classics and a *GSOH*. I was all for protecting our flagship species for future generations, but in reality, judging by her baggy throat sack and tendency to forget names, I suspect she'd been quite creative about her age when filling out the application form.

Now, you might suggest this kind of harlotry sounds like easy money for a tortoise of my pedigree, but I would soon discover that being prompted into position by gloved hands and forced to mate before a live audience wasn't really my thing. It's far more exhausting than it sounds, especially at retirement age. I daresay it was a sorry sight to behold as I clambered around upon her slippery shell in the name of conservation, unable to maintain a steady grip whilst she rolled her ancient eyes in disappointment and lit up a post-coital cigarette with resentment. And just to add further insult to my prowess, the squeals tortoises are known to make whilst in the throws of passion are downright humiliating as many Internet meme will reveal, though I beg you not to go searching for them.

Little Hitler loved the zoo however, and one lazy afternoon decked out in the vibrant colours of summer, our paths would first cross. I'd often seen him and his younger sister Paula visiting on occasion, stumbling around on unsteady feet, nibbling rice cakes and talking childish gibberish (no surprise there) as they gazed in awe at all the exotic animals whose original home was far removed from their own slab grey country. But on this remarkably pleasant day, we were to finally meet face to face as he pressed his snotty nose up to the glass of my enclosure, raised his arm, and waved at me with his little infant claw.

I've never been a supporter of captivity as you'll later discover, but this particular zoo was one of the nicer places for a four-legged gigolo such as I to ply ones trade. This being the case, on quieter days -when I'd skip my carnal duties by faking a headache- I helped the impoverished keepers earn a few extra deutschmarks by toeing the line as they invited giddy children to enter the enclosures to pet and feed the animals (though not the lions obviously). And that day the future Führer, in his dribble-stained cardigan and schoolboy shorts, had entered mine clutching a handful of lettuce leaves and wearing a dimpled smile that could warm places the sun would never reach. I've since discovered that this angelic act had been nothing more than a guileful ruse, but at the time I was completely taken in.

Everything had seemed perfectly normal that clement afternoon as the infant Adolf fed me the greens and stroked my beak in an awkward display of tenderness before, with the aid of one of the keepers, he climbed upon my back for a little ride. I was fine with this. It was a routine I'd carried out a hundred times before so nothing seemed untoward as I began a gentle lap of my patch, drinking in the summertide scenery whilst the swallows circled freely in the corn-flower blue skies above. I took it easy, stuck to the paths, and never once exceeded the speed limit.

"Everything ok up there?" I'd asked the little mite as we passed the zebra enclosure, about halfway around my regular route.

"Nein, nein, nein," he'd replied in a lively manner, which in German means yes if I'm not mistaken. Over the years I've done my ample share of globetrotting, from wandering the Grand Trunk Road of the Indian subcontinent, trekking the Darien Gap in South America and even exploring the towering majesty of Birmingham's Bullring, so I pride myself on being fluent in many diverse languages and patois, especially Austro-Bavarian. "Nein, nein, nein."

"That's splendid," I'd smiled, nibbling on a few dandelion heads as I marvelled once more at the birds above as they circled in their eternal holding pattern.

"Hilfe. Hilfe," he'd yelped again in native tongue, his little corned beef coloured legs swinging eagerly back and forth. I presumed this joyous outburst meant he was appreciating the bounties of nature, but I must confess I was getting annoyed with the constant distractions. Seconds later however, as I rounded the grassy bend and waved at the monkeys who seemed to be waving back frantically, hell decided to slip its leash and swiftly broke loose without even the slightest of warning.

"Muuuuuuttttteeeeeeerrrrrrrrrrrrrrr," shrieked the strippling upon my back as he cried out for his mother in what can only be described as a chillingly tyrannical tone. I stopped dead in my tracks, a pool of dark crimson now coagulating at my claws, just as the child slipped listlessly from my shell. The monkeys covered their eyes in horror as the boy clutched at his crotch with sticky little fingers, and in that moment, as the young fellow let out another bone-chilling scream, my hyper-sensitive animal instinct told me something must have gone terribly wrong.

"What have you done, you animal?" screamed Mrs Hitler as she came racing towards me, her face a blur of ferocity as rage sprang to life behind frost bitten blue eyes. "What have you done to my poor little baby?"

"Eh?" I'd replied with a bewildered look spread upon my tank green face. "I haven't done anything." She barged straight past me and scooped up the limp infant in her arms, glaring at me with her features arranged in a look of undiluted loathing. I had no idea what she was yelling about despite my being well versed in the Germanic dialect, but there did seem to be rather a lot of icky blood coming from somewhere. I quickly checked myself over thoroughly but could detect no obvious signs of injury, much to my immediate relief.

"He's bitten my boy!" the stricken mother had yelled at the peak of her voice, and in no time, the keepers came rushing into my enclosure with dinners down their fronts and guns in their hands. In only a matter of minutes, the situation had escalated from a peaceful stroll through the countryside into an armoured stand off as a barrage of zoo staff with searching eyes surrounded me, their rifles tilted like *LAPD* and all aimed squarely at my head.

"That despicable animal has mutilated my poor little Adolf,"

"I did no such thing, don't shoot," I'd pleaded as I held up my claws against the greenery, but my appeals were quite ineffective and they shot me anyway. As a quiver of sedative darts whistled through the air, I heard the keepers congratulating themselves on such an impressive aim as my vision became soaked in shadows and my limbs grew heavy and slow, even for a tortoise of my advanced years.

Unfortunately for little Adolf, on disembarking from my shell that day it transpired he'd somehow managed to catch his 'unmentionables' in the awkward gap between my plastron and nuchal shield. I still maintain it was a freak accident, a one in a million chance you might say, but the fact he'd injured himself whilst on my watch was regrettable, and still is. Throughout my life, I've always adopted a chummy disposition and I'm not a dangerous animal as I'm sure you'll agree, but mummy and daddy Hitler hadn't seen it that way at the time. I could see where little 'H' would later inherit his nasty temper.

"That vicious beast should be put down immediately!" roared Mr Hitler in an accusatory way, jabbing his finger towards my yawning face whilst someone raced to find an ice pack and call an ambulance. He crammed the remainder of his hot dog into his mouth before continuing his tirade. "We will sue this place for every single last penny, just mark my words."

"It wasn't my fault," I'd insisted like a drunken guttersnipe, before my faculties finally gave way and my wrinkled knees buckled beneath me. As the heavy sedative pumped its way around my cold-blood stream, my movements became as sluggish as a wasp in winter as my body entered its hypnopompic state. I remember hearing the distant wailings of sirens and the squall of tempers rising before I hit the deck in a heap of lettuce leaves and unconsciousness. It was the height of summer, months until hibernation season, but I slept for nearly a solid fortnight afterwards.

The zoo almost lost its licence over the incident, but I suppose little Adolf lost a lot more that regretful (though accidental) day. No word of a lie, this was how the future Führer came to be unattached from his right testicle. It wasn't blown off during The First Battle of the Somme (1916) and nor was it an urban myth or birth defect as some would have you believe. It was simply an accident, though unfortunately, the families' disdain of me didn't lessen over time. The Hitler's put in an official complaint about my unstable temperament, which meant because of my infraction of the zoo's rules I was labelled a 'problem' animal despite my appeals for mediation. Before I'd had the chance for any goodbyes I was swiftly relieved of my Don Juan duties, packed up in a box of straw, and transferred overseas. In truth, the breeding programme had been nothing short of disaster and I was glad of the rest, but I was sad that my character had been tarnished so unfairly by an unintended maiming. I wouldn't see

Hitler again until many years later, by which time he was all grown up and invading France.

In the years between, I discovered he'd taken up a keen interest in painting as a teenager, but on failing the entrance exam at the Academy of Fine Arts in Vienna twice (1907 and 1908), he'd developed a mean temper and an interest in the right wing workings of Karl Luger rather than the usual; girls, snooker halls and heavy metal music. Although it was said he did have some capability at the canvas, it was agreed his human figures lacked character or empathy which with prior knowledge is no real surprise. Perhaps if the academy had shown a bit more leniency towards his talents then history could have been saved a whole lot of heartache, but I guess that's the art crowd for you.

As it was, Hitler found himself reduced to eating from soup kitchens and sleeping on park benches as he wandered the winding streets of Vienna as a homeless vagabond, forced to sell his under-par watercolour paintings for pennies just to get by. With no money in his pockets, and no pockets because he didn't own a winter-coat, Adolf Hitler soon renounced his Austrian citizenship, had grown a daft toothbrush moustache, and over the next few years, would set out on a new career path that would make a job with HMRC seem charitable in comparison.

As a young Hitler rose through the ranks of the Nazi Party to become its leader, I'm sorry to say that the arrogance of youth had given way to the bloodlust of adulthood. With his head filled of homicidal tendencies and territorial expansion, that stainless child I'd once carried upon my back in blazing sunshine had now found another outlet for his anger, and he began mapping out his ungodly uprising from the serenity of a clandestine base in the foothills of the Bavarian Alps. This wasn't mere sabre-rattling, the man was completely nuts even if his own were not, and under the illusion of genetic superiority this lunatic would quickly turn Germany into a war state by smashing the nations democratic institutions, promoting genocide, and taking over the world. I sincerely hope the Vienna School of Arts is reading this.

Like most sequels, World War II (1939-1945) was even more costly, bloody, and violent than its predecessor. With bigger tanks, noisier explosions and more blood spill than in the original, the *Wehrmacth* would advance into Europe and rain death from the skies, sinking its ships in ruby coloured seas and ethnically cleansing anyone not of Aryan race. Clearly disillusioned, this rabid *'monorchid'* (the correct term for an owner of one testicle, so I'm told) firmly believed he could make his fatherland a world power once more as he pulled the strings from his Wolfs Lair headquarters in the forests of Masuria, but I often wonder what could have become of him had he not decided to climb upon my shell that day at the zoo? Perhaps he would have turned out to be a more relaxed, well-rounded individual? Could he have become a youth pastor or even followed a career as a correctional psychologist maybe? I suppose we'll never really know, but despite my feeling a sense of blameless guilt for what came to pass, you can't live your life by 'what ifs' forever now, can you?

I must say though, in all my time crawling this earth never have I met a race so eager to inflict suffering upon one another with such venom and revulsion as the eternal bin-fire, that is humanity. I'm sorry that- if as a biped reading this- you are offended by my bluntness, but peace seems only a mere interval between the main-attraction of war for you uprights. I'm just a simple creature of the Cryptodira suborder, but I still maintain that men and fighting go together rather like mosquitos and malaria. As my experiences have so far shown me, bickering is what human primates seem to do best besides turning the seas into plastic soup and conversing on the weather.

Hundreds, if not thousands of books and movies have already been written about the shameful atrocities of WW2, so I don't intend this memoir to be one of them. It's not my place to constantly remind you of the dark evil of which man is capable, or to finger wag like a wiper blade at your misdemeanours. I'm not whitewashing here either, it's just that once you start bringing the mood down with stories of genocide and the like, it's hard to win back the room. That's why I don't endeavour to needle these old wounds or give Adolf Hitler anymore column inches here than are obligatory, just so we're clear. Instead, before we move on to more uplifting episodes of my life, I'd like to enlighten you on a lesser-known act of heroism during the war. An act that I may have played a little part in, and here is exactly how it went.

During the conflict, whilst the Germans occupied France in 1940, I was approached one war-torn afternoon by my dear friend Pierre-Jules Boulanger (then chairman of the Citroën Motor Company), who was beside himself after being forced by Hitler and his camarilla, to build a fleet of trucks and jeeps to be used in his campaign against the allies.

"I just can't do it Jonathan," he'd sobbed in anguish, and in French. "But what other choice have I got?"

"I know, right," I sympathised.

He managed a weak smile. "Please Jonathan. You have to help me. I don't know what else to do."

I gave his predicament five seconds of thought because I was on my dinner break. "Then go ahead and build their trucks," I'd said indifferently, poking at the rations in my mess tin. "I really don't see the big deal, Pierre."

"What?" he'd replied, unable to keep the angry tremor from his Gallic voice as he stood, surprised, in his grease monkey overalls.

"Just give them whatever they want," I'd shrugged.

"But I will be a traitor to my country. I'll be tarred and feathered for sure."

"Not necessarily," I offered, looking up from the gloop that passed for war cabbage back then. "One man's fish is another man's poisson, after all." I winked, but he didn't look amused, far from it in fact.

"You're seriously suggesting I should sympathise with their plight, like I'm flipping Edward VIII or something?"

"That's not what I meant," I replied.

'Then I'm afraid I don't follow…"

"Build Hitler his trucks," I'd whispered, as I grabbed his arm and took him aside. "Even paint them panzer gray if he insists. But before they are built; inform your engineers to set the oil level indicators -on the dipsticks- just a little higher than usual during manufacturing, you know, to suggest the trucks contain more oil than they actually do."

"Eh?" he said.

"Set the oil level indicators -on the dipsticks- just a little higher than usual during manufacturing." I repeated, slower this time.

"Eh?" he'd repeated once more. Although he'd been a First World War reconnaissance photographer with the French Air Force, he certainly took his time in seeing the bigger picture on this occasion. "Sorry Jonathan, I still don't follow."

I sighed impatiently, already worried they'd be no time left for dessert before I returned to my post "This is how we can do our bit to defeat Hitler. Just trust me, ok?" I kissed him on both cheeks, as is the Continental way with the French, before bidding him a pleasant afternoon and a safe farewell.

Pierre was confused, but to his endless credit he did as I asked. He returned to the factory and told his workers to alter all the oil gauges on the production line to my specifications. A week later, when the Nazis marched into town to collect their new convoy of vehicles from the dealership, they hadn't suspected a thing as they drove off the forecourt with satisfied grins upon their ignoble faces. Within a matter of days though, German mechanics began scratching their heads and wondering why the newly acquired trucks continually overheated and broke down without any indication or warning. In many cases, leaving hundreds of hungry troops stranded on the hard shoulder in the middle of nowhere with engine seizure and a long walk home, even though the oil indicator told them they still had plenty left in the tank. Not only did this masterstroke cause huge tailbacks and lower morale through the core of the German army, I also believe it played a climatic key part in what was finally to come.

On 7th March 1945, the guns fell silent, the brandy was spilt and the skies returned to nature once more. As German defences crumbled and once loyal commanders now abandoned their posts, Soviet allies were closing in on the Nazi oppressor like a pipe vice and had made their way towards a secret bunker near the Reich Chancellery, hoping to put an end to Hitler and his agenda once and for all. Ultimately, inside that cramped concrete cube beneath the earth, the demonic overlord had beaten them to the punch. Rather than face the consequences of his appalling actions, he'd scribbled a will, swallowed down a cyanide capsule and then shot himself in the skull with his own service pistol.

The murderous dictator had claimed himself as his final victim, leaving in his wake a palisade of innocent bones from both sides, and the promise from world leaders that something as barbarous and inhumane as this should never be allowed to happen again. With Hitler dead, the war, instigated by the mundane flaws of man, was over. The healing process was just getting started.

At the Nuremberg trials in the long months that followed, I watched on with revulsion from the public gallery as Hitler's tyrannical regime was disgraced and dismantled for all to see. His once beloved fatherland was carved up and shared out between the allies like cake at a birthday party, but there was little cause for celebration. The revoltingness of war had taken its toll on everyone and the devastation left in its wake was bruising and immeasurable. The world would lick its wounds and the thin veneer of civilization would slowly be rebuilt, together with high concrete brick walls that would stretch the length of Germany and divide its nation. But the threat of war forever bubbled below, poking at waiflike peace as if invariably spoiling for another fight. Believe me when I tell you that the days after the war were almost as bleak as those spent whilst in the thick of battle. With rationing and grave mistrust at every corner, it would take decades for peace and normality to return to the globe, if it ever truly has.

I was asked a question years later by the very talented actor David Hasselhoff as we stood atop of the Berlin Wall, just before it was torn down in 1989 to finally unify Germany once more. If, had I known who that little child Adolf would go on to become, would I have attempted to kill him that day he'd entered my enclosure, doing the world a favour and sparing everyone from the misery and massacre that he'd go on to create?

I'd thought long and hard about this for a few minutes. It was a good question and deserved a thoughtful answer. For years guilty thoughts had jabbed at my conscience like accusing fingers on this very subject, but finally I replied. "No I would not. I don't believe anyone is born of evil. If I would have known what that child would have gone on to do, I'd have taught him right from wrong and steered his life in the right direction."

The Hoff had looked at me blankly. Blaming World War II on bad parenting wasn't the reply he was expecting.

"However," I'd added pithily, despite my being vegetarian. "I would have made sure to chew the little clackers fingers and toes off too."

'Never thinks that war, no matter how necessary, nor how justified, is not a crime.' Ernest Hemingway once memorably remarked, and although I've never really seen eye to eye with the bear-hunting novelist, I have to agree he has a compelling point. An estimated seventy-five million people tragically lost their lives in the atrocities of World War II, all started by a man who was sloppy with a paintbrush and short in the trouser department. The scars Hitler left on the world remain to this day. As do his paintings, which now fetch thousands at auction. I still don't like them.

I was right.

The drizzle outside begins to fall, and I watch with casual curiosity as the silvery droplets trickle and twist down the tall fenestra windows of the restaurant as if alive. The pattern they leave behind distorts the view below of the Thames, the river I'd often pillaged in my youth. I curse myself for not bringing along an umbrella.

"They say a storms on the way," remarks my dining partner as he chases the last of the broccoli stems around his plate with an eager fork before popping them into his mouth. Only at that point does he decide to speak again.

"I bam babeeve boo bot bickonbs ."

"What?" I ask.

He swallows. "I can't believe you met Dickens."

"So you don't believe me?" I snap.

"Just a figure of speech," he replies with hands held up defensively. *"You do seem to know a lot of people on bank notes is all I'm saying. But he sounds awesome."*

"He was." I reply fondly, as I watch him continue to chew his food at volume.

"Darwin not so much though," he says through another mouthful of greens. *"He sounds like a total ass, and I'm sorry to hear about your family."*

"It was all such a long time ago now, but thank you and yes he was."

The drizzle is turning heavier now and I'm thankful to be indoors as I watch one of the waiters scrambling to bring in the chairs and tablecloths from outside as he battles against the rain. There had been no mention of a storm on the weather report that morning as I recall.

"So, did you really get put in the slammer for sitting on a bus?" enquires my guest keenly, as he swats away another fly that must have been attracted to his heavily lacquered hair. Jet-black hair, scraped tightly over a shining forehead to make

him appear as if a mix between Dracula and a young Midge Ure in his Ultravox days.

"Indeed I did," I explain, as I grab a cocktail stick and attempt to pick remnants of lettuce from my toothless gums. I hear a rumble of thunder far off in the distance and the airy room suddenly grows overcast, even though my company keeps up the bright smiles and dark glasses.

"And you castrated a child?" he asks with a snake-oil salesman's smile as I watch a fly take rest on the lapel of his slick suit. I say nothing as the waiter approaches starchily at my side to pour more water, but as he refills our glasses my nostrils stand to attention like little soldiers and my senses are sparked by a familiar putrid stench that overcomes me.

"You ok?" my guest asks with a suspicious grin.

I stare at the filthy brown liquid offered up as refreshment, which now swims in my glass like dirty toilet water. The sickly stink reminds me of an event in my life that I haven't thought about in a very, very long time. I've heard it said, that the sense of smell is the next best thing to a time machine, but I'm in no mood for sentiment as I glare at the water waiter in disbelief.

"What on earth are you doing young man?" I fluster with a shake off my head. "We can't possibly drink that filth?"

"Oh. Would you prefer sparkling sir?" the waiter replies with a concerned raise of his handsome eyebrow.

I'm about ready to kick off (especially at these prices), when momentarily I glance back at our glasses and notice they are now brimming with the purest, gin-clear Scottish Mountain water money can possibly buy. I can feel my ancient face crumbling in confusion, like an old dissipated relic, as I try to register my thoughts. What on earth just happened?

"Don't worry about my friend, we're good with the still," my dining partner reassures the waiter with a light snigger, as he waives him away.

As I warily pick up the glass and take a cursory sip, I'm beginning to wonder if perhaps I need to start getting more sleep, and that maybe we should have gone to Magic China for the all-day buffet instead.

CHAPTER SIX

London in the 1850s was still a cramped, unsavoury hovel and the stink of infection from the Thames forever lingered in the sullied air, meaning consumption and pleurisy were never far from lung-shot. On the plus side there were far fewer fried chicken shops along the high street and obesity then was reserved for the rich and influential, not just families wearing breakfast vests and tracksuits.

As rickety streetcars clattered by throwing up a foul dust and nomadic livestock competed with vermin in the streets for scraps, the air held thick with profanity and racial tensions. London wouldn't become electrified until the 1880s, but as the surrendering sun threw up shadows to reveal the cities dark underbelly I saw it's true face, and unlike mine it wasn't so classically handsome. The sprawl of the inner city had become a noxious place, packed tight with gambling dens and violent saloons where murder was looked upon with sullen indifference, social etiquette was swiftly dismantled, and even the children got drunk. As I'd crawl the night-soiled streets, stepping over dead horses denied the decencies of death, it seems obvious to me now that the capital was a squalid axis of disease casually checking its watch, drumming it's fingers, and waiting patiently for a pandemic to arrive.

Autumn was in its final throws and old man winter was planning a big entrance as the bitter wind niggled and nipped as I strolled the cities breezy thoroughfares. It was a grey and joyless afternoon that seemed a million miles away from the cheery Galapagos with its predictable abundance of glossy palm trees and sunny disposition, and as I struggled on with my beak chattering in the breeze I could feel the satisfying crackle of frost underfoot as I picked up my pace, already late for my appointment.

I'd developed a stubborn sniffle that I was convinced was something more sinister (well you do, don't you), so had decided to pay a visit to the local surgery that very afternoon. My routine doctor had been called away on some urgent business or other, so when finally I'd arrived at the small practice on Harley Street that was flanked either side between a caretakers parlour and a gunsmiths, the locum had gone about a cursory examination of my sodden beak with piggy eyes hidden behind half moon glasses. He stroked his greying beard with an air of authority as he prodded and poked, an authority almost as heavy as the vinous drinking fumes I could smell on his disagreeable breath.

"So, how long have you been feeling ill?" he'd enquired through thin lips, almost knocking me flat despite my beak not being in the finest of fettle.

"I started feeling a bit peaky last Tuesday after supper with Edward Elgar, when ...*Achoooooo!...Achooooooo!*"

Before I could explain any further, the doctor had risen from his chair with apparent concern and was squinting at me unevenly as he stumbled awkwardly across the filthy curvilinear carpet. "You do look a bit green."

"That's because I'm a tortoise," I shrugged, watching as he bounced off the mildew stained walls in his white surgical shirt, disappearing for a few noisy moments behind a mountain of files before returning with my medical notes clutched in unsteady hands. He blew away a layer of dust and pretended to study them, then simply gave up and cleared his throat to speak.

" Mr Shelton," he'd declared solemnly as I braced myself for his prescription of damnation, "I'm afraid you might have a case of Autosomal Dominant Compelling Helio-Ophthalmic Outburst Syndrome."

I certainly didn't like the sound of this, but I was impressed that in his current state he could say it. "And is it fatal?" I asked, now quite concerned.

"Do you shave with a cut throat?"

"Of course not. I'm a tortoise. Reptiles don't posses hair."

"Then you should be fine," he garbled, rummaging through his bag to retrieve something resembling a murder weapon. "You just have a common sneeze, but let me give you a check-up, just to be sure at your age."

"Achoooooo!" I replied.

The doctor had tapped at my shell with a toffee hammer the size of a small child and listened to my wheezing chest with his filthy ear, before taking all of six seconds to reach his professional prognosis. "Sniffing this mouldy old sock thrice daily should cure it," he'd said with a hiccup, as he began the fumbling task of unrolling one of his own crusty foot garments to hand to me as a prescription. "You'll feel right as rain in no time,"

"Say again?" I'd tittered in a pitch higher than I would have liked. Surely he was pulling my tail about snorting second hand socks to feel better? Or perhaps he'd had more to drink than I thought? Nowadays medical experts would be struck off for boozing on the job, but in those dispiriting times surgeons were so half cut that it wasn't unusual for them to turn up for theatre and amputate the wrong limb during surgery because they were either seeing double, or drinking one.

"Trust me, I'm a doctor," the none-too bright man had slurred with an air of self -importance before lighting up a cigarette to relieve his asthma. "Now if you could just remove your shell and bend over…"

I removed myself from the surgery that afternoon, about as fast as a tortoise with a suspected heavy chest infection possibly could. Since that day, I've always been vigilant of the medical fraternity and the warped beliefs they hold dear. This kind of guidance however, I'm sorry to say, was customary in Victorian Britain when modern medicines like antibiotics, ibuprofen or even the humble Fisherman's Friend had yet to be discovered. Instead, doctors had placed their trust in the ludicrous four humours theory (blood, phlegm, black bile and yellow bile) that they believed controlled the wellbeing and temperament of individuals. To maintain this chemical balance they considered beards to be a health benefit, relied on socks to cure colds, baked potatoes held against the ear were thought to ease an earache, and a dead mole hung around a baby's neck was a bona fide way to alleviate teething pains. No word of a lie. It was even believed that sitting inside a dead whale carcass could cure rheumatism, though luckily (for both whale and patient) there weren't many of them splashing about in the Thames at the time.

With such nonsensical presumptions, it will come as no surprise to learn the average life expectancy in those days was a measly thirty-eight years old, if you were lucky enough not to be hung for stealing fruit or flattened by a horse. These flimflammer doctors with their diabolical potions and cures were the sick ones in my opinion, and you didn't want to be falling ill whilst under their care if you could possibly help it. Miserably, a lot of two-leggers were doing just that, none more so than the very neighbours I was nestled amongst on a crowded street in the filthy heart of Soho.

Broad Street was well located for commuting, with the shops only a stone's throw away and good parking, but what the estate agent had failed to mention was that it was also a hotbed of malady. Toilets were still waiting to be invented by Thomas Crapper (with a name like that I'm sure he was bullied at school) and the Soho cobbles were awash with human droppings rather than the hipster types of today in their sand shoes and top buns. You could say the neighbourhood has changed for the worse in some respects.

There had been Cholera outbreaks in the capital previously of course, but I remember the one that cut through its main artery in the summer months of 1854 to be particularly fierce, with even the rats avoiding the place like the plague they'd once helped carry through those same streets. Despite warnings from the government to wear face coverings, stay at home and regularly wash your hands, residents of every age were either going the way of all flesh, or at the very least, becoming quite concerned that the likelihood of rising death figures would begin affecting house prices.

The usually affable working-class community were becoming increasingly spooked by this invisible menace too. Any sniffle, snuffle, or splutter was regarded with grave suspicion at the time. People would cross the street or pull blackened scarfs up to their faces at the drop of a sneeze, whilst shops would be stripped bare of their tinned bully as survivalists prepared for the impending apocalypse. Nobody knew where the disease had come from or how it was spread, and the government, despite following the science, were as clueless as anyone in trying to bring down the curve.

Cholera is a particularly cruel and humiliating disease. It lurks wherever sanitation tends not to, and the symptoms can read like something from the pages of a gory horror novel. It was referred to at the time as the 'blue death,' because people would develop sudden vomiting and diarrhoea so acute that dehydration would turn their skin a transparent blue before they met a very slow and painful end on the pot. Often, these sorry souls would be discovered the next morning with underwear around their ankles and embarrassed panic etched forever upon their lifeless eyes.

The medical fraternity had scratched their heads (and whiskey-scented beards no doubt) as to why so many people were falling ill in such close proximity to one another on Broad Street, but they remained baffled. Many believed this deadly sickliness was an airborne disease or was carried by rodents, but even then I'd harboured doubts. I found it unfathomable that whilst my friends and neighbours were turning a sallow sunken-eyed blue from infection, just a few streets away the people were positively rosy cheeked in comparison, skipping disease free along the cobblestone. I must admit it was a head scratcher. How could it be that within the space of just a few streets the illness hadn't spread? And why was the R number only skyrocketing expediently amongst the impoverished lower classes?

The answer my friends, came quite by accident one day as I pumped water for my monthly bath from the communal well at the top of Broad Street when, without warning, the rusted handle had snapped clean off in my claw. I had no intention of reporting it to the authorities and was about to hide the evidence I held, when at that moment, John Snow the neighbour came frolicking down the street swinging his bucket to fill. He'd seen me with the handle in my claw before I'd had the chance to dispose of it and now I'd been rumbled. Worst still, although he was a doctor by profession and had taken the Hippocratic oath, I knew John had a mouth on him.

"What you got there then?" he'd asked, his searching eyes as sharp as claymores as they fell upon the broken well, before immediately, they flicked back to my guilty green face. I had to think fast.

"Nothing," I'd stuttered, holding my claws behind my back as I performed the weak diversionary tactic of pretending to notice something in the distance. It didn't work, and instead he eyed me with suspicion stamped all over his eighteenth-century face. As you may have already surmised, I've never been a great liar or fabricator of inaccuracies.

"It's the handle to the well isn't it?" he'd scoffed with asperity as he stood with disapproving hands on hips. "You've broken the well haven't you Jonathan? Nice one. So how on earth will the street get their fresh water to bathe in now?"

"It wasn't me," I'd whined, because in those seconds I could think of nothing better to say, "It was like this when I found it."

"Don't try and make a stuffed bird laugh Jonathan," the busybody doctor had leered disparagingly, revealing uneven teeth and a testing manner. "You're really suggesting that some other person vandalized the well, then put the evidence in your claw, before instantly vanishing into thin air?"

"That's about the size of it, yes,"

"Is that so?" He sounded annoyed, pressing me more hotly.

"It is so."

"So the real perpetrator has disappeared in a puff of smoke I presume?" he'd quizzed accusingly, waving his hands around like an amateur conjuror as he did so. "Swear on your life you didn't break the well Jonathan?"

"I swear," I mumbled, realising I was likely going to hell.

"Unbelievable," he huffed with a shake of his self-righteous side whiskers, before he'd muttered some expletives and stomped off to the shabby tavern on the corner to enjoy his rip-roaring social life. He really was a man of limited charms, and I knew immediately I was in big trouble. I was also in little doubt that he'd soon inform everybody in the pub of what I'd just done. The locals were already fretful of catching something deathly on the fecal streets, and although they weren't the cleanliest bunch I've had the privilege to live next door to, I knew that with tensions running high it wouldn't take much to tip them over the edge and create civil unrest.

I shuffled back to my abode and kept a low profile over the following days, hunkered down in my bedsit seeking anonymity and fearing an angry mob every time I peered out from mullion windows at the cobbles below. I became quite convinced the unwashed would be coming for me now I'd broken their well and deprived them of water. At the very least I'd expected a brick through my window or a dirty protest through the letterbox, but all I received in the post was a leaflet advising me to stay alert, control the virus and save lives. The silence was torture.

The following evening, as the gas lamps flickered into life on the street outside and exposed my home from the cover of shadows, there came the knock on the door I'd been dreading. I tried to ignore it at first, thinking it may have been a mistaken caller or perhaps a wayfaring traveller selling sponges, but the rapping on the woodwork became incessant so with a resigned breath and nervous claws, I twisted at the lock and opened it with a chirr. It was the doctor John Snow.

"I've been knocking for ages," he said.

"Sorry. I was in the bath."

"Bath? But we haven't had water for days?"

"Yeah I know. I just like sitting in the bath," I lied. He looked confused at my explanation, giving me an opportunity to inch my head further out of the door and see if he'd brought a mob along to help dish out a customary shellacking. Fortunately he hadn't.

"Listen Jonathan," he'd clucked in a jovial tone that sounded more in keeping with an invite for a few tins and a bite at a barbecue gathering. "Just thought you should know that people have stopped getting all poorly and blue, and *that*." He shuffled apologetically.

"Is that right?" I replied with a stroke of my wrinkled chin. Already I'd put two and two together in my clever green head.

"Yes. It must be a miracle," remarked the physician, offering his unwanted professional opinion.

"Or not?" I said, a trifle cryptically.

"I'm not sure I follow you Jonathan."

Without wanting to blow my own trumpet again (though I shall), I'd just made the connection that would forever change the course of history in medicine. It wasn't vermin, poor hand hygiene, or even bad air that had spread this vicious illness and killed so many eighteenth-century unfortunates. It had come from the water pumped from the well on our very own doorstep. I had not so much single-handedly, as heavy-handedly discovered the cause of Cholera. It was a waterborne disease.

"There's something in the water John," I explained.

"What? Like an eel or something?" he said.

"No, the deadly disease John. It must be coming from the water. Ever since that day I broke the handle off the well the deaths have dwindled."

"Ah…so, you admit it was you then?" he'd grinned with a satisfied glee he didn't try to disguise.

"Just think about it John," I continued, ignoring his childish recriminations. "The curve has dipped dramatically since last Wednesday, has it not?"

It was his turn to stroke his chin as he gave it some thought. "By Jove, you could be right little tortoise!" he'd squealed, agreeing it must surely be more than coincidence. "We'll leave the handle off the well for the rest of the week and keep a close eye on things, don't you think? We call it observation in the medical profession…so, fancy a pint then?"

"Sure, why not?" I'd agreed, a little taken aback, but happy to be free from the house after days of self enforced lockdown. "I'll just grab my keys."

"Splendid," he replied absently, rubbing his hands together against the cold.

"Oh, and by the way John," I'd added, as we stopped in the middle of the road to let a horse pass whilst John Snow filled the bowl of his foul pipe.

"Yes, Jonathan?" he asked, as his teeth clamped down on damp pear wood.

"Nobody likes a grass."

Cases of Cholera dropped dramatically on Broad Street in the days that followed and by the Friday, John Snow was telling anyone who cared to listen that he had discovered the source of the heinous disease and that everyone should stop drinking water pumped from the well, and instead buy him a well earned drink for saving their lives. They did more than that. They decided to name the pub after him too, which still stands on the same spot today as it did all those years ago. If you happen to be passing and can squeeze by all the media luvvies outside, you'll even be able to see the old well with it's handle still removed…or at least I hope it is.

The name John Snow would go down in the annals of history as being one of the major reasons to changes in world sanitation, fundamentally saving millions of lives by looking at how we deal with our waste and water systems. Quite high praise for someone who carried a bucket, stole my thunder, and then grassed me up to the homebody for his part. I hold no grudges though. He's been deceased for years now, so I guess we know who the ultimate winner is there. Curiously though, over the centuries I've often found humankind's appetite for the limelight to be quite bemusing, and although I get little credit for saving all those lives long ago, it's still nice to know I did the neighbourly thing.

With the discovery of modern medicines, doctors like John have come a long way in the last hundred or so years. Today, they can achieve incredible feats like creating vaccines, reattaching limbs, and even growing ears onto the back of mice, although personally, I think mice have enough ears already. The next time you have to visit the doctor to get your prostate poked, or you begin to moan about the grossly under funded NHS, this story should serve as a sobering reminder of how much worse off you could have had it in the 1800s with drunken doctors, dysentery and sock remedies. Of course the best way to avoid the white coats altogether is to eat your greens, do the Lorraine Kelly workout video religiously, and cut down on processed meat. I'm not saying you'll live as long as me, but it can't hurt.

CHAPTER SEVEN

I've always felt at home in showbiz circles, so when Orson Welles rang one evening in the autumn of 1955 and invited me to join him and a few friends for dinner at the Villa Capri, of course I accepted. I was well accustomed with high life at this stage, but I much preferred these indoor social affairs to the torturous annual celebrity golfing galas organised by the likes of Bing Crosby at the Riviera Country Club. Mostly, I should confess, because I'd regularly be thrown off the green for nibbling on the boundaries when I got a little peckish. It's often mooted that golf is a good walk spoiled, but for me it is an all-you-can eat buffet with far too many club rules and regulations. The Villa Capri, with its high-ornate ceilings and white-gloved wine waiters was certainly more up my street.

I'd first met Orson several years previous when he used to earn $25 a day dressing up as Peter Rabbit and standing in the window of a famous Chicago department store. Even then I knew he'd go on to do great things such as writing and directing Citizen Kane, starring in Touch of Evil, and providing the voice of Unicron in the 1986 animated film: Transformers The Movie, for example. I found Orson possessed clarity of vision way beyond that of the other plastic trees who'd already stuck their hands into wet cement along Hollywood Boulevard, and I was also impressed that he was something of a Ladies' man too. In fact, it wasn't at all unusual for him to take me along to social events just on a whim, to provide splendid company and to act as his wingman for the evening. I'd had an uninterrupted stream of success with the women at that point, and he'd parade me around at parties together with the white rabbit he kept in his overcoat (Orson was a big fan of magic) as he worked the room with a flourish, hoping to seduce the ladies with his quips and parlour tricks as though he were an early incarnation of the Fonz.

"We make a great team, don't you think kid?" he'd often say, despite me being over a hundred years his senior, but he had a point and I enjoyed his company nonetheless. As we'd reached the restaurants grand marbled entrance that evening, we skirted the queuing rabble (as is any celebrities given right, apparently) before ducking effortlessly beneath the velvety rope like high-fliers fuelled by sex, drugs and (in my case) rocket leaves. He was right of course, we did make a great team, and my role in this impromptu double act was to play the straight man, disarming admirers with my knowing eyes whilst Orson would attempt to charm them with his magical repertoire and sleight of hand. He was a member of the International Brotherhood of Magicians so wasn't too shabby when it came to wizardry, but on this particular night in question Orson had failed to ring ahead and the restaurant was so busy even the great man himself couldn't conjure up a table for at least an hour and a half.

"Couldn't you make an exception, dear boy?" Orson had moaned to the stolid doorman, delving into his trouser pockets that were overstuffed with dollar bills. He waved a wad beneath the nose of the bouncer as though he were a Geisha with a folding fan. "Don't you know who I am?"

"Yes Sir. You're that fat chap off of the telly." he'd replied disinterested, as Orson clicked his meaty knuckles and looked to the skies in annoyance.

The restaurant was packed tight that night, a place of grandeur and bon viveur that was renowned for filling the modified faces of the rich and famous of yesteryear. It was here, beneath the warm glow of camp chandeliers, that the glitterati would inhale Continental cigars held between manicured fingers as their voices competed with a cacophony of others in this gladiatorial arena, also known as the main dining room. Of course, that was if you were lucky enough to get a seat.

Fortunately for us, we were. A young actor by the name of James Dean had spotted Orson remonstrating with the staff and had graciously stepped in before someone got hurt, kindly inviting us to join him and his entourage at a reserved table by the window. I must say, at the time I didn't know the young man from a hole in the wall, but with angst filled blue eyes and skinny good looks I was in no doubt this man-child would go on to become a major mainstay on the bedroom walls of teenage admirers for years to come. No word of a lie.

The tenderfoot Dean instantly warmed to the gregarious Orson, who in turn seemed delighted to join the group and impart his acting wisdoms upon the young actor over pints of bourbon and a plate of calamari rings. As we pulled up our chairs to join with the Hollywood smart set, all bleached teeth and hair, I noticed one person who didn't quite fit in with the rest of the guests as he sat with a quiet dignity and arms neatly folded. His hair wasn't particularly smart and unlike the others, his teeth were far from immaculate. As you've probably guessed, he was British. Orson leaned across the table, his hulking freckled hand outstretched over the gingham tablecloth like a pink fleshy bridge, as he introduced himself in his usual mercurial manner with a tip of the frowzy straw Panama he often wore.

"I'm a huge, huge fan," Orson boomed with delight, before grabbing the dainty hand within his pithy palm. The owner, to his credit, took it admirably in his stride with a thin smile.

"And I too, am a big fan of yours," said Alec Guinness politely, before wiping his hands with a damp napkin and enquiring if anyone was having a starter, or whether we should all just skip straight to the mains.

"I think I'll go for something off the kids menu," announced the young James Dean, and in that moment I was reminded of his probity and youthfulness. As orders were placed and pockets of cordial conversations struck up around the table, Orson began his usual grandstanding of pulling rabbits from hats and plucking pennies from behind people's ears in his monopoly for table attention. Meanwhile, a gracious Alec Guinness feigned surprise and even lightly applauded the impromptu 'Orson Wells' show.

"Is he always like this?" Guinness had whispered to me from the corner of his mouth, whilst Orson was busy pretending to take his thumb on and off.

"I'm afraid so," I apologised.

The esteemed actor sighed inwardly and took a huge glug of wine before sinking into the fabric of his seat. "Who is the more foolish? The fool, or the fool that follows?"

I laughed heartily at this, wanting to give the illusion I was quite the Bohemian, until I realised he was talking about me. But before I could question his snarky swipe, James Dean had taken it upon himself to jump up onto his chair, and playing to the crowd like a circus pantaloon, he declared that he had a few tricks of his own he'd like to share. Orson had seemed a little put out that this upstart should be muscling in on his eminence, Guinness simply looked fed up, but I thought it only proper we should give the young actor our due attention. Dean seemed like a nice fellow to me (he had gotten us a table after all), and despite dressing for dinner barefoot and clad in filthy jeans worn so tight I feared he might have future fertility issues, it turns out he did have a few impressive illusions that were worthy of our profound consideration.

"Check this out, Orson," he'd squeaked excitedly, eager to please the veteran actor as he wobbled unsteadily on his chair. He reached deep inside his mouth and removed his two front teeth, much to the surprise and delight of everyone in vicinity. He smiled back at us all with a gummy grin, taking an exaggerated bow to the gallery as he did so.

"How impressive," said an unimpressed Guinness.

"How you do that?" howled a very impressed Orson, slapping the table with a plump palm and demanding to know how he'd achieved such witchcraft.

"They're false ones." James Dean explained with a wink. "I knocked them out in a motorcycle accident."

"That's the funniest thing I've seen…ever," screeched Orson, as tears rolled down his flushed face. "You look like a hillbilly at a bus station."

I'll admit it was amusing to see, but it wasn't as funny as my fat friend had made out and technically, it was dentistry, not magic. I later learned the young actor had in fact knocked out his choppers as a child after messing around on a trapeze swing in his uncle's barn, but I suppose the trick was still pretty neat all the same and his fan club need never know the truth.

As a tortoise, I've always made do with the toothless gums I was given, so it was quite refreshing to see the young actor not taking his image so seriously. Most human celebrities nowadays (and some animal ones too) really are the worst when it comes to dealings of narcissism, wouldn't you agree? Even before the emergence of scientology, I've found household names to be a superficial and detestable lot. As I'd looked around at the other tables that evening, their Botox foreheads shining and their teeth gleaming as white as fresh photocopying paper, I remember contemplating why I even bothered to entertain such a shallow social circle. Then in that very moment my complementary mint julep arrived, the thought escaping the cage of my mind like an unencumbered canary as I sat back to enjoy more smoke and mirrors provided by the fresh-faced actor.

Dean slotted the fake teeth back into his handsome face, took another slurp of Chateauneuf-du-Pape, and prepared us for his next performance. One that would involve him placing an unlit cigarette and a fresh match into his mouth, before taking out a lit smoke all in the blink of an eye. It was an impressive display and

I could see Orson watching on with a cow-eyed gaze as his mouth lay wide open like a toddler tasting their first snowflake. A smatter of applause travelled around the table as I took a generous slug from my free drink and Dean took another bow.

"Show me that again," boomed Orson, almost setting alight to his suit in an attempt to try the trick himself. "Show me that again, why don't ya!"

"Oh crumbs," uttered Alec Guinness beneath his breath as he too took a large swig from his drink, followed by another. "It's going to be a long night,"

The tricks went on for quite some time that evening to be fair, until thankfully, the food arrived at our table and a pint of scotch and two rare beefsteaks were plomped, ready in position, before Orson's considerable gut. The doctors were always warning him about the sticky sludge that bottlenecked in his veins, and in turn, he always ignored them. "So anyway, how's business kid?" he'd asked the young actor from behind a thick plume of cigar smoke.

"Funny you should ask," winked a gallant Dean, as he clambered down from his chair and popped a chicken nugget into his grinning mouth. "Being a good actor isn't easy. Being a man is even harder. I want to be both before I'm done. That's why I've just signed up for a new movie."

"Really?" said Guinness, looking up from his lettuce with disdain. "Another of those preposterous space capers, or a pouting period drama no doubt?"

"Actually, it's a biopic called *Somebody Up There Likes Me*."

"I see," replied the thespian, a tinge of envy evident in his tone.

"Somebody Up There Likes Me?" mused Orson, sucking in his sizable lips as he gave it some consideration whilst he stroked an impressive collection of chins. "Well I don't know about that kid, but I guess you're not dead yet, so you must be doing something right, right?"

He extinguished his cigar and tucked the napkin into his wide neck with a chuckle before getting to work on his supper plate as the rest of the table were forced to endure the sound of his undying devotion to food. But the repulsive cheek sloshing and lip smacking wasn't what had bothered me in that moment from across the table. What disturbed me most were those choice words he'd spoken, the ones that could turn sugar sour, the ones about not being dead *yet*. Those words still send a shudder right down my tail, and as banal conversation struck up around the table once more, I half listened without taking in a thing.

I attempted to shake the nagging thoughts of looming misfortune resolutely from my mind. It was a road I certainly hoped wouldn't rise up and meet anyone soon, and besides, dark ponderings like that do tend to put a bit of a dampener on dessert and are a definite vibe killer. Perhaps I should have listened more carefully to my instincts right then, but in my infinite wisdom I simply swiped them aside with a dismissive claw, the unease I felt in my marrow begrudgingly taking a backseat to my ignorance.

After an enjoyable yet pricey meal, Dean had insisted on ordering more wine for the table as he began to brag of his many hobbies that included bullfighting (points deducted there), watercolour painting and racing fast cars. The one thing he was keen to show off more than anything that evening sat outside in the parking lot.

"How fast does it go?" Orson had asked as we made our way out into the chilly night as a quartet, all gathered around the brand new sports car bathed in the saffron miasma of the streetlights.

"One hundred and fifty miles an hour," Dean announced proudly, his breath dancing in the cold air as he stroked the bonnet of the silver 550 Porsche Spyder with the gentle caress of a lover.

"Wow. She's a beaut," cooed Orson, who, like most men knew little about cars but pretended to all the same. In fact, at that time he'd travelled most places around the city in a rented ambulance so he could be guaranteed to get to his appointments on time. That was just the type of guy he was.

"Have you driven it?" Alec Guinness asked, his face growing ashen.

"No, it's just arrived." Dean had replied.

"Whatever you do, don't drive that car. That car is sinister." Guinness warned, taking a hesitant step back.

"What?" the boy Dean, had asked.

"Does it have that new car smell?" I interjected, trying to lighten the mood that had taken a sudden dark twist, but Dean wasn't in the mood for listening. Instead, he'd look at Guiness.

"What you mean, sinister?" he demanded with actorish swagger as he ran a smooth hand through his perfect hair.

"Don't drive that car," Guinness repeated without a hint of humour.

"Don't worry," Dean shot back. "When I'm on the highway I'm always extra cautious,"

"If you get in that car you will be dead in a week's time."

Dean had waved away this comment and Orson and I heartily laughed.

A week later we weren't laughing.

CHAPTER EIGHT

"Bllllaaaaarrrrrgggggggggguuuuggghhhhh."

I think that's the distressing sound that escaped me on the 17th of December 1903, as a green vileness left my mouth and landed in my lap, but I'm now realising it's a quite difficult noise to articulate, especially on the page.

Perhaps it was more of a: *"Yerrrcccchhhhhuuugghhhh?"*

Either way, it's not a pleasurable experience, sitting covered in ones own regurgitated breakfast whilst flying low over the hills of North Carolina. That frost bound morning I'd discovered, much to my surprise, that I was a quite nervous and jittery passenger. Though I guess anyone might be a bit jumpy when they've just been strapped into an aeroplane made only of spruce wood and bound together with modelling glue and a large dash of hope. The death trap was called the Wright Flyer, and at the time, it was the epitome of flying economy class.

"Pass me my bag." I'd muttered, as I heaved up more green leaf brunch into my favourite satchel and inadvertently invented the sick bag. Strapped in besides me -and looking equally as green- was my friend Orville Wright, who now stared at me through the fog of his goggles as he hurriedly drew a sign of the cross upon his heaving chest with a sorry groan. He looked down at the ground below, and although I couldn't relay what emotion was in his eyes at that moment, I knew they bulged with uncertainty and there was little left of his nibbled fingernails. It had been his bright idea to 'take some air' that morning, but right then, as the wind whipped at his hair to expose a bald patch fit for a hen to lay eggs, I could sense he was having creeping doubts about the capabilities of his latest invention as it stuttered on through woollen grey skies.

"We're all going to die!" he'd screamed through rattling teeth, his hands gripping the arms of his seat as his knuckles turned a brilliant white.

"Pull yourself together, man!" I'd shouted, dispatching a sharp slap across his quivering chops that brought him to his senses with a start. We hit another air pocket and both shrieked, embracing one another like lovers.

"I'm too young to die!" I sobbed.

"Jonathan, you're in your nineties," Orville reminded me, now taking his turn to slap my green cheeks with the sharpness of a guillotine as little black points of pain swam before my eyes and attempted to restore some orderliness to our inbound flight.

His brother Wilbur sat up front, wrestling with the controls in the rudimentary cockpit as his concerned hands pulled at wooden levers and nervous fingers tapped the little clocks. He was fighting hard to keep us in the air against a freezing headwind, but it was a battle against gravity he was losing as The Flyer creaked and groaned like an old man with rheumatism, ploughing through thick clouds and threatening any second to break up in mid air, sending us hurtling towards the ground with an undignified splat. As we encountered another wave of turbulence, Orville began to pray and my stomach began to rebel against breakfast once more.

"This is your captain speaking," hollered Wilbur, who was now barely audible over the howling wind and noisy propeller. " Hold onto your hats."

I'd already lost my hat to the wind before long take off, and as the flying machine dipped and shook in the vault of heaven, fresh fear pinned me to my seat and I pined for a stiff drink to take the edge of the buffeting. Typically though, there was no refreshment trolley on board this short haul flight destined for certain death. Nor was there any in-flight entertainment, life jackets, windows, emergency exits, lemon scented wipes or black box. All it carried were three terrified passengers and lots of second hand porridge that had come back to say good morning.

David Warren, the man who'd first invented the flight data recorder (black box), passed away in 2010, and was buried in a casket with the words: 'Flight Recorder Inventor. Do Not Open' emblazoned upon its side. Up in the sky that morning, I wondered what might be the eulogy written upon my grave as I headed towards it at worrying speed.

"We're going down!" shouted Wilbur as I adopted the brace position and kissed goodbye to my tail as the flyer began to shake and shudder violently, jostling us around in our seats like bottles in a crate. The trees below had grown dangerously close and the squirrels took cover as we attempted to come in for a safe landing. I didn't think much of our chances.

"May Day! May Day! May Day!" I'd bawled, despite it being December.

"Blurrrghhhhhhhh." was all Orville could manage as vomit clung to his thick moustache like a needy child who refused to let go. In those seconds before impact, just as the right wing tip brushed the trees and I readied myself for death, I saw my life flash before my eyes. Regardless of my age, it didn't take as long as expected.

The Wright brothers had chosen Kitty Hawke airfield to conduct their insane aeronautic experiments because of its gusty weather and soft earth, but that did little to lessen the impact as we met the ground with a tail-jarring bang before we skidded to a blundering stop in a cloud of North Carolina dust. I unbuckled myself as soon as the seatbelt sign blinked off and rushed for the exit, just like people always do on holiday aeroplanes. Don't ask me why they choose to do this, because the chances are they'll still be stood right besides you at passport control anyway. I imagine these are the very same imbeciles who insist on reclining their seats on short-haul flights and smoke in the toilets.

"We're alive! We're alive!" I'd gushed, kissing the muddy ground at my feet like a relieved reptilian priest. No word of a lie, it had to have been the longest fifty-nine seconds of my entire life. To this day I'm still a bad flyer, and I infinitely prefer to travel by boat or train wherever I can in most cases. I have that maiden trip and those two brothers to thank for a life span of aeroplane anxiety, smothering cabin fever and airport runny tummy. I can only assume it's the underlying reason that I act a little bit out of sorts on aeroplanes.

I'm the passenger who, before take off, always watches the safety demonstrations intently whilst everyone else browses the duty free magazine or shuffles around looking for their headphones. I also ask questions that cause hardened cabin crews to exchange nervous glances too, lots of questions. Like for example; where would be the best place to sit if we were to crash? Who would fly the plane if both the pilot and co-pilot were to, lets say die, because of food poisoning or a bomb? Where would you even get a bomb? And where might be the best place to even store a bomb on-board if you had a bomb, anyway? Believe me, it's these kinds of prying questions that they don't like, especially from shifty-looking nervous characters of exotic origin like myself. These sun-tanned princes and princesses are more at home wheeling perfume carts down the aisle's or pretending to blow air into useless life jackets than of informing people on how to act in a real life emergency, I feel at least.

Once I'd finished smooching the floor, I saw Orville climb from the wreckage of the Flyer and rip off his goggles, throwing them aside as he raced across the runway towards his brother who was still struggling with the zip on his flying suit. "You!" he'd shouted in anger as he stabbed a finger at Wilbur. "You are still dangerous," both brothers squared up to one another preparing for the inevitable sibling ruckus, before a smile curled on Orville's hairy lips. "You can be my wingman anytime."

"Bull," Wilbur had replied before they'd embraced. "You can be mine."

I felt a sudden surge of air rage in that moment as I stomped towards them on wobbly legs. "You two are both dangerous. You could have killed me!" As the ground crew did their best to pull us apart, expletives tumbled from my beak and the sun decided to go and hide behind thick grey cloud.

I look back now, with great fondness on that day. That blustery morning two Bishop's sons from Ohio had triumphantly gotten their invention off the ground and had glided into the history books by flying the world's first successful motor operated aeroplane. The late Sylvia Plath once wrote; *'There is nothing like puking with someone, to make you into old friends.'* I'll firmly stand by her solid, if somewhat disgusting hypothesis too. I'd know the brothers since they were boys, and it had been their lifetime's aspiration to imitate the birds and navigate the skies. In fact, it was perhaps I that had ignited their passion for flight when I'd gifted them a small helicopter toy brought back from my travels in France, years before that momentous day. No word of a lie.

"If birds can glide for long periods of time, then…why can't I?" a six-year old Orville had enquired with eyes full of wonder whilst he and his brother squabbled for turns and played for hours with the wooden flying machine.

"One day you shall." I'd assured him, a patronising smile dwindling on my beak-like lips. Of course at the time I'd never believed it, the very thought sounded surely inconceivable, but as you're no doubt aware I'd definitely underestimated their persistence.

When news broke of their mammoth achievement, their claims were met with much scepticism and scoff in aeronautical circles. Many thought it impossible that man could fly (it still sounds unorthodox), but as the siblings travelled the globe and demonstrated the feats of their collective endeavour to fields of fascinated thousands, any curious doubters were soon silenced into an innate sense of awe as these masters of aerodynamics took to the clouds, the sky their canvas upon which to paint the future of travel.

Their father (Milton Wright) had insisted the brothers take a vow never to fly together again for fear of losing both sons at once, so finally on September 9th 1908, Orville completed the first-hour long solo flight at Fort Myer, Virginia, which lasted sixty-minutes and fifteen seconds. Their reputation and international fame was now indisputable, although unlike Orson Welles, neither brother seemed overly keen on red carpets or limelight. Wilbur though, not to be outdone by his siblings efforts, had flown the length of the Hudson river on his return to New York, circling the Statue Of Liberty a few times much to the delight of the million strong crowd who looked to the skies in astonishment. Despite his quiet demeanour, Wilbur could actually be something of a show off at times, although in fairness he had just co-created a contrivance of great significance and importance to the world, so I could forgive him his flaunting. He was a lovely lad nonetheless, and it warmed the cockles of my heart to see him navigate the wild blue yonder that notable day all those years ago.

Sadly, it would be one of his final flights.

Only a few years later I received doleful news whilst overseas that Wilbur had passed away, not in an air accident as I'd often imagined might be the case, but after eating some bad shellfish. After a short struggle with typhoid fever in 1912, he'd died at the tender age of forty-five, unmarried and without children. He'd always remarked to me he didn't have time for both a wife and an aeroplane, and I guess, in the end he ran out of time to enjoy either. With the help of his ever faithful brother, we'd carried the coffin made of fitting spruce wood into church the morning of his funeral as their father delivered a heartfelt eulogy to the rest of the congregation, unwieldy tears bursting from the surface of his face like hot geysers.

"A short life, full of consequences. An unfailing intellect, imperturbable temper, great self-reliance and as great modesty, seeing the right clearly, pursuing it steadfastly, he lived and died."

It was a sad spectacle to witness a father bury his own son, but perhaps more regrettable was the fact that brother Orville would go on to live to an impressively ripe age of ninety-one, impressive for humans at least. But why is this sad you may ask? Well, it was sad because he would survive to see the invention he and his brother had so brilliantly created, bring great destruction and death upon thousands when it was used to drop deadly bombs on towns and cities from the skies, during the conflict of World War II. I have to assume this certainly hadn't been the intention.

"We dared to hope we had invented something that would bring lasting peace to the Earth. But we were wrong. We underestimated man's capacity to hate and to corrupt good means for an evil end," Orville explained to the St. Louis Post Dispatch in 1943. "I don't have any regrets about my part in the invention of the airplane, though no one could deplore more than I the destruction it has caused."

Neither myself, or the brothers could have envisaged on that cold day in 1903, with our hearts full of cheer and faces smeared with spew, that such an amazing feat of invention would be used to deliver devastation on such a grand scale. I know it made Orville profoundly sad in later life before his heart gave in, although there are still huge positives to glean from all their hard work. The billionaire Bill Gates even said of their achievements:

"The Wright Brothers created the single greatest cultural force since the invention of writing. The airplane became the first World Wide Web, bringing people, languages, ideas and values together."

I don't usually hold much regard for the words of multi-wulti billionaires, but on this occasion he's right of course. It's been universally acknowledged that the Wright brothers glorious invention has changed the way our world works forever. Up in the skies at any one time, there are half a million people thousands of feet above our heads, all struggling to open little bags of peanuts with their teeth and listening to screaming babies whilst they breathe in others flatulence.

This is called a holiday.

Those big machine-driven birds that can take us on flights of fantasy to far-flung places like Ayia Napa or Torremolinos, are today made from metal and fibreglass rather than the glue and spruce wood of yesteryear, but the intention remains the same. They travel vast oceans, soar the tallest mountains and the mere fact that mankind looked up at the birds one day and thought to himself; *'Hey, I wanna do that too'*, is a testament to the tenacity and industry of your kind. It's those brothers we all have to thank today for the joys of flight delays, Ryanair, and baggage handlers.

CHAPTER NINE

Now call me old fashioned, but ever since Charles Babbage (1791-1871) first mooted the idea of *'the difference engine'* I had reservations. I think I'd known from the sense of unease in my belly, that it was a concept I was planning to hate on principal all along. I suppose it just goes to show you should always go with your gut and never trust a man who considers algebra to be one of his favourite pastimes.

"You worry too much Jonathan," this father of technology had mumbled to me through a mouthful of stewed meat one evening towards the backend of the nineteenth century, as he'd galloped through supper. I'd been invited over to his Marylebone man-cave to discuss, in excruciating detail, his latest invention that would lay down the groundwork for what was to become the modern day programmable computer. You might think me a luddite, but even then I suspected it would bring a heap of spam and stress into my inbox.

"Babs, are you sure this new brainwave of yours is such a good idea?" I'd warned him at the time with a gentle touch of diplomacy, but he'd seemed far more interested in choosing what to have for pudding than of listening to my sage advice on dabbling in the digital world. Although a true Englishman, he could eat like a modern day American, and I recall his ratty purple waistcoat looked fit to bursting as he sucked up the vestiges from his plate before answering in a quite snooty manner. This was often the case when interrupted from his plate.

"I see, Jonathan. Perhaps it would be better for science, that all criticism should be avowed," he'd sniped with intimidating grandeur between mouthfuls, adjusted his neck collar so he could better work on his sweat. I nodded blankly, not having understood a single word the man had just said.

"What if there's a glitch in the system, or something goes wrong?" I'd remarked, with amazing hindsight as it turned out.

Babbage was still busy eating with his grabby hands, as if any second someone might appear from thin air to snatch away the crumbs from a plate the size of a hubcap. "Errors using inadequate data are much less than those using no data at all," he scoffed (quite literally).

As you can clearly see, this was becoming a conversational vacuum, but supressing a yawn, I decided against my better judgment to persist with my point all the same. "Still, we ought to be careful what we let out of the box, don't you think?"

"Mmmm…" he'd dwelled thoughtfully. "Are you going to finish that summer pudding, or can I have it?"

That evening, as the genius mathematician brought my unfinished dessert towards the largest hole in his face, how could either of us have possibly imagined that his futuristic concept, basically a huge mechanical calculator that could compute tables of infinite numbers, would one day bring with it near Armageddon many years down the line, towards the turn of the millennia? Of course, Babbage had been long in the ground by then (renal inadequacy finished him in the end, whatever that is?) and his rudimentary computer has now evolved into something way beyond even his comprehension, but I would have enjoyed wiping the grin from his grease-smeared face, or at the very least, trolled him on social media about his algorithmic failings.

I don't mean to give the wrong impression. Babbage had a number of annoying surface traits, but despite a tendency for over eating and shouting pompous obscenities at street performing organ grinders (whom he loathed), I mildly liked the man. Absolutely, he could be offensively uppity in his manner, especially when it came to lambasting the recreations of the working classes, but there was no denying the man had an ocean of genius inside that unfeasibly large brain. But don't just take my word for it. At this moment it's floating in its very own tank on proud display at the London Science Museum, so go take a look for yourself.

Without question Babbage was an inspiration for the adaption of the modern technologies that surround us today, but though it's true that mathematicians might be good with equations and eliminating human error, I've yet to meet one who lived with a foot in the real world. As the infamous mass murderer Charles Darwin once remarked: *A mathematician is a blind man in a dark room looking for a black cat that isn't there.*

Lost felines aside, the world has since learnt to its cost that there *were* data errors in his machine of modernity…tonnes in fact. And the biggest fly in the ointment that Babbage had failed to recognise all those years ago wasn't actually a fly at all. It was a bug. A particularly devious one that would swarm the modern globe in the year 2000, sparking an epidemic of fear and mistrust that hadn't been seen since the Conservatives first came back into power in 1951.

The Millennium or Y2K bug as it was termed, was a programming hiccup that concerned the limitations of the clocks that lived inside computers. Fascinating stuff, and please forgive my lack of technical jargon as I'm not a nerd, but to save on memory most computers read only the last two digits of a year which was all well and good, until some clever soul asked the question: what would happen when we reached the year 2000? It was a good question too, but one of the trickier kinds that nobody really had an answer for.

When the digits hit 00, it was feared that the mechanics of many computers would go back in time and interpret this as the year

1900, causing them to meltdown, reset or perhaps even start wearing Herringbone flattened caps and shovelling coal. I'm being facetious of course, but the truth of it was, not even the pimply mathematicians knew for sure what might befall the planet if the machines were to fail on the strike of midnight, in the year 2k. Nobody had seen it coming, or knew how to handle it when it inevitably came. I'd already lived through 1900 once (a quite disheartening era) and I had no appetite for going back there again. I felt clammy with unease at the prospect, and it was clear something had to be done before it was too late.

Governments of the late 1990s thankfully agreed, and went about spending gazillions globally in trying to paper over their shortcomings and avert potential disaster when they realised this overlooked error. If these temperamental machines (first imagined by Charles Babbage) decided to wipe their memories of the last century and began acting up, it was feared that global business would grind to a halt, planes would fall from the skies and computers would turn on their reliant owners like delinquent children, ripping us limb from limb with emotionless disregard. Nobody really wanted that, so the planet began making feverish preparations to avoid catastrophe, prompting many people to pop out for a quick haircut whilst they could, too.

Tony Blair, then UK Prime Minister since 1997, described it as: 'one of the most serious problems facing not only British business but the global economy today'. And like all serious threats that British governments are faced with, they decided to tackle the issue head on with a very strong leafleting campaign and door-to-door surveys. Meanwhile, we hurtled carelessly towards the end of the world as the clock ticked down and people unplugged their peripherals before bed, just to be on the safe side.

The day was soon upon us and I remember with great lucidness, December 31st 1999, the night before potential disaster, previously known as 'New Years Eve' in better times. Under duress, the world had hoped for the best and had extended a lukewarm welcome to the festivities with colourful cocktails, a cannonry of ready-to-go fireworks and heavily crossed fingers. Everyone was poised on tenterhooks that evening as a queer mix of forced-fun, hard partying and sheer panic filled the dance-floors of the globe as the new-year countdown began. I won't lie I was getting twitchy.

10…9…8…7…

As the last seconds of potential peace fell away and 1999 grabbed its hat and coat, people hovered restlessly, side-glancing their fellow revellers with party poppers in one hand and baseball bats in the other (for protection, not sport). I felt a hopelessness wash over me as we stared heedfully at the blinking clock, anxiously awaiting the outcome as we prepared to welcome in the noughties through gritted teeth (or gums in my case). Had enough been done to avoid half-demolished cities crashing down around our ears in smoking ruin? Would satellite stations hurtle down at us from space, drowning out the festive bells and sparking a chain of events that would terrorize all our collective psyches? I looked at the goading clock once more, a single bead of sweat (or perhaps a tear) running down my cheek as the delicate hands tumbled towards midnight, and very possibly Armageddon.

6...5...4...

At this point I expelled a foul, mordant smell and a distressed hiss as unease sat as heavy as a bears breakfast in my reptilian tummy, my throat becoming as dry as ancient dust. The prospect of what might befall our susceptible planet raced through my mind at incredible speed and left a trail of worry in its wake. Were maleficent computers about to wipe out bank accounts and corrupt the already unreliable transport system? Could corrupt programming errors create floods and fireballs, turning us all into puddles of gloop or worse still, block people from updating their status on Myspace? You do remember Myspace, right?

3...2...1...

Happy New Year! I closed my eyes and took the best part of my gin in one gulp as though it were my last. I gripped the hand of a stranger (I still don't know whose) and not for the first time in my life I prepared for a difficult, messy death. Then inconceivably, as the bells chimed their midnight toll and the crowd became unsettled, to my utter disbelief absolutely nothing happened. I warily opened one eye, then the other, but all I could see of any note were popping disco lights and a drunken man throwing up into his hands. Its momentous moments in history like this that make documenting them in this book so worthwhile, I find. I suddenly remembered to breath again, and I'd never been so glad to hear the dulcet tones of 'Auld Lang Syne' belting out through the fizzy speakers before the dance-floor exploded, but in a good way of course.

As you might have already guessed, the digital threat had been greatly exaggerated. Their century long plan to take over the world had been little more than a mere dress rehearsal. National armed forces lowered their weapons and wished one another good tidings before they were quickly stood down, the red buttons were packed back into their glass cases, and eminent leaders around the world poured themselves a large one and breathed a collective sigh of relief, thankful after having just dodged a Babbage shaped bullet.

The year 2000 had rolled on in without so much as a squeak, shriek, blip or bleep, despite the civil servants and politician's worst fears. The nasty bug embedded inside these impish computers had little impact on infrastructure in the end, and the spheroid remained unscathed as most of these super intelligent, billion pound computer systems managed to cope with the confusion of which century they were living in. Although it all came to nothing in the end, the amount of fear it stoked in the civilized world shouldn't be dismissed or underestimated. For months proceeding events, our minds had been colonised by an assortment of blind panic, impending dread, discouraging horror, and then more blind panic. I remember that the constant doom mongering had certainly tempered the New Year's Eve celebrations that year, and it won't go down as one of my better nights out by a long stretch.

After this near miss on the cusp of the year 2000, I'd wrongly assumed that the two-leggers faith in machines would become corrupted and that they'd be more responsible when deciding to lay their trust in these disingenuous cocktails of circuitry again. But if anything, people have now become modern day evangelists of the digital era, happy to bestow more faith into these esoteric virtual hands despite their snooping algorithms, psychotic bents, and murky track record. Personally, I think we need to look again at the dubious relationship between people and computers, as we've become a global species. These shifty little processors have been handed the tasks of today that we're far too important, or perhaps too busy to perform in our chaotic lives. From dishing out a glut of prescriptions and choosing whom we date, through to doing our weekly shopping and handling matters of national security in a veiled manner We've surrendered our privacy, giving these computers the keys to our towns, cities and bank accounts. It doesn't exactly strain the imagination to understand that should something go terribly wrong again then we've brought this failure upon ourselves.

Babbage was right when he'd said: *'The economy of human time is the next advantage of machinery in manufactures,'* if that is, you regard modern slavery as an advantage? Perhaps it's no coincidence that the word robot comes from the Czech "robota" which translates into forced labour or work? Yes this book is educational, and I'm about to give you even more of an education. Tortoises are the longest living of all vertebrates, and this particular one has lived long enough to realise that these microprocessors, no bigger than a speck of dust, are fast becoming the true taskmasters of humanity. Manipulating how we vote, shaping the way we think and coaxing us into buying products with crypto-currencies that we don't particularly want or need. Personally, I don't trust these new guardians of data. In fact, I don't even trust the Sat-Nav on my mobility scooter anymore.

Just like people, computers aren't infallible. But I'm afraid unlike humans, (most anyway) they refuse to apologise for their mistakes. Forgive me for sounding like a fully fledged member of the tin-foil hat brigade, but a lot can go astray as we sit like desk flesh behind glowing screens, our fingers flying over keyboards that act as maligned portals into our alternate lives. These terminals are susceptible to a whole scope of viruses and malware that can hack into entire networks and bring embarrassment to celebrities, manipulate social behaviour, and bring corporations to their knees. These cyber attacks are becoming ever more frequent too, as I found out to my own cost recently, when my cloud was hacked and some rather intimate videos of myself and a tortoise friend of mine called Georgina were leaked online. This resulted in many unfortunates having to see previously unobserved parts of one-self, and the footage was meant for David Attenborough's latest documentary series, so he wasn't best pleased.

Perhaps this is why I've become paranoid and untrusting in my ripe age? Or maybe I'm just overreacting and there really is a deceased beneficiary or Nigerian prince out there in cyberspace who wants to share their inheritance in exchange for my help? Either way, it does seem we've already become slaves to Facebook, technobabble and twitter (the little bird is actually called Larry, so more education), posting pictures of our food online and sharing our opinions and lives in a vacuous attempt just to appear more popular and interesting than we could ever hope to be. Granted, computers can serve a worthwhile purpose and I don't want to be a stick in the mud. I too have an online web presence: -jonathantortoise.com-but the next time something similar to the Millennium Bug of 2000 arrives on our touchscreens, I fear the Trojan horse may have already bolted.

I dearly wish Charles Babbage had left well alone in the invention of the computer and simply stuck to filling his face in frankness. I long for those bygone days when nobody swiped, clicked or poked one another. I think you'll attest we've all become too reliant on social media, algorithms, and artificial intelligence organising our daily lives. If this is the precursor of tomorrow, then it's quite a relief I'm almost at the automated exit doors.

Alexa…Add quilted toilet roll and lettuce to my basket.

"Well Jonathan, I must say your stories of plane crashes, car accidents, and insidious computers have cheered me up no end," remarks my luncheon guest without even the slightest hint of irony.

"I suppose it is all a bit doom and gloom," I agree, as the waiter pirouettes around the dining room like a spinning top with his silver tray. Finally, he delivers the soup to our table.

"Well, I'm sure it will brighten later," my companion reiterates, as he points outside at the inclement weather.

"No, I meant my stories." I retort, with perhaps too much eagerness. "Don't you think maybe I've painted mankind in rather a bad light at times?"

"Well that's humanity for you, I guess. Otherwise history would be full of people giving up their seats on buses and handing out lollipops to children, instead of the usual greed, treachery and fly tipping."

He has a point.

The rain is still hammering hard against the window and the rumble of thunder grows closer, but I attempt my best to ignore them as I dig deep within my memory for any morsel of empathy or kind gesture that humans may have extended to the world. My soup has grown cold by the time I finally pluck one out from the realms of obscurity, but hopefully this next story can redress the balance and bring a little light into the room of humanity once more.

CHAPTER TEN

"Well tonight thank God it's them...instead of youuuuuuuuu," I
crooned into the microphone before Midge Ure yelled cut for the
fourteenth time. The year was 1984, and I was participating in a
charity single to help raise money for starving children in Africa.
I'd seen pictures on television of the distressing famine in
Ethiopia, and as I watched those small African kids with
potbellies, too weak to wave the flies from their eyes, I knew I
had to do something. I also knew what it was like to be hungry.
Due to our metabolism tortoises can go for months without
food, but I'd been in New York at the time of the Irish potato
famine (1845-1849) and I didn't want to see another pelting of
the peckish, at least not if I had anything to do with it.

Musicians Bob Geldof and Midge Ure, had appealed for help
with their plight to feed the starving and had formed a collective
super-group called 'Band Aid', comprised of musicians who were
to record a charity single wearing oversized jumpers and
highlights in their hair. All the proceeds were to be given to the
hungry, so I eagerly picked up the phone, and at the nineteenth
time of asking (and the promise of a substantial donation), I was
invited down to the recording at Sarm's Studios in London, to
add my voice to the cause.

I've always taken pleasure from singing and on many occasion I've brought people to tears with my mellifluous mezzo-soprano, but once I was there in the booth performing my vocal before such music royalty as Bananarama and Jody Watley of Shalamar, it seemed neither Ure nor Geldof were completely happy with my contribution as they sat in the studio with their ears covered.

"Maybe we should try him with the 'clang' instead?" Geldof had suggested in a suspicious way, his scruffy head in his hands.

"What's the clang?" I asked, sensing the tension in the room. Paul Weller and George Michael had already been at each other's throats earlier in the day, so I didn't want any more confrontation. This was for charity after all.

"The 'clang' is only the best bloody bit in the song." Midge had explained with a light Scottish lilt and a smirk. I noted he was going quite thin on top as he bent down to stuff his gills from a selection of biscuits that could have sufficiently sustained an African village for a month.

"Doesn't Boy George want to do it then?" I readily replied.

"I honestly think it's a part best suited to your vocal range," Geldof had mumbled, scratching at something else in his unwashed mop.

"Sure, ok, the clang it is." I'd smiled absently, secretly rather chuffed to be given the best bit of the song by all accounts. I've always enjoyed the idea of being part of a band and sharing in the camaraderie of likeminded contemporaries as we created rhythmic harmonies together, but what I didn't envisage was the part in the band I was to play seemed equivalent to being handed the triangle at the school concert, when all along, you'd had your hopes set on being the enigmatic lead singer. I'd often dreamed of having my own mic-drop moment standing on a smoke-lit, but that's kind of hard to do with a triangle…or a clang.

"Do I at least get one of Midge's digestives?" I'd asked hopefully, before Simon (the bouncer) Le Bon quarterbacked me out of the studio quite unnecessarily.

Now, if you've ever heard the original recording of this goodwill single with its ensemble cast, then you're no doubt familiar with the glum 'clangs' at the beginning of the song, intended to make you feel all warm and Christmassy inside. In case you were wondering, it's the part just before a young Paul Young chirps in with his first line. Well friends, that 'clang' was yours truly.

Whilst everyone else was belting out their verses and having a good old celebrity giggle as they knocked back the egg-nog and swapped hair tips, I was left to my own devices to hit an over sized cowbell continually with a percussion stick in a dimly lit room near the fire escape. It wasn't exactly the rock n' roll lifestyle I'd imagined, and I'd secretly hoped to use this opportunity to get to know Jody Watley a bit better too, or at least get her to sign my albums. As it turned out, that wasn't to be the case.

The day went from bad to worse when I wasn't invited to join the rest of the stars as they gathered for the joint chorus, Geldof insinuating my erratic dance moves on the rostrum were putting him off. I later discovered they'd even cut me from the video, which was something I'd really been looking forward to being involved with. I'd already pre-warned my friends to keep an eye out on *Top Of The Pops* that evening, so I was furious to be left as a memory on the editing floor.

"Bob. What's going on?" I'd asked Geldof, once I'd caught up with him in the corridor after the recording. He'd been thrown off-guard and he looked at me with a sideways-tilt of his head.

"What do you mean?" he'd squirmed skittishly, his eyes reminding me of my fathers as they skirted his surroundings looking for the nearest escape. "Don't be a prima donna."

"You've cut me from the video, you've cut me from the song. How on earth can I contribute to a good cause and raise my profile like the others, if nobody even knows I was involved?"

"They don't do it for their careers. They do it for charity," explained a naive Bob.

"Yeah, right," replied an angry tortoise.

"Stop it Jonathan. That is so unfair," Bob moan in a damp voice.

"Stop it Jonathan. That is so unfair," I mimicked, unfairly, imitating his voice in a display of intelligent hounding. I was hot with anger but also embarrassed to have been made such a fool of.

"Look, I'm dead busy. Can you talk to Midge about it?" he'd said, as he barged past me and went off to his next live television interview with ripped jeans that appeared almost as filthy as his potty mouth. He'd never really looked like the pop star type to me anyway. More like a bin man doing some cheap impersonation of a pop star who was trying to look like a bin man. And of course, in saying that I mean no disrespect to bin men, or bin ladies. You guys (and girls) do a terrific job.

I passed Martyn Ware of Heaven 17 in the corridor and asked him if he'd seen Midge, but he just shook his head guiltily and stank of cigarettes. Those eighties synth icons were a *clique-y* bunch believe you me, an impenetrable force field of outlandish hair and plastic trousers. Nobody seemed interested in pandering to my diva demands, so given up, I crawled home from the studio that evening with a deep feeling of dejection and loss, although at least I can say I did my bit. Bono got my line in the end, with his self- righteous warbling's, but this story isn't really about me. It's about the kids in Africa. Really though, my vocal was way better. Even Paul Young said so at the time.

The single went on to be released in the UK on the 3rd of December 1984, and was called 'Do They Know It's Christmas?' I'll admit it was a pretty catchy ditty, but its plastic production quality wasn't really to my taste. It went straight in at number one and stayed there for five weeks, making it the fastest selling single of all time (at the time) and was soon released worldwide, totting up an estimated eight million pounds to fight famine and put food in bellies.

That's more food on plates than even my uncle Brian or Charles Babbage could manage between them, and soon the Americans followed suit (or simply copied) the idea with their own charity single spearheaded by Michael Jackson called 'We Are The World.' This saccharine ballad went on to become an even bigger hit with sales in excess of twenty million, but I didn't make the cut for that video either sadly. This was due to an argument with the country legend Waylon Jennings when I'd suggested the song be sung entirely in Swahili. A simple misunderstanding I'm sure.

I do think this short story offers hope for your kind and demonstrates that you aren't all bad. Sometimes, when humans get together they can achieve some pretty amazing things. I offered to donate my services to Band Aid II, 20 and 40 over the following years but never heard back.

Surprisingly, Status Quo did.

CHAPTER ELEVEN

One of the strangest gigs I've ever attended would have to be seeing Shalamar performing live at the Camden Roxy in 1987. The American R&B vocal group were promoting material from their new LP, an album filled with potboilers that seemed quite disjointed to me at the time, but one that I have since grown to cherish. The second would have to be the occasion myself and Nikola Tesla (1856-1943) went to watch Thomas Edison on tour in 1903. You won't be surprised to learn I didn't buy a t-shirt.

I wasn't much of an Edison fan in all sincerity. Just what was all this fuss? I thought the light bulb overrated and doubted it would ever catch on, but Nikola was very keen to see what his adversary had been up to in the years since they'd acrimoniously fallen out over money. I've never been one to stay in the same groove, so I'd agreed to accompany him to The Luna Park Arena that afternoon just to see for myself what all the talk was about in the trade press, though I can't say I was especially looking forward to it. Nikola had confided in me that Edison still owed him a substantial amount of money for numerous inventions he'd created whilst working at The Edison Machine Works, but so far all the inventor had endeavoured to stump up were lame excuses and rubber cheques.

"Tesla my man. You don't understand our American sense of humour," is all Edison had offered when he'd asked for what was owed. That's according to a destitute Nikola, at least.

"I don't care that they stole my idea; I care that they don't have any of their own." Tesla had grumbled that evening as we made our way to the gig, navigating the muddy fields and stepping over acid casualties in our welly-boots.

We'd arrived there late, neither of us that bothered about the support act, and by the time we'd found the main stage the place was already thick with people as a thousand bodies, all pushing and shoving against one another in a wriggling mass, got themselves pumped up on dopamine and cheap drink like fans at an Iron Maiden concert. They were all here to see the headline act that evening, an act billed as *America's Greatest Inventor.*

"America's greatest con merchant, more like," Nikola had sneered, suggesting we make our way over to the beer tent. He was an exceptional man in many respects, and it bothered me deeply that his marvellous work went largely unnoticed at the time. Despite his obvious intellect and creative flair, inventions like the AC motor, the Rotating Magnetic Field, and the Tesla coil just didn't catch the public imagination as he'd hoped. But I guess what niggled him most was the simple truth they all failed to match the recognition or financial rewards of his nemesis. He just couldn't get a break, and it's a sad affair he would never receive the coveted Nobel Prize for his work, which in my opinion, was nothing short of robbery (although today there is a statue of him in Silicon Valley that emits free Wi-Fi as a homage to his vision for wireless communication). In later years, with his mental health failing, Nikola would live out his days talking to pigeons in the park and obsessing over the number three, but right now his obsession was focused solely on the man about to take to the stage.

As we drained the last of our drinks, the lights dimmed and a huge roar sprang up from the enthusiastic crowd as the inventor from Port Huron, Michigan, strolled arrogantly across the boards twenty minutes late with arms outstretched, like a returning Messiah to his fandom. I wasn't at all impressed with his relaxed attitude towards the clock. He may have been a precisely dressed man, but his time keeping was anything but.

"Just who does he think he is?" Nikola had bristled boorishly through narrow eyes. "I mean, what has he ever done?"

I could certainly sympathise with Nikola's frustration, but his uncompromising opinion of his antagonist seemed a little unfair. Without turning this whole circumstance into a familiar Monty Python sketch regarding the Romans, he had achieved rather a lot in his career, as I was about to discover when the curtain went up and the central stage was illuminated by a thousand electric light bulbs that blazed and dazzled.

There stood Thomas Edison, bathed in the glow of his most magnificent invention and the adoration of his home herd. He flicked the bulbs on and off a few more times as the crowd went wild (unlike when Dylan first went electric in 65) and I'm sure a woman in close proximity wet herself. Now, it's an unspoken rule in rock circles that any artist worthy of their salt should save their biggest hit for the encore and leave their audience on a high, but this man had just torn up that particular script. Instead he'd gone early and unveiled his number one hit with the confidence of an inventor who knew, without qualm, he was at the top of his game. I tried my hardest to look on unimpressed as Nikola scowled at the white haired, well-dressed figure on stage, but in truth, I'd been blown away by this first-rate performance. I couldn't take my eyes off Thomas Edison as he began fist pumping the air to work up the already delirious writhing masses.

"Let me see those hands in the air!" he'd sang to the crowd, and it took all of my strength to keep my claws at my side. The wizard of Menlo Park (as he was affectionately known to his fans) whispered his thanks, as if not wanting anyone to know he possessed manners, before ripping into his next hit effortlessly, as he whipped away a white dustsheet to lay bare the phonograph that sat beneath. A collective intake of breath went up from the audience, immediately followed by emphatic applause and delighted howls as Edison dropped the needle and the crackle of music began to leak out from somewhere deep within the innards of his latest contraption. Heads bobbed, feet swayed and if the cigarette lighter had existed at that point, now would have been its big moment. Even Tesla couldn't help tapping his foot a little, much to his annoyance.

"Scream for me Luna Park! Scream for me!" a sweat drenched Edison had yelled to the sell-out crowd, and thousands of compliant mouths happily obliged with waves of appreciation. The excitement was palpable and he made for a pretty good front man with the looks, the swagger and the nifty inventions. I've since seen The Stones at Altamont, Elvis playing the Pontiac Silverdome in 1968, and even witnessed four young lads who shook the Wirral performing a live set on the rooftop of Apple records in 69', but not one of them came close on the decibel scale to the ear splitting noise that rang around the walls of the stadium that evening. The place literally shook from within as Edison continued to bombard the horde with a constant stream of hits that included the motion picture camera, fluoroscopy, and the mimeograph. People straddled the shoulders of strangers for a better view, American flags were waved and one or two women even exposed their upper halves as Edison tore through his impressive back catalogue with masterful poise and showmanship.

I was being won over by this father of invention despite my loyalties to Tesla, and in a time long before Instagram or mobile phones, it was nice to see people actually watching the stage rather than filming it. I felt a dizzy euphoria wash over me, an emotion I wouldn't experience again until Woodstock in 1969, as I swayed on rhapsodic claws with the doting crowd, all of them praying at the alter of this iconic man. I was rather enjoying myself, and it was only when Edison announced he'd like to try out some new material that things began to take a sharp downturn. As any seasoned gig goer will tell you, this is the perfect opportunity to head for the toilet when the suggestion of a new song is mooted. But I didn't need to go, and neither did I like the look of the queue.

"I'd like to dedicate this new one to my dear friend, Nikola Tesla." Edison had crowed into the microphone with peculiar sentiment, a flagrant smile stretching across his face as he sneaked off stage, leaving Nikola to stew in his own anger.

"What's Teddy up to now?" Nikola had groaned, his fists like balls and his jaw tightly clenched. He really wasn't a fan of the headline act, and without being privy to the published set-list we were both similarly stumped.

"Perhaps he's trying to make amends?" I suggested. "Maybe he wants to finally give you the recognition you deserve?"

"I'd prefer to take a cheque," he retorted.

Minutes later, when Edison returned to the stage sipping a bottle of mineral water with a towel draped around his neck, I couldn't believe what my eyes were telling me. I'd turned to Nikola for confirmation and he simply shrugged in allied bewilderment as we watched Thomas Edison lead out a full-grown Asian elephant on a chain. He turned to the crowd with a disquieting grin and introduced *'Topsy'* to the audience, just like George Michael announces Elton John midway through the song that has momentarily slipped my mind, but that I shall Google later. Was this to be a duet perhaps? In that moment, I honestly hadn't the foggiest.

"Well, this is certainly different," I'd remarked to Nikola, who looked equally as puzzled as me as he placed me up on his shoulder so I could get a better view over the thousands of bobbing heads. As we watched in curious bafflement, our faces slowly turned to that of horror when Edison made clear his intentions to the waiting audience.

"Ladies and Gentlemen. For my next number, I'd like to demonstrate both the power and dangers of electricity by electrocuting this elephant, live on stage."

"I think I preferred his older stuff," Tesla remarked absently, with a dumbfounded look.

I too, was horrified. Was this idiot really going to electrocute six tonnes of elephant live on stage, just for a five star review in the papers? To make matters even worse, he'd decided on filming the whole barbaric episode with one of the motion picture cameras he'd recently invented too, no doubt to sell to his fans as a memento of the day. No word of a lie. If you don't believe me, search *electrocuted elephant* on Youtube and take a look for yourselves, but don't forget to clear your browser history later or people will think you're barbaric.

"What's he planning for an encore? Human sacrifice?" Tesla whispered.

I was speechless. Years later, in the cut and thrust of the nineteen-eighties, my friend Ozzy Osbourne would accidentally bite the head off a bat whilst live on stage during a frenzied performance. Although I don't condone this belligerent behaviour, that's all people remember him for nowadays. Thomas Edison was about to murder an innocent elephant in front of a thousand people and produce a live souvenir DVD of the event, and all that's said about him in history class today is what a very clever man he was, and how we should all pay enormous tribute to a real American hero.

I disagree entirely. Unlike most people (because I have four legs and am not like most people) when I hear the name Thomas Edison, I don't immediately think of the light bulb, kinetoscope, or even the phonograph. No, I think of an incorrigible, cold-blooded elephant assassin who should have spent the rest of his years behind strengthened glass. Nikola had a much more unsavoury term for the man, but as it's not age-appropriate I'm sure you can use your imagination.

I decided not to stay to watch the fate that would befall poor Topsy. Instead, I pushed against a conveyor belt of people and stormed past the merchandise stall without making a purchase as I headed towards the exit, my face twisted in anger and my usually cold blood at boiling point. As I waited outside the Luna Park stadium that evening, I was anticipating a tsunami of hisses and boos from those inside the venue who were forced to witness his macabre display, but much to the shame of humanity all I heard were gales of laughter and deafening cheers.

Nikola later informed me that Edison had shot Topsy with 6,000 volts of raw electricity whilst she was subdued with heavy straps. She'd shook a little and lifted a foot, before toppling to the floor dead. The whole pathetic act had lasted ten seconds. Well done, Thomas. Good luck with the DVD.

Edison died in 1931, although I doubt that's much comfort to Topsy and her family now. People around the world had dimmed their light or turned off the power to commemorate the passing of this famous inventor, but I certainly wasn't one of them. I'm very much in the Tesla camp if we were to put an 'Oasis' v 'Blur' spin on things, although it is difficult to avoid Edison's lifetime of work unless you want to sit in a darkened room in silence all night. Nevertheless, I'm always very careful whenever I switch on the light, as I know its inventor had a nuance for electrocuting animals in the most execrable ways.

Shalamar were much better to watch live.

CHAPTER TWELVE

Now before I go any further, I should probably address the other elephant in the room, and I'm not referring to my time in Barnum's circus in the early 1900s. I'm talking of course, about my ill-fated appearance on Blue Peter in 1978. An episode that still makes my scales blush at the unfortunate way events unfolded. It's been well documented that I made rather a fool of myself that day on national television before the watershed, and because we now live in a time when you can rake up any misdemeanour of the past with the simple click of a finger thanks to the museum of embarrassment that is the internet, I'd like at least if I may, to put forward my version of events.

Blue Peter -for those unaware- is a factual children's television programme first launched in 1958 by the BBC, and now holds the accolade of being the longest running show of it's kind in the world today. A child friendly affair, it's fronted by a cluster of straight-laced and tirelessly bouncy presenters, which makes what I did all those years ago even more regrettable, I suppose. I'd been invited along to the live recording at White City, to appear alongside the late Johnny Morris in a segment involving the conservation of creatures and to highlight the destruction of their natural habitats. I was over the moon to partake in a cause so dear to my heart, and Johnny was always a joy with whom I'd worked with on several occasions. In fact, we shared many interests and preoccupations in happier times.

He was a keen zoologist who loved animals and he was always campaigning for their welfare, featuring them regularly on his own television show 'Animal Magic'. Personally, I thought the idea of talking animals quite ridiculous, but he would dub over footage of lions and monkeys with silly voices and quirky catchphrases just so the kids could feel more attuned with wildlife and learn of their on-going plight. The show soon became an overnight success meaning Johnny was always warmly received with open arms by the echelons at broadcast centre.

It wasn't at all unusual for animals to be regularly featured on Blue Peter in those days too, perhaps to help push up the viewing figures and appeal to the 'after school' audience. *Shep,* the excitable border collie dog, was already a permanent fixture on the sofa alongside her owner John Noakes who, together with Simon Groom and Lesley Judd, made up the trio of human presenters who would inform kids about stranger danger, the fireworks code, or demonstrate the wonders of sticky backed tape. Elephants, donkeys, and even parakeets had all appeared on the show without incident over the years, so I'm ashamed to say I rather let down the animal kingdom that day.

I think perhaps I'd eaten too much complimentary fermented fruit in the green room beforehand, which has always been a peccadillo of mine. Because, once summoned before the hot studio lights by a junior producer, I was already tottering on unsteady feet as I bowled out onto the stage floor. I could see that presenter Simon Groom looked rather uneasy as he stood in his hideous caramel jumper before the cameras, the final touches of make-up having been applied to his vainglorious face as the bearded floor manager signalled we were only seconds away from going live.

"Oh, Jaysus…" Johnny had muttered under his breath, his cheeks turning the colour of raw beef as he caught sight of me stumbling towards him with a sideways tilt and a half filled carafe. He'd looked far from impressed at my wobbly state, but there was very little the Welsh animal lover could do to stop proceedings, as the cameras began to roll and both men eyed me with a frisson of panic as we went live to the nation.

"Live in three…two…one," shouted the director with his clipboard, as nautical music filled the studio and immediately I began to feel rather queasy. I'm usually a natural in front of the camera so it had nothing to do with last minute nerves or stage fright, I might add.

"Hello, and welcome to Blue Peter," beamed a bubbly Groom straight into camera 1, once the jolly opening credits came to an end. "Coming up, we'll be learning how to make a model of the Taj Mahal using empty washing-up liquid bottles, and later we'll find out what happened when Lesley Judd spent the day with Pan's People. But first we have a guest. Now, who have you brought along for us to meet today, Johnny?"

Johnny Morris looked a bit hesitant as he stood beside me in his zookeeper's hat, but ever the professional he afforded his warmest smile to camera 3 and tried his best to carry on regardless. "Well…this is my friend called Jonathan," he beamed under duress.

"He's a Galapagos tortoise, isn't he?" asked Simon Groom stating the obvious, as the camera zoomed in on my gormless face. Already I could hear the producer, Biddy Baxter, shouting through the earpiece of the director to get me off set and pour me black coffee.

"That's right, Simon," continued Johnny, with an over compensating smile. "And did you know he's an indigenous reptile over a hundred and…"

It's at this point, around 01:32 on the clip, that my behaviour becomes disappointing. Tortoises are famously shy and reserved creatures, and even today I can't quiet believe my awful behaviour. The footage still often appears on video compilation shows like: *'When animals misbehave.'* or the equally cheap to make: *'When animals attack'.*

"WIIILLDDDD THANGGGGG…" I suddenly began to sing at the top of my drink-slurred voice, blatantly emboldened by alcohol, as I cut across the floor like a reptilian version of Oliver Reed on stomping feet. I stuck out my tongue for the camera with my claws outstretched and my head held to the skies. *"YOU MAKE MY HEART SING!"*

"Maybe we should go to a break," Groom had spluttered with an over smile, forgetting for a second we were on the non-commercial BBC. I doubt Peter Duncan would have made the same error, but there you go.

"Jonathan. Pack it in," Johnny had pleaded with a desperate whisper, but I was far too gone to care at that point. Many sheets to the wind, I'd carried on prancing around the studio like a merry-andrew, fudging the words as I moved in time to my own internal beat. Despite my inebriation, I could sense the crew weren't wholly on board with this new programming format and their patience waned as they chased me around the studio with their cumbersome cameras, constantly tripping over random cables as they went.

" YOU MAKE EVERYTHING…." I'd continued to garble much to my eternal shame as I swayed like a real imbecile, gyrating my hips and sweating profusely under the glare of sizzling lights. *"GROOOVVEEEYYY!"*

I remember not feeling terribly well right then, but I was as surprised as anybody when straight out of the blue, I felt my bowels plunge south and I defecated on the pristine studio floor before a million innocent school children watching at home. I've always found aged fruit goes right through me like a steam train, and this gastrointestinal catastrophe wouldn't have been helped by the natural progression of age.

"Oh deary, deary me," was the best a flushed John Noakes could muster from across the studio, before the floor fell as silent as a moonbeam and the delightful Lesley Judd went to find a mop and bucket.

The enormity that I'd just soiled myself before millions had failed to register in my addled head, but the look on poor Johnny's face told me everything I needed to know. He had his head in his hands and was spitting tacks. I imagine in those dreadful moments his television career must have flashed before his eyes at the shortcomings of my dirty protest. "You've ruined me tortoise. What have you done?" I remember he'd growled into my ear, his face full of upset as he tried his best to keep me upright.

"Followed through…I think," was my confused reply.

At this point, the inquisitive *Shep* had decided to have a sniff around my backend and I'd reared up on hind legs with a cautionary hiss, believing I was under siege from the wet nosed assassin. Groom (ever the hero) stepped in to restrain me, and at this point I swung my claws around aimlessly, and rather aggressively it has to be said. Although I have no recollection of the incident thereafter, the footage clearly shows my foul use of language and the two studio producers prising me off the squealing blonde haired presenter, just before Biddy Baxter cut the feed to a pre-recorded piece on steeplejacks in former northern cotton towns.

Of course, this meant I was spared the indignity of the nation seeing me throw up all over Lesley Judd's blouse as she'd raced over with a bucket, but I had just pooped myself live on air and that's not something you want to read about yourself in the morning papers. Though I'm by no means perfect, even I'm surprised at my behaviour that day and with the blessing of hindsight, of course I could have handled the whole thing with more aplomb, but what is a life without regrets?

I would even suggest that the unapologetic dandy; Groom, got off lightly. A few superficial scratches requiring no more than a tetanus jab would be needed, but otherwise he'd survived unscathed. Much unlike my own afflicted television career, which now lay besmirched in a steaming pile of ruin beneath white-hot lights on a studio floor somewhere in west London.

"You'll never work in TV again," screamed Biddy Baxter from the gantry as she decried my professionalism, but by then I was impervious to her ranting and wasn't really listening. Still under the influence, I'd staggered off to the Blue Peter garden to throw up again, then passed out on the sofa to sleep off the rotten effects of the fruit. I'll be the first to admit it wasn't my finest moment.

"Oh, deary, deary me," John Noakes had repeated later that day, once I'd awakened on my back in studio 3 with a hangover the size of a whale calf growing between my eyes. The considerate presenter had passed me some painkillers, a mug of black coffee, and his judgement. "I think someone might have blotted their copybook," he giggled with a chummy wink. I think he was right too, as it seemed my drunkenness was akin to devil worship in the eyes of the holier than thou BBC.

Johnny Morris never spoke to me again afterwards. Despite my letters of apology and the promise of adopting a donkey, I was shunned from his social circle and banished from helping with his animal charities for life. Even the usually affable Terry Nutkins was quite offish with me too, as I remember. Thankfully my behaviour had no lasting damage on Johnny's televisual career, and he would go on to make some enlightening and essential programming as he continued to introduce animals to generations of audiences worldwide, before his sad death in 1999. Many say he was the thinking man's Attenborough, and though I was probably the only animal he wasn't so fond of (apart from spiders apparently), I hold no grudge.

In an attempt to smooth things over with the network, I offered to foot the dry cleaning bill for Lesley Judd's dress and reluctantly paid for Groom's medical treatment, but despite this, the BBC banned me from all future programming and it would be a long time until broadcasting house saw my shadow once more. In fact, it wasn't until the early nineties that I was invited back to appear in the opening and closing titles of their hilarious sit-com hit: *'One Foot In the Grave'*.

Needless to say, I'm still waiting to receive my Blue Peter badge.

CHAPTER THIRTEEN

Years later, I would make a far more sober appearance on Desert Island Discs, where I redeemed myself in the eyes of the public as I recounted the sad loss of my family and the various scrapes that have been the hallmark of my long and eventful life. Unlike my unfortunate parents, those chosen songs had been my rock throughout the highs and lows of life and I'm not talking the soft, heavy, or alternative kind.

It was an enormous compliment to appear on the show, tainted only by the fact that the programme was one of the few that were wiped following transmission. I had become victim to a brutal round of BBC cost-cutting measures that sought to recycle tape-stock instead of just buying more. It was an act of broadcasting vandalism that saw myself and a whole swathe of gems lost forever, such as classic episodes of *Hancock, Round The Horne, Not Only But Also* and *Cheggers Plays Pop.*

A national disgrace, which I remind the producers of on a regular basis as I make frequent requests to make another appearance on the show. If Monkhouse, Wogan and Fry (Stephen, not Martin or Barry) can all have several bites of the cherry, then surely this geriatric tortoise can take another nibble? Until that day arrives here's my discs, book and luxury item that I shared with Sue Lawley on that lovely morning we spent together in 1998. The

BBC didn't think it was worth preserving but thankfully my memory did, so you can take my word for it. For rights reasons, the music is shorter than the original broadcast but I hope you enjoy listening. Cue the music…

By the Sleepy Lagoon- Eric Coates.

I'd chosen this sedate orchestral piece purely because it was the introductory music to the show and I'd included it in a transparent attempt to curry favour with the producers and applaud their taste in music. It hadn't worked, and today it only reminds me of the fact that my appearance can't be enjoyed in podcast form.

To Be Young, Gifted And Black- Nina Simone.

Nina had a temper to match my aunties, but boy could she sing. I met her once when I worked in a shoe store and she'd forced me at gunpoint to take back a pair of sandals she'd already worn. This song was considered an anthem of the Civil Rights Movement, and although I'm of a different colour myself (green), it resonated with me. Whenever I feel a bit down, I dig it out. When you feel really low. Yeah, there's a great truth you should know. When you're young, gifted and black. Your soul's intact. Amazing stuff!

Blow The Man Down- Woody Guthrie.

I can't listen to this without thinking of my time at sea after escaping death and sailing towards freedom. This roistering sea-shanty was often sung on deck by the cheery crew, as they reeled in their heavy nets to its rhythmic verses. It's an ancient song that still fills me with hope for the future. I've chosen Woody's rendition of this classic over the Spongebob Squarepants version, as I think he brings more emotion to the piece.

Makin' Whoopee- Bing Crosby.

What can I say, Sue? This song reminds me of the many times I've been involved with breeding programmes over the years. Some fun, some not so much, though most were highly inefficient.

At this point in the proceedings Sue, dressed in Levi jeans and a faded Dead Kennedys t-shirt, was repeatedly nodding her head in quiet admiration at my music taste (as I presume you are doing right now) before prompting me for my next choice with a gentle coax of her smile.

I Don't Wanna Dance- Eddie Grant.

Oh, but I do. The eighties were a time of great musical discovery for me, and this number one reggae hit was never off the radio in 82. I much prefer it to his later hit, Electric Avenue, and obscurely this song reminds me of seeing the Thames Barrier first publicly demonstrated and the popular soft drink Lilt. (Other soft drinks are available).

Walking Slow- Jackson Browne.

For obvious reasons that need no elaboration…

Joy Division Oven Gloves- Half Man Half Biscuit.

As you will soon discover, I have left my own mark on the world of fashion and this satirical take on the monetisation of merchandise tickles my tail no end. I like to listen to it when I'm baking a vegan quiche. I wonder if you can buy Shalamar oven gloves?

I Can Make You Feel Good- Shalamar.

You knew it was coming. To be honest, it could have been any song by my favourite band, but I chose this 80s smasher because it does indeed make me feel good. It's infectious beat also makes me feel young once more. Oh, to be a hundred and sixty three again…

With my desert island disc selection at an end, Sue smiled warmly as she wiped a tear from her eye before asking the penultimate question. "I'll allow you to take one book with you onto the Island. What will it be?"

"The Adventures of Martin Chuzzlewit." I answered without even the slightest hesitation.

"And your luxury item?"

"Anti-aging cream," I grinned, as Sue giggled and the natural frisson between the two of us smouldered through the airwaves.

"Jonathan Shelton, thank you for sharing your Desert Island Discs."

"Thank you Sue."

Myself and a young Hitler circa 1893, before he turned nasty

Rosa. Banged up just for not standing up.

Me just before I boarded the first recorded flight. I'm bricking it.

An aborted publicity shot of Abe that's in no way photoshopped.

Poor Topsy taking a topple thanks to a national treasure.

Why you should always listen to a Jedi master.

Who ate all the pies indeed?

Forty Elephants and one Jonathan. 1917.

An ad for 60's fashion. Thank god it's in black and white.

A vintage advert for arsenic soap. Proof that 19th century doctors had no clue.

With Bananarama on the set of Band Aid 1984

Chilling with my man Benjamin circa 1935

Am I boring?

The reason I ask is because for the last ten minutes, my dinner guest hasn't stopped looking at his watch.

"Am I keeping you?" I ask him.

Annoyingly he glances at his watch once more. "Well I am a little behind schedule, but the other engagement can wait for now, I guess."

I'm not sure I believe him, because nobody in their right mind would go out in weather so torrid as this. Another rumble of thunder shakes the windows and I'm starting to wish they weren't so tall, or made of glass.

"Did you really cack yourself on live television?" he asks me, crudely.

"Yes I did," I reply, as I look out once more at the sideways rain and note the Thames travelling faster than a sports car as it

threatens to break its banks. I haven't known a storm like this since...

"An interesting choice in music you have Jonathan," interrupts my company as the flies buzz around his head like a character in a cartoon. It's as if every bluebottle in London is sheltering from the rain today.

"Thank you." I say.

Suddenly, the lights above flicker like a disco strobe before going out completely, and in the darkness I can hear the waiters bumping into tables and asking people to remain calm as they hand out candles for the customers to use.

"The storm must have knocked out the electricity," observes my guest with a smile, as he lights a candle and his face is bathed in an eerie glow. "I'm more of a Death Metal fan myself by the way, if truth be told."

"Really?" I reply. "Well, I know what to buy you for Christmas then." I quip.

"Oh. I wouldn't be worrying about Christmas, Jonathan." he mutters before picking up the knife and fork and getting to

work on the rare steak that swims in its own blood on his plate.

I look out at the rain again, but my mind is elsewhere. The mention of Christmas and the sight of blood, sparking another long forgotten memory in my mind as the candle on the table flickers and dies.

CHAPTER FOURTEEN

As dawn broke on Christmas Day morning in 1914, the first thing that struck me was that the guns were silent. The endless shelling had instead been replaced by a distant hum, which to my ears wasn't much of an improvement. I hunkered down in one of the many lines of trenches that ran along the Belgian countryside like scars upon the face of the earth, hoping all would soon be quiet on the Western Front.

"What is that racket?" I'd asked the young soldier next to me who could have been no more than a boy. He wore a face as if puberty had left its job half done, rudely interrupted by the onslaught of war.

"It's the Germans," squeals the youth, sucking on a rolled cigarette whilst the ominous hum grew louder.

"Are they using some kind of new sonic weapon to obliterate us?" I asked.

"No. I think they're singing,"

"I think I preferred the shelling,"

People are often surprised to learn that over sixteen million animals fought in World War One (1914-1917), and sadly many would never return home to their baskets, paddocks or cages. Creatures from both sides of the fighting were called upon as an essential part of the war effort dubbed the war to end all wars, although as we now know, that denomination was someway off the mark. Horses were charged into battle like beasts of burden, dogs carried messages to the front lines and dependable camels would carry off the injured soldiers under a hail of enemy bullets. Brave canaries would sniff out noxious gas, titanic elephants transported munitions across Africa, and even monkeys, crocodiles, and lion cubs would play their part in the national effort by keeping up morale as mascots in the trenches, providing familiarity and companionship for the troops during those dark days of war.

Even goldfish had lain down their lives with great hardihood in the bloody conflict begun by man. After a gas attack, the infantry gas masks would be washed and rinsed, before being placed in their tanks and left overnight. If the fish were found belly up in the morning, then it meant the masks still contained traces of poison so should not be worn. So far as I know, no goldfish ever received a posthumous Military Cross for saving thousands of lives, but I thought I'd share this interesting fishy fact all the same (educational remember).

I was part of the Indian Labour Corps stationed in Belgium. I'd been drafted to serve my adopted country (and spiritual home) on the front lines, by digging trench systems designed to protect the troops from the constant barrage of enemy artillery fire. I've always loved a mud wallow, it kept the ticks away and provided useful for camouflage, so with industrious claws (ten at the front, eight at the back) I would crawl in the mud and I never gave up. It might have had something to do with the quantities of amphetamine supplied to British soldiers by the government to suppress our appetites due to food shortages (true fact), but I also like to think it was national pride that kept me going in those trying times. We eat to enable us to fight, we fight to enable us to live and so on and so forth, until eternity shall fail.

I'd excavate Belgian poppy fields and tirelessly construct kilometres of deep, narrow ditches, which were to become our subterranean homes for so long as we could stay alive. Meanwhile, rifles cracked like horse whips and bullets whistled overhead, as opportunist rats fed upon the flesh of the fallen below. Crouching in cold fields and slinging lead at one another in the thick fog of war, is perhaps not the nicest way to spend Christmas, though for some I suspect it beat visiting the relatives.

"Are you sure they're singing?" I'd asked again with brevity, wiping the crusted mud from my claws as I took a snifty nip of whisky from my hip flask.

"Listen," said the boy as we lifted our helmets and cocked an ear towards No Man's Land. The strains of Stille Nacht had travelled upon the morning breeze, the gloomy hymn reaching the rest of the British troops holed up in their miserable muddy enclaves that I'd helped construct as shelter during the shelling. After some initial confusion, they'd responded with carols of their own and soon, both sides were yelling out Christmas greetings to one another across the fog filled fields as thoughts of warm fires, family and roasted goose leftovers lingered in their minds. And amongst the singing and messages of goodwill that day, there began tentative calls from both sides to meet up in No Man's Land, as if they were no longer bitter adversaries, but simply cordial neighbours chatting over a barbed wire fence about their plans over the festive period.

"You must pop over for eggnog," Fritz might say.

"Of course," Tommy would reply. "We'll bring the mince pies."

"Are we still doing secret Santa this year?"

"But of course. It's Christmas."

"I love your novelty jumper by the way."

"Vielen Dank."

War is tiresome, and I for one was sick of all the constant fighting. The overflowing latrines, dead comrades and lice infestations could easily be traded for a spry morning stroll and a few shreds of festive peace. I just remember hoping it wasn't some underhand impish tactic the Germans had deployed to play to my better nature. I took another large snifter from my flask and straightened my helmet with a steady claw. "I'm going over," I'd announced to the young private still crouched beside me.

"Eh? Are you mad?"

"It has been said," I smiled with the kind of heroism you might encounter in a black and white war film. I sincerely hoped the Germans invite of reconciliation, if even for a short time, wasn't mere smoke on the wind.

"Then take this," he'd insisted, handing me his bayonet with a miffed look still lingering on his pubescent face.

"I shan't be needing that." I declined, as I climbed the makeshift rope ladder, ducked the angry barbed wire, and prayed to a God I didn't believe in that I wasn't about to become morning target practice for our noisy neighbours across the way. Like a helmet with legs, I emerged from the trench and took my first prudent steps onto the torn up land that was strewn with the sorry remains of wasted youth, mere boys whose lifeless eyes now looked up vacantly at a splendid morning sky they'd never get to appreciate.

It was Plato who'd said 'Only the dead have seen the end of war', but I so hoped he was wrong. How can it be that mankind, a creature considered the most intelligent of species, allows itself to succumb to such atrocities as this? How could a dustup escalate to such an extent and get so out of hand, that blowing each other to bits with lumps of metal seemed the only viable option? War doesn't determine who is right-only who is left.

 I can't have been the only one craving peace that yuletide morning either. As I worked my way slowly onwards through a cruel contrast of still bodies and blossoming flowers, I saw men from both sides now clambering out of their boggy pits and shuffling cautiously towards one another, both conveying understandable wariness in their eyes. Attempting to kill each other had been easy. Making small talk however, was proving to be far more socially awkward. The two sworn enemies hovered around self-consciously in the quaggy morass, staring down at their boots and fidgeting with their hands as if quite unsure of what to do next. After a few moments of clumsiness, small gifts like cigarettes, whisky and chocolates were exchanged as wallets were opened and photographs displayed of loved ones and families that they hoped to see again someday.

Peace had begun to spread elsewhere along the lines too, as more men climbed out of holes in the ground like heedful moles, guardedly exchanging seasonal greetings with the enemy instead of the usual gunfire and lobbed hand grenades. This truce was a warming sight to behold and allowed both sides to retrieve the bodies of the recently fallen, providing them with a proper burial. Despite the strong stench of death that permeated the chilly air, I felt oddly comforted by this display of humanness. As I crawled amongst the poppies, munching on a few for sustenance, I was moved at the sight of funerals taking place with sombre soldiers from both sides gathered around graves together, reciting Psalms before lowering their lost into the hard, cold ground.

'All war is a symptom of man's failure as a thinking animal,' John Steinbeck once said (I know, I know, another quote) and with thoughts of the fallen fresh in my mind, that failure had been of epic proportions.

As the Germans and British mingled freely that morning, it had the feel of an extended family reuniting but like most family get-togethers over the festive period, this one was not short on disagreements as I overheard two opposing soldiers begin an argument that threatened to sour the day.

"What's going on here, Potter?" I heard a passing Sergeant ask the wiry Tommy, who was already squaring up to his counterpart as they stood in the mud with splattered boots and furrowed brows. He looked like your typical unintelligent human.

"Fritz here insulted me sir." the soldier named Potter had replied.

"What did I say?" the German, whose name was actually Gunther, was asking in his native tongue as he pleaded innocence.

"I showed him a picture of my sweetheart, Millie," spluttered Potter.

"Then what happened?" asked the Sergeant, who was trying his best to diffuse the situation seeing as it was Christmas.

"He said something quite despicable, sir."

"Go on." prompted the Sergeant.

"He called her bewundernswert sir."

"What!" the sergeant had asked, as he stared down the German.

"I showed him a picture of the girl I am courting back home, and he described her as bewundernswert." Potter repeated as his voice quivered.

"Let me tell you something, Fritz," the sergeant said to the German soldier, "I don't know what that means, and I'm not sure I want to know what it means, but it sounds downright bloomin' awful."

I watched all this from a distance as the argument unfolded and a crowd quickly gathered at something finally worth watching over Christmas.

"All I said was that she's a perfectly fine looking, lady," explained Gunther in German, still perplexed by their overreaction and pugnacity.

"There. He said it again," blurted out Potter, who began rolling up his sleeves.

"He's certainly got a mouth on him, this one," the sergeant observed.

"Permission to punch him, sir?"

"Let me see the picture first Potter," the Sergeant had ordered, as Potter fished it out of his wallet and handed it over to his superior.

"I can't see what he's on about," the Sergeant had agreed as he studied the photograph. "She's a perfectly handsome woman, and not in the least bit bewundernswert. Permission granted."

I'd decided this piffle had gone on long for enough. The jejune bickering was becoming a sharpened pain in the hoop, and it was time to interject before the harmony of Christmas spilled over into yet more senseless violence. I yearned for a life with a lot less blood in it, so I'd retreated to my digs and retrieved the weapon from my camouflage kit bag (the one I'd lost on many occasion) just in time to see the Englishman with fists cocked and ready to strike.

I set my sights, took aim and shot.

As the stuffed leather pigskin hit the Private squarely in the privates, he crumpled to the floor with the wind knocked out of him, the look of a wounded animal set upon his grimacing face. "What an underhand bosh tactic," he'd groaned, but nobody was there to hear his words as he lay in the mud. The men, that moments ago had surrounded him, were now in the middle of No Man's Land playing football with the very ball that had just felled him. The ball I'd just booted into his particulars. I'd evidently lost my touch, because I'd been aiming for his head.

These men had witnessed enough fighting of recent and could happily forego a punch up in exchange for a kick about it seemed. As the accused German soldier had helped Private Potter to his feet, both men shook hands before the Englishman gestured they should go and join the others, and soon a full blown game was underway. Not for the first time in my life, I thanked whatever God was up there for the beautiful game.

Perched on a line of sand bags in full battle-dress, a single crystalline snowflake fell from above as I took out my flask and settled down to watch my first match in years that frosty Christmas morning. That being said, it wasn't one for the purists. Under soil heating and a proper drainage system would have improved playing conditions no end, and the absence of a proper referee meant that at times the match could be something of a free for all, but both limitations applied to either sides so they couldn't really be used as an excuse by the Tommies after they lost the match 3-2. In the trenches afterwards, an inquest was held amongst the English ranks as it was felt that a number of big name players had simply gone missing during the game and hadn't really justified their selection.

A pattern that was to repeat itself for the next century.

CHAPTER FIFTEEN

I still remember the utter outcry in 1963, when it was first revealed that women actually had legs. The fashionista Mary Quant was staging a London fashion show to promote her new boutique on the Kings Road and somehow I'd been roped in to helping, not as a model as you might expect (the catwalk would take me days), but as an extra pair of claws to help get the girls in and out of their outfits backstage at the prestigious Chelsea fashion show. No word of a lie.

Being a tortoise I rarely wear anything but the shell upon my back, which is likely a good thing as buying shoes for four feet must get rather expensive, but that's not to say I wasn't mesmerised by the flagrant clothes and fustian tastes that humans like to garnish themselves in at the time. I've always believed the vagaries of fashion are something to be revered and enjoyed with posterity.

There's a whole generation of people out there today who shiver with cold regret whenever someone reaches for the family album and they are reminded in an unthinking moment, of how preposterous they must have looked back in the 60s, leaning against Morris Marinas with beehive hair or captured forever in polaroid aspic with their long hair and even longer ruffled bell-bottoms flapping against the wind. I doubt even Darwin could have predicted what humans would have evolved into in this decade of undiluted debauchery, but I adored the era. That's why, on that decisive day in 1963, when Mary had asked if I'd had any previous experience in the fashion industry, of course I'd lied.

"Don't worry, darling," I'd said frivolously, hiding the truth behind an oversized pair of aviator glasses and a paisley patterned neckerchief. "I won't let you down, darling." I think by saying 'darling' enough times, she'd been taken in by my deception.

"Great. Well we might as well throw you in at the deep-end then," she'd smiled, a cigarette dangling fantastically from her lips. "The Autumn-Winter show starts next Monday, don't be late."

I was looking forwards to learning more about the fashion circuit and perhaps the opportunity to meet some of the girls backstage (though in a plainly platonic way) but when Monday came around, I was ill prepared for the hustle and bustle of fashion and just how hard I would have to work. The venue was a human assemblage of girls in voluminous dresses and sickly mustard shades, each waltzing through the curtains on a constant, unrelenting conveyor belt of outfit changes. I began to feel like a chef at the hotplate of a busy London hotel, barking out orders and sending out girl after girl wrapped hurriedly in Mary's creative designs, rather than bacon or Parma ham. Working at that frantic pace, it was only going to be a matter of time before mistakes were made.

Anyone who was anyone in the fashion world was in attendance that day, and Mary was hoping this show was going to put her on the map and show of her designer skills in all their resplendence. I remember her quiet clearly telling me she'd had a lot riding on this launch, and was relying on me as a stagehand to make sure things ran smoothly behind the wizard's curtain. Predictably, when you mix reptiles and reliability, well that's where trouble always begins to show up. We all have our flaws, right?

As the next girl came waltzing off the catwalk and threaded her way through the crimson curtains to change, I grabbed her allotted outfit to swiftly throw on and get back out there, but in my hurry the material must have accidentally snagged on an unkempt claw that I'd failed to keep under review. Once the model had wriggled into the dress and was about to head out into the spotlight once more, I noticed the large gaping rip across the hem of the ankle skirt and shrieked with campy despair.

"Stop! Do not move another inch!" I yelled at the model Jean Shrimpton, as she turned her head and froze in fear.

"What is it?" she asked, nervously glued to the spot. "Is it a wasp? Or an escaped snake, like the one Penelope Tree was wearing around her neck earlier?"

"No darling, it is much, much, worse. It's a tear in your skirt."

"Oh, I see," sighed Jean with relief.

I could feel myself beginning to hyperventilate. "Mary is going to kill me. What shall I do?"

"Dunno," shrugged Jean, who was a lovely girl but not much help in a crisis. "Do you think she'll even notice?"

"Duh!" I said, unnecessarily. "Of course she'll notice."

Jean giggled at my misfortune but it wasn't funny, and even if it were, it was about as funny as an episode of Mrs Browns Boys. I was running out of time and already I could mentally visualise Mary shuffling impatiently in her seat outside, wondering what on earth the delay was and why the stage was deserted. I had to act quickly so I took a deep breath and a leap of faith, grabbed the dressmaker's scissors and channelled my artistic spirit and accumulated wisdom.

"Hold still," I told Jean as I crouched down and began to snip away, but between my panicking and her wriggling, I cut the skirt shorter than Mary had ever intended. Far shorter, in fact. "*Jonathan*, you complete fopdoodle," I muttered to myself in a low voice, something I find myself doing quite often.

"It's a bit short isn't it?" Jean pondered self-consciously, as she looked herself up and down in the full-length mirror.

"How observant of you Jean," I'd snapped, as I peeked through the curtain to see the next gaggle of models in lampshade dresses and swirling patterns approaching the pits for an attire change. "We might get away with it though. It just looks like a really, really short skirt."

"A mini-skirt!" Jean giggled.

It seemed my sense of humour had deserted me by this point. "Look Jean. If you're going to keep taking the mickey, I can always book Twiggy next time."

"Sorry Jonathan," she said genuinely, and I felt immediately bad.

The clock was ticking as a backlog of models in various states of undress were bottlenecked on the other side of the backstage curtain, and right then I had no other option but to go with it. "You're on Jean." I said, pushing her towards the curtain. "When you're out there, just act natural and look as though that's the way Mary intended it ok?"

"I can't go out like this?" she'd spluttered. "I've seen new-born babies wearing more."

"Don't be a wet wipe Jean," I'd groaned, looking at the clock.

"Well you wear it then!" she retorted.

"Black isn't really my colour. Now go, go, go," I urged with one final push, sensing the audience were becoming restless behind their sunglasses and blank expressions. "And good luck."

It had been a huge risk and I've never been good with scissors, but the fashion Gods must have been looking down on me (or at me) that day and somehow I think I got away with it…kind of. Unbeknownst at the time, my ineptitude would go on to gain notoriety that resulted in global uproar, domestic unbalance, and ultimately the grounding of a million teenage girls for an eternity. That certainly hadn't been the intention when Mary had first drawn up the blueprint and fired up her sewing machine but sometimes in fashion you've just got to roll with the punches. On that day in 1963 the mini-skirt was born, albeit accidentally.

As it transpired, instead of seeing it as a behind the scenes mess-up of huge proportions (which I guess is true), when Jean had tottered out onto the walkway under hot lights that day of the premiere, the skirt was received with riotous applause by the fashion sheeple, most of them misinterpreting the skirt as an expression of sexual freedom and liberation against the fustiness of the 50s rather than a gaffe. This hadn't been the original intention, but I'll take it over a thick ear from Mary, any day. I was filled with relief to hear the whoops of delight that resonated around the auditorium from the spectators that afternoon, but sadly, like any creative soul who decides to put themselves out there into the wider world, the haters are still gonna hate.

With its daring style and unintentional design, the skirt would go on to summon waves of outrage and fluster amongst the puritanical mind-set of the era. Many prudish dampeners would deem the shortly cut garb a form of witchcraft, whilst other reactionaries simply decided it was a work akin to devil worship. I guess there's no accounting for taste, but either way I've always thought this feedback quite excessive. Yes it was plucky, but if you've ever met Elton John, you'll know that the mini-skirt wasn't the worse crime committed against fashion.

"Where is he?" boomed Mary after the show as I attempted to make a quick exit through the fire doors, but as you know my exits are rarely quick and she soon caught up with me.

"Mary, darling!" I announced, with feigned delight. She was dressed up like a pink marshmallow, which wasn't at all unusual in the seduction of the swinging 60s. "Everything ok? I heard the collection was warmly received."

"You've really gone and done it this time, Jonathan?"

"I'm so sorry Mary," I pleaded, shielding my handsome face with my claws as I suspected she was about to tear me a new hoop.

She opened her flat palm as I prepared for impact, before grabbing my wrinkly wrists and drawing me close to her mallow chest with a hug. "You're a green genius!" Mary had screeched in felicity, before showering me with a bombardment of wet kisses and lipstick smudges. "A greenius! The crowd just loved it Jonathan, and pre-orders have gone through the roof."

"Really?" I asked warily.

"Of course really," she'd beamed. "Even Ralph Lauren liked it, and you know how splashy and pretentious he can be."

"Not too short then?"

"Well, I like my skirts short," Mary had said in defiance of our joint creation. "So I can run and catch the bus to get to work,"

"Quite right Mary," I agreed, as we grabbed our coats and headed off down the King's Road to celebrate. "Quite right."

I suppose the mini-skirt seems quite tame by today's outlandish standards but not long after, in some European countries the skirt was promptly banned from being worn in polite society for fear it might corrupt or cause scandal, although personally I'm convinced this censorship only served to bolster its popularity amongst rebellious youths hell-bent on annoying their parents by baring their bottoms to the neighbours.

"The real creators of the mini-skirt are the girls, the same that you see in the street," Mary had famously said at the time, and I have to agree that without them I don't think its popularity would have exploded in the way it did. It became such an icon that in 2009 the Royal Mail even issued a stamp dedicated to the skirt, and June 6th has since been declared World Mini-skirt Day, dedicated to women supressed by the system.

I did try and follow up my accomplishments in the fashion world years later in the 1980s by announcing to the world 'the shell suit' with varying degrees of success. This looked nothing like a regular suit and even less like a shell (I should know), but its banana yellow and pepto-pink combination would light up the once grey industrial cities in the north of England and was quite popular, for a time at least, amongst those seeking more casual loungewear. Although garish in style and highly flammable, to its credit I expect its neon design drastically cut down on the amount of road traffic accidents.

Much like the mini-skirt, it is often resigned to the wardrobe of obscurity nowadays, hanging up besides the lime leggings, pastel coloured blazers and dusty parachute pants of the past, but I've since learnt that if you hibernate for long enough, everything comes back in to fashion eventually. Sort of…ish.

CHAPTER SIXTEEN

Abraham Lincoln was a lovely fellow. Most American Presidents I've met over the years have been about as friendly as sandpaper, but I can safely assume that he was by far my favourite and I grew so fond of him I still carry his picture with me in my wallet wherever I go. Granted, it's in the form of a one dollar bill, but every time I unfurl that tattered note and steal a look at his worn but affable face, it transports me back to the last time I saw him in the spring of 1864. A Tuesday I think.

We were lounging in the gardens of the White House, sipping honeyed tea and accompanied by birdsong that sounded just as sweet now the swallows had ventured back into the promise of summer after a long winter away. Their chorus brought with it memories of the finches back home, and I was reminded just how much I missed the place, with it's unspoilt sands and warm sunlight that slanted through lime green palms.

"Everything Ok?" Abe had asked, likely sensing the melancholy as he topped up my teacup and passed me the sugar.

"I'm fine."

"Biscuit perhaps?" he offered kindly. I was trying to cut down on sugary snacks after recently developing a muffin top, but who doesn't like biscuits?

He was a wonky looking man with large ears and the hint of an under bite, but his slouchy blue eyes shined with kindness. Despite his ferocious reputation as a formidable combatant in the political arena, this 16th President of the Untied States was really just a soft lump at heart. He was a big animal lover too, as it goes. One who'd refused to hunt or fish and instead, collected up stray cats from the local shelter and allowed them to dine at the White House table with him. He even confided in me once that his pet cat, Dixie, was more intelligent than his whole cabinet. I so wish politicians of today could be as transparent as he was.

"You just seem a little down Jonathan, that's all," the President suggested in a tone that was soporific and deliberate, but don't let that mislead you. The man was as sharp as a button.

"I'm ok, the mood will pass," I replied through a mouthful of Earl Grey and custard cream. "I'm just thinking, that's all,"

"It's good to think Jonathan. My best friend is a person who will give me a book I have not read."

"Am I your best friend Abe?" I asked with underlying desperation, silently kicking myself for not bringing along a book to lend him. I saw Fido, his faithful yellow mongrel dog, curled up at his owners feet as he cocked an ear towards our conversation, suddenly interested and all that. Why is it dogs always presume to be man's best friend?

"Yes Jonathan, you are." Lincoln had smiled through tea-dampened whiskers as he began cleaning his gold mounted rifle. "My best friend ever in fact."

Fido let out a vengeful squeak of bum gas, but I pretended not to notice. Nonetheless, I wasn't here to float a business proposition to the President about becoming a lending library to the senate. I was here with an offer of something that could prove far more lucrative, for both parties. I'd already gone to great lengths to strength-test my strategy and now I was ready to set out my stall and pitch him my inventive idea, although I could tell by the nature of his mood that it wasn't going to be an easy sell.

"Fancy shooting some rifles?" he'd asked.

"Maybe later," I declined, guns not really being my thing. "So, how's this presidency malarkey going anyhow? Getting any easier?"

"Meh," he'd laughed miserably with a shrug of his considerable shoulders. Heavy is the head that wears the crown, and I felt sorry for the man as he removed his infamous black hat and peeked inside as if looking for an answer that wasn't there. Finally he spoke again at his leisurely pace. "Actually, not so good really. I've had the unions on my back all week, and it looks like this Civil War thing isn't going away anytime soon."

"Bummer." I sympathised.

"People are already accusing me of being two faced."

"Oh, come now Abe." I said, trying to diffuse his mood. " If you had two faces, would you really wear that one?"

With his gentle sense of humour he'd chuckled at this jape, forcing out a jet of tea that Fido wasted no time in lapping up with his lolling pink tongue. It was nice to see the President smile again, and now that I'd greased the wheels of friendship this seemed like the perfect opportunity to proffer my ingenious business proposal.

"Ever thought of packing up with all this work nonsense, Abe?"

He stopped polishing the stock of his rifle and looked quite taken aback at my suggestion. "But my people need me, Jonathan. My country needs me."

"I suppose," I'd tutted with a token sigh. "But you're not getting any younger. You shouldn't have to deal with all this stress at your age."

"Jonathan, in the end, it's not the years in your life that count; it's the life in your years." He had an answer for everything which I imagine is why he'd made such a good politician, but I was far from given up.

"How about semi-retirement then?

"And do what? Gardening?" he scoffed.

"Not exactly."

"Then what?"

Now was my moment to talk turkey. The plan was fool proof. I finished my biscuit and took a deep breath. "Superstar wrestling." I announced with a flourish. He spat out more tea; which wasn't the reaction I'd been hoping for.

Now it may come as a surprise to many, but before taking office in The White House, Abraham Lincoln's first call in life was flexing his muscles, growling a lot and making silly faces. No, he wasn't a member of the Conservative party, but instead he'd worked as a professional wrestler. No word of a lie.

Growing up in Kentucky, Indiana, he'd began working the ring at an early age, learning most of what he knew from his uncle Morde who was a very equipped wrestler in his own right so I believe. At an imposing six-foot four inches (even without his hat) a young Lincoln had been a worthy match for anybody inside the ropes, and with his frontier style of wrestling it wasn't long before he was making a name for himself on the circuit of New Salem County. He'd built up considerable support as a safe bet to plonk your hard earned greenback on, and many punters were left crying into their tall hats and were considerably out of pocket once he'd left the limelight. I'd heard delightful stories of how he'd strut through the crowd on fight night to the soundtrack of 'America The Beautiful', as he de-robed down to his stars and stripes leotard, made tiger claws with his fingers and tossed his hat into the cheering crowd like a modern day Hulk Hogan. As he strutted around the ring his quivering opponents would look on with fear in their eyes.

"I'm the big buck of this lick," he'd roar as he stood on the top ropes and worked the crowd into a total frenzy. "If any of you want to try it, then come whet your horns."

Only the foolish ever did dare to whet their horns (whatever on earth that meant), but I was sure his loyal fan-base still remained and would have loved to see him make a return to the sport. His contests were the stuff of legend and with me in his corner, I believed we could make a comeback and return the championship title belt back to its rightful owner. I was convinced crowds would turn up a million strong across the northern state to see their former President dish out neck chops and pile drivers in his ankle boots to any unfortunates who got in his way. In over three hundred grapples he'd only lost the once, and rumour had it Hank Thompson's camp were keen on a lucrative rematch. It was indeed a genius plan, but it was obvious Abe still needed a little working on.

"Have you totally lost your mind?" he exclaimed.

This wasn't my first rodeo and I'd anticipated there might have been some resistance to my outlandish proposal. I smiled and dipped into my satchel for what I believed would be the deal sweetener.

"What on earth is that?" he'd asked, as Fido let out a canine snigger before returning to the more important task of licking his bits and bobs.

"It's a Mexican wrestling mask," I beamed, holding up the brightly coloured sequined apparel proudly. " I thought we could rebrand you as *El Abrahimo* and add a bit of mystique?"

"I'm not wearing that, I'll look a complete fool…I'm not even Mexican."

"Well, how about you keep your own hat on and we call you *The Stovepipe Hat Destroyer*? Or *President Pummel* if you'd prefer?"

"Most certainly not." he said, firmly.

"How about *Bam! Bam! Abraham*." I offered, now clutching at straws.

I began to regret booking out the Capitoline Grounds Stadium for three Saturdays in advance, and thought better of showing him the little figurine I'd whittled in his likeness. I'd intended to sell them on the merchandise stall alongside the oversized foam fingers and key fobs I'd procured in a job lot (I was way ahead in terms of monetising the sport), and I'd already secured image rights on his behalf. I could really have done with him getting on board with my intentions. Regrettably, much to my shame, I adopted another approach as I began flapping my arms around like poultry.

"Are you chicken, is that it?" I baited him as I began to cluck. "Are you a big chicken baby?"

As I circled the President with this dance of provocation, I saw a fleeting flicker in his eye for a second. Perhaps a momentary desire to pick me up and hold me above his head before bringing me down across his knee with a sickening crunch, leaving me sprawled on the canvas like a villain in the morality pantomime that is wrestling. Then the flicker was gone, replaced by that placid glaze that reminded me how he'd always been kind to animals. Interestingly, I later learned he was born on the exact same day as Charles Darwin in 1809, a man who didn't show quite as much compassion towards animals, as you know. I thought this an interesting educational tit-bit to include, just so you haven't completely wasted your money in buying this book under false pretence that you might learn something.

"Do I not destroy my enemies when I make them my friends?" he'd reasoned in a tone that made it difficult to argue, though I tried all the same.

"But just look at the pay per view forecasts," I pleaded, holding out a kind of eighteenth century spread sheet, but to no avail.

"I'm afraid America still needs me Jonathan," he'd declared, staring into his hat once more. "My days of camel clutches, curb stomps and glam slams are over."

"But, surely you can't hang up your leotard just yet?"

"I must." he said with a resigned sigh and drooping eyes. "And let that be the end of this silly talk of making a comeback."

I don't know whether he genuinely didn't fancy it or whether it was bad timing on my part, but either way my aspirations of being a wrestling promoter had been delivered a fatal choke-slam. The sipping of cocktails in the penthouse suites of desert hotels would have to wait, but the honeyed tea wasn't all that bad. I heard the creaking of knees as Abe rose to his feet, grinning his warmest of smiles and glancing at his pocket watch, before stooping to shake my little claw with his huge hand. Although I'd rather stretched my welcome, it was more than I deserved in fairness.

"Take care my friend, won't you."

"Call me if you change your mind," I said, despite the telephone having not yet been invented. It was just a term I coined well before its time. He straightened his hat with a wink, brushed the biscuit crumbs from his crisp Brooke Brothers suit, and walked across the parched lawns of The White House with his rifle at his side and Fido at his heels. I never did much like that dog.

In hindsight, I'm relieved he'd turned down my offer that day. Otherwise the uniting of the country and the abolition of slavery might never have happened. I'm also glad I didn't spark a trend in Presidents deciding to take their chances at becoming the next 'Jake The Snake' or 'Stone Cold Steve Austin', although Donald Trump did take down WWE chairman Vince McMahon at WrestleMania 23. Mercifully he didn't wear a leotard. If you care to look, you'll find Abraham Lincoln's name has been inaugurated into the wrestling hall of fame today, alongside such greats as "Macho Man" Randy Savage, and Rick "The Model" Martel. A fitting tribute if ever there was one for a great man of our times.

That day would be the last time I saw him alive. If he'd heeded my advice and stepped back into the ring, the worst harm he would have come to was getting hit over the back of the head in the ring with a folding plastic chair. Instead, he ended up being shot in the back of the head by actor John Wilkes Booth on April the 14th 1865, whilst enjoying an evening at the theatre with friends. Apparently his bodyguard (John Frederick Parker) had snuck off to the bar just before it happened.

Not even a fair fight if you ask me.

CHAPTER SEVENTEEN

"I wouldn't go opening that if I were you, Howard," I'd warned in earnest to a sweaty man in 1922 whose name was, as you might have guessed, Howard.

"Chill your beans, Jonathan. What's the worse that can happen?" he'd responded with a shrug, mopping the perspiration from his eager eyes and sharing a rare smile through well-kept teeth.

"Oh, I dunno, a lifetime of bad luck, illness and sudden death maybe?" I'd joked with my signature stinging humour, and we'd both reeled helplessly with extended bouts of laughter. As it turned out, I wasn't far off the mark.

We were kneeling in the blistering heat of the Valley of the Kings, squinting against the sun with our frazzled skin as we sucked in the oven warm air of the Egyptian desert that stung like embers in our throats. The famous archaeologist crouched beside me in a battered Homburg and rolled up sleeves, continued his digging in the sand with the determination of a man who'd lost an expensive pair of sunglasses at the beach. His name was Howard Carter, and the thing I wouldn't go opening *'if I were him'*, was the elusive hidden entrance to a dead Egyptian's tomb. An ancient resting place remained undisturbed beneath the hotplate sands for almost thirty centuries.

At least that is, until we had come along.

It belonged to the boy King himself; Tutankhamun (1342-1325 BC), and though I was no spring chicken myself, this pharaoh was ancient and already I was anticipating the unpleasant smell that would greet our nostrils on the hottest day of the year as we'd balanced precariously on the precipice of plunder.

A hurricane of dark thoughts swept through my faculty at the prospect of what skullduggery we were about to commit. Desecration of the dead didn't seem the most noble of deeds in my eyes, and I wasn't very comfortable with us becoming known as a modern era Burke & Hare, a repulsive pair who'd ransacked and murdered with a similar *modus operandi* years before. And what would my mum think of all this digging up of the long gone?

But this wasn't the only reason for my apprehension as we cut through the sands at pace that afternoon. I could already see the camels were becoming increasingly spooked with each strike of the archaeologist's heavy mattock, moaning and spitting their objections as if they could somehow sense an ominous force lurking deep beneath our feet. The camel's natural inklings were right. Something was certainly amiss, and as I watched them close their thick eyelids (a camel has three on each eye) against the sand as the wind picked up, the familiarity of unease rose in my tummy.

"Are you sure this is a good idea?" I'd asked a sweat-sodden Howard, for at least the fourth or fifth time that afternoon.

"Don't worry your little green head," gasped Howard, not stopping for breath or water, as he kept scratching at the barren earth on a hunch. But naturally I was worried. It was getting hotter than a training ground in hell out there, and if were to carry on digging in this golden cauldron much longer without protection (against the sun and against evil entities) then I feared for both of our welfares. As I dipped my head into a nearby bucket, the lukewarm water provided scant relief and I began to suspect this little treasure hunt was a worse idea than the time I suggested filling the Hindenburg with hydrogen.

I'd first met Howard Carter whilst sharing a shisha pipe in Thebes, and later over Turkish tea, he'd invited me along on his exploration to help dig the scorching sands of Luxor and to serve as his water boy whilst in pursuit for long lost, long dead royalty. I'm a natural forager as you know, but I'd had reservations about this expedition involving the 18th Dynasty Egyptian Pharaoh long before my claws had touched the sand in Giza. The problem with Howard (as with most uprights) was that he was of a stubborn nature and rarely listened. Although I was standing right beside him that day in the desiccant desert as I voiced my reservations, he might as well have been stood on the moon. With his unmovable stance my concerns fell upon deaf ears, and some say this led to what followed. In fairness, I'd have to agree.

This was to be our last chance at finding the hidden tomb, as Lord Carnarvon -who was funding the whole expedition- was growing impatient with our lack of success and the relationship between himself and Howard had grown frosty, even in the extreme heat of North Africa. To be fair, he had stumped up mass amounts of money to support the quest, and so far, all he'd received in return was a tonne of sand, a mountain of bottle tops, and the occasional abandoned flip-flop. It's with deep regret that I have to confess it was in fact myself who had unearthed the ancient steps leading to the entrance of King Tut's tomb, that sweltering Saturday afternoon.

"Hurry Jonathan," Howard pleaded desperately, his nose a burnt red from over exposure. With his panicked hastening I felt as though I was down to the last few seconds in my attempts to deactivate a nuclear bomb, so I kept grubbling around in the sand at his insistence. I continued my digging until at last my claws had hit upon the limestone brick of a doorway, and I'd never seen Howard so ebullient as he'd jumped around and high-fived me with an hysterical whoop. This was long before the ridiculous gesture was adopted by people who attend team-building workshop Wednesdays, which by the way is a very sad thing to do, even on a Wednesday.

"After years of fruitless searching, finally, I've succeeded." Howard had cried with emotion caught in his throat. "At last, I have found it."

"We've found it." I reminded him.

"Whatever," he whispered, his eyes now glazing over with greed as we began clearing away more of the sand like rabid corpse dogs.

Once we'd stumbled upon the entrance inscribed with ancient symbols and the seals of the royal necropolis, there was no stopping Howard or his chisel. Together with Lord Carnarvon and his daughter Lady Evelyn Herbert, we'd entered the darkened burial chamber that evening to be greeted by a thousand years of cobwebs and a warm stale air, which rushed past us in a bid to escape its lengthy prison sentence. I lit my candle with unsteady claws and waited for my eyes to become accustomed to the darkness within, but already I was on edge and suffering some mild intestinal disruption. My neurosis intensified with each tentative step deeper into the stagnant chamber, the sneaky shadows providing a united front to cloak the potential blue devils and danger that lay ahead.

"Ouch! That was my toe!" squealed Lady Evelyn.

"Haven't the Egyptians ever heard of light-switches?" moaned Howard.

I went first, as we ushered one another forwards like giddy teenagers in a haunted house attraction. I held aloft the flickering flame to cast light upon the centuries of the past and I was quietened by the resplendent spectacle that lay before us like a carpet of ebony and gold lavishly patterned with jewels. "Can you see anything?" Lord Carnarvon had asked.

"Yes, wonderful things," I'd whispered.

The chamber was awash with a wealth of shimmering treasures that the deceased king had supposedly needed for the afterlife. Ceramic canopic jars lined the dusty walls, jewel encrusted scarabs winked at our feet, and gilded statues looked down at us with disapproving eyes as we trespassed amongst the antiquities of Egyptian history on clumsy feet. I tried to ignore their constant glare as we shuffled deeper into the darkness like inquisitive rats, but I felt apprehensive nonetheless. Something just didn't seem right with the place, and as I ventured further forth, a nameless, choking dread began to soak into the shadowy recesses of my mind.

"I'm going to be rich," pronounced Howard, quite unnecessarily, as he marvelled at his gleaming surroundings by candlelight.

"I'm going to be richer," said Carnarvon.

"Have some respect. This isn't a competition," I hissed. "And please stop prancing around with that golden garland on your head, Howard."

As we pushed onwards through the half-light, being careful not to knock our heads upon the low stone ceilings as we went, we eventually came across the very thing we'd been searching for all this time. Following a labyrinth of narrow corridors and dead ends we'd managed to reach the main burial chamber, and in a darkened corner amongst the shadows sat a large sarcophagus (posh coffin) that held dead cats, mummy bands, and the King's own sorry remains. As I made a start towards the gilded golden casket decorated with lapis lazuli, I felt a sudden barbed chill run through my body, sharp enough to cut me in half. It was as if all the heat of the day had been sucked out of me in that very moment and I remained frozen to the spot, startled into something closely resembling unease. In the darkness, I could have sworn I'd heard a disembodied croak in some long forgotten tongue as it flitted snakelike past my ear. It hadn't appeared particularly friendly either. I don't speak Coptic script, but it sounded to me like a hateful warning from something that was, and would be again. Turns out I'm a bit of a pantywaist when it comes to the malevolent un-dead.

"Did anyone else hear that?" I shivered nervously, preparing to bolt for the vaults exit if indeed they had, but the others didn't reply. They were far too busy rubbing their hands in delight before prising the heavy lid from the boy King's coffin with an exerted effort. Once they'd ceased with the huffing and puffing and the centuries of dust had settled, a childlike face, cast in tarnished gold, stared back at them with a neutral expression. It was the face of Tutankhamun.

"Oh my," exclaimed Lady Evelyn, the dollar signs shining in her piercing blue eyes that had a definite air of Meg Foster about them. Oh my indeed. In the sombre shadows, I saw a tear trickle down Howard's dusty cheek as he gripped Lord Carnarvon's shoulder, but I was in no mood for sentiment.

"Can we get out of here now, please? This place gives me the fidgets," I'd implored, dubiously backing up towards the entrance from whence we'd just came. I could see by the look on Howard's face that he had no intention of going anywhere, and he tried his hardest to convince me to do the same.

"Down here, it's our time," he pleaded with reason. "It's our time down here. That's all over the second we ride up those stairs."

But I wasn't buying this goonish bunkum. With my beak at a quaver, I'd listened out for the sinister voice once more amidst the dusty shadows and was thankful that it never spoke aloud again in the living world. At that point I'd had enough grave robbing for one day if not a lifetime, and I was anticipating a cold bath to cool down and rid myself of the chaffing sand that seemed to get into intimate places I'd forgotten I possessed. It had taken us five painstaking years to find the entrance to the lost royal chamber that had lain buried deep beneath the Egyptian sands in Luxor. It took me exactly 8.7 seconds to find the exit.

Later that same evening, after a light supper and some moderate to heavy drinking, I hunkered down in my sleeping bag and attempted to disregard the haunting voice I'd heard inside the depths of that unswept chamber. I'm not usually of a goose-bumpy nature, but whatever those things are that do go bump in the night, well I didn't want them to go bumping into me. I kept the lanterns burning bright in my tent and it took me forever to settle, but when finally my body released its tension and I began to drift, my slumber was black and filled with terrors. I dreamt of digging in slow-stirring sands, searching for my own death with greedy eyes glinting like stolen gemstones, whilst a mysterious voice echoed inside the chamber of my subconscious in a long vanquished accent, warning me to stay away, stay away, stay away.

Now you may laugh and call me a stupid old fool, but without a scintilla of doubt in my mind, on opening the chamber that day I fear we'd summoned something forth that we shouldn't have. *'Flapdoodle!'* you may cry (or possibly not if you were born after 1914), but in truth we'd had no business in being there and I now believe that the 'something' was an ancient, execrable curse. You really do find out what you're made of when it comes to apparitional un-dead vexations, but though by nature I've never been a creature troubled by superstition, some of the malignant events that plagued those who'd assisted in looting the kid kings valuables on that excursion…well, let's just say they aren't easily explained away. In fact, some of them would make my blood run cold if it wasn't already. As you're aware by now, I never tire of that analogy, but let me divulge before you make up your own judgement on the fragile state of my sanity.

Some might think I'm being over-sensitive, but I'm totally not. Not long after the chamber had been opened to accommodate our pillaging, Carnarvon contracted blood poisoning from a mosquito bite not far from the tomb itself. He'd nicked the bite while shaving and it had become badly infected. Coincidentally, an autopsy on the body of King Tut later revealed a lesion on the cheek of the long expired pharaoh, in the exact same place. Carnarvon died a few days later in Cairo, and at the time of his death all the lights mysteriously went out across the city, his son back home in England reporting that the Lord's favourite dog had let out a dolent howl, before instantly dropping dead. Now I've never worn underpants as a rule, but it's around this time that if I had they'd be starting to fill as whispers of a curse began to spread amongst the taverns and firesides of Luxor.

Just a few days later a cobra snake, believed to be the symbol of Egyptian monarchy, was found inside the cage of Howard's pet canary. The golden bird that Carter had brought with him from London and believed would lead him to the dead kings tomb (it didn't, I did), had been gobbled up by the serpent. I was starting to get quite freaked out by all this disturbing activity, but Howard just scoffed at any mention of a curse.

"There is something down there. Something not us!" I warned one evening, as we took supper in his safari tent.

"You don't believe that tommyrot do you?" he'd laughed with a cursory flap of his hand, as if batting away a pestering mosquito rather than some sepulchral jinx. "You watch too much TV Jonathan."

As I studied his moustachioed face for clues I was still undecided, but became far less convinced of his bravado when it was rumoured he'd kept a tablet of stone hidden from the rest of the party, inscribed upon it a harmful curse which read: *'Cursed be he who moves my body. To him shall come fire, water, and pestilence.'* I didn't like the sound of any of those options in all truth, and call it animal instinct if you choose, but I sensed a dark pall hanging over the expedition as our insecurities grew.

The final straw that broke the camels back was plucked one afternoon when a rich American businessman called George Jay Gould, collapsed and died from a fever he contracted after visiting the tomb, and I had declared right then, that my time with the expedition was at an end. I returned to my tent, packed up my belongings and drank the entire contents of the mini bar

dry, before bidding a fond farewell to the others with whom I'd
shared the last five years of my life. I was adamant on getting out
of there before the curse could get its sinister intentions on me,
dishing out a dire punishment I no doubt deserved for my
brazenness. It had been fun to be a part of one the most famous
findings in recent history, but now a shadowy force had ruined
that fun and escaping with my life was a major incentive. I might
not have always made the right decisions in my time, but I've
come to recognise when danger is jumping up and down and
waving its red flags at me.

I'd begged with pleading exhaustion for Howard to put the
pharaoh's belongings back where we'd found them, allowing us
to forget the whole sorry episode. I tried to convince him to
reseal the chamber, bury the unholy spoils beneath the sands of
time, and to join me on the next available camel out of there, but
Howard being the man he was had insisted on finishing up the
macabre work of cataloguing our ill-gotten gains and his resolve
couldn't be shifted. As it turned out, it would be a job that would
take him several years to complete. It seemed we'd pretty much
wiped out the boy King's assets, along with the nest egg he might
well need going into the afterlife.

"Are you sure you must leave, Jonathan?" Howard had asked
with a despondent pout as I sat atop the humps of my ride, all
packed up and ready to go. "All we have to do is peel the shrine
like an onion and we will be with the King himself,"

"But what about the curse you failed to mention to anyone?" I probed.

He couldn't meet my gaze. "Doesn't ring any bells," he'd spluttered, suspiciously sticking his tongue against the inside of his cheek. I knew he was lying, because even I could hear the bell towers chiming in his head.

"You've lost your marbles," I mumbled back through my head turban. "Like most men, you've let greed get the better of you. I wish you a great life Howard, but you're on your own from here on."

I took one final look towards the cavernous entrance of the catacomb, and though probably just a trick of the light, it appeared like a tortured mouth set in eternal objection. With those parting words and a shake of the camel's reins I made haste on borrowed hooves, keen to put some distance between myself and the unholy excavation before the sun sank into the sands. Soon, I became just another distant speck in the vastness of the desert.

We pretty much lost touch after that, not even the occasional Christmas card or apologetic pocket-dialled exchanged. Over the years that followed, countless naysayers have tried to debunk the myth of a curse of course, some even accusing the media of sensationalising the whole affair to sell more newspapers, but these doubters hadn't been there or had witnessed what I'd seen. I know myself how sneaky journalists can be as they dole out their dross, but even after I'd returned to the sanctity of England and had moved on in life, strange occurrences continued to happen to the people complicit with the invasion of the tomb and it's long deceased occupant.

Houses were mysteriously burnt to the ground. Jackals with heads resembling Anubis (the Egyptian God of Death) had returned to the Luxor deserts for the first time in almost thirty-five years, and unexplained deaths from mysterious illness and misadventure, were a plenty. Sir Archibald Douglas Reid, who had first X-Rayed the coffin whilst inside the chamber, died of unexplained circumstances in 1923. Carter's secretary, Richard Bethel, was found smothered in his bed a few years later, and poor Arthur Mace- part of the excavation team –bit the dust from suspected arsenic poisoning in 1928. Surely this can't be just coincidence, can it? For years I've laid awake at night in fear of what was might become of me, and the rest of us despoilers who had dared to meddle with things that best belonged forever buried.

If you still remain unconvinced by my dark account, then perhaps I should quickly share with you the story of the malevolent pair of trumpets, engraved with decorative Gods and recovered from a large chest in the antechamber whilst on the dig. Silent for over 3,000 years, the BBC decided it a good idea to sound these instruments for a live international broadcast on the 16th of April 1939, to an audience of millions. For the BBC, this turned out to be an even more damning decision than revoking free television licences for pensioners like myself, because only weeks later World War II broke out across Europe and many pointed the finger towards the shudder-some brass section responsible. It is thought whenever these trumpets are blown, their chorus will summon unrest and war will imminently ensue.

In 1991, a student at the Egyptian museum decided to test this equivocal theory once more and blew heftily into one of the trumpets, accidentally kicking off The Gulf War. Although when you consider Tony Blair was Prime Minister at the time, I suppose this aspiring musician can't be held solely responsible for that one. If you remain in any doubt to my claims regarding these archaic weapons of mass destruction, then please consult the fountain of present day knowledge that is Wikipedia, which will confirm all of what I've shared. As a brief side note, I've often been accused of lifting historical fact from the aforementioned website, but I'd like to reassure you that when you've lived the past as I have and you're almost as old as the trees, you don't need a Wiktionary to tell you how it was.

Howard died in 1939, almost two decades after opening the tomb, so perhaps there wasn't a curse. Or maybe he just got lucky. Nevertheless, no word of a lie, when we'd entered the tomb that day I could have sworn there was something else inside of there with us that wasn't of this regular world. I think our poking around and general disregard for the deceased had awoken this devilish force and stirred its dander, and for that, I am sorry. Life is full of regrets, and when you've reached an age like mine you'll understand I have more than most. For certain, if given the choice again I'd have left the dead King in peace and shown more respect for the dead, because the morally ambiguous career of grave robbing doesn't look good on anybody's curriculum vitae. But no matter how deeply you bury the skeletons of your past, they often have a painful habit of coming back to bite you.

Today, now virtually blind in one eye, with worn out bones, relentless urinary infections and only Alexa for company, I often wonder if perchance I was cursed that fateful day under the watchful eye of Egyptian gods. Cursed perhaps, with eternal life and the foul essence of despair. Destined to watch on through thick glaucoma as the fat lady stifles a yawn with appetence and everyone I've ever loved dies away. I remain here alone in regret now, age having eaten away at my once handsome face and my body no longer fit for purpose. This truly is a curse, and it continues to punish.

I haven't returned to Egypt since, and I don't expect at my age I ever will. One of the last remaining wonders of the ancient world (and I'm not talking about myself) will forever live on in the squall of my memories, but, if there's anything you can learn from my apathy, it's that one should never underestimate or dabble in dark powers of which they have no comprehension. And that camel's do indeed have three eyelids.

CHAPTER EIGHTEEN

The 2nd of November 1982. And unlike the day JFK was shot to bits in the backseat of his dark blue Lincoln Continental in Dallas, Texas, I'll never forget where I was that remarkable afternoon when my world was about to become changed forever. The weather outside was in gloomy mood and the sky struggled to take on colour, but I didn't give it much thought as I sat snug and warm as toast, inside the comforts of a semi-detached living room in deepest Doncaster, England.

Myself, and the Patel's (my foster family at the time), were huddled around the mammoth wood-finished television set that took up one whole corner of the small front room like a square-shaped squatter. We sat in silence, eagerly watching the static bounce around the screen with thick anticipation, which in normal circumstances would have been quiet peculiar, but not in this instance.

We didn't care that it was beginning to drizzle against the single glazed window, or that the streetlights outside had melted from red to orange by 4pm, because ourselves and the rest of the nation (except for perhaps the most enthusiastic of dog walkers), had no plans on going anywhere that afternoon. Something extraordinary was about to happen before our very eyes that would make the moon landings or a televised royal wedding (yawn), melt into pallid insignificance. Britain was about to be gifted a new television channel.

Now this might not seem much of a hoo-ha nowadays, but in a time when anachronisms such as Blankety-Blank and The Russ Abbot Madhouse qualified as prime-time entertainment, it was welcome news. The soon to be launched Channel 4-as it was imaginatively titled-promised a plethora of cutting edge drama, in-depth nature programmes (my favourite), cosy daytime chat shows, and approachable newsreaders who no longer sat behind stuffy desks, but instead adopted a more casual approach as they informed us of the miners strike and Margaret Thatcher's proposed budget cuts to further punish the working classes.

Television was like a religion in our house at the time, the lumpy box in the corner our church (or in the case of the Patels; their Mandir Temple), and this was to be the UK's first new channel in over eighteen years. The public in their millions could barely contain their excitement as they readied themselves for a slew of fresh entertainment about to enter their woodchip wallpapered worlds from this most magic of boxes.

It seemed we'd been waiting for an eternity in beigey blandness (or at least for a very, very long time), but at precisely 4:40pm, we watched in a collective trance as an assemblage of colourful blocks broke through the static and came together on the TV screen to ingeniously create the number *four*. This was met with rapturous applause from the sofa, and just a few seconds later the channel let out its first lungful as a new-born; "Good afternoon. It's a pleasure to say to you: Welcome to Channel Four," went the seductive tones of continuity announcer, Paul Coia.

As Mrs Patel pumped her fists keenly in delight and the children hurriedly stowed away their spud guns for another day, you could sense in the central-heated air, that we were about to witness immortal history in the making. We perched on the edge of our gaudy eighties sofa like eager blue jays awaiting a fat televisual worm to appear on screen, as we were teased with a montage of all the amazing shows and attractive presenters to feast our eyes upon in the forthcoming days…but then Countdown came on.

We'd been looking forwards to this moment for weeks, and it was as though the wind had been sucked right out of us as we watched in bafflement and inadequacy at a disconcerting army of jumbled up numbers and letters populating the screen. I couldn't for the life of me, work out the nauseating format of the show, or why it needed a corner dedicated to *dictionaries* of all things? It made absolutely no sense at all. Mr Patel puffed out his troubled cheeks whilst the rest of us scratched our chins in wonder at this cyclopean anti-climax. This wasn't what we'd been promised.

"I just don't understand Asif," Mrs Patel had sighed to her husband with a note of joyless desperation, especially seeing as she'd even done her hair for the occasion. With a confounded look, she'd pointed at the conker brown television set with a befuddled finger. "What is this? What is *happening?*"

"I'll tell you what's happening," Mr Patel had grumbled, throwing his coveted copy of the TV Times at the screen. "I'm missing Grandstand for this load of tosh?"

The dog began to howl, the kids began to howl louder and Mrs Patel was beginning to regret cancelling her Tupperware party, because quite frankly, this obscure first offering wasn't up to snuff. It had been a huge anti-climax and I was most disconsolate, a bone lodged firmly in my craw at having to watch a maths lesson thinly disguised as entertainment. Ever since time began tortoises have held a deep-seated loathing for water hemlock, hungry sea-hawks, and television game shows. I just can't imagine why any sane person (or indeed insane person) might enjoy watching a Tony from Pontefract or Pamela from Daventry, answering mundane questions and conundrums set by overly-cheery hosts, and then clapping themselves, yes *themselves* after each correct reply. They really are one of humanities worst creations, don't you think?

"Can't we watch *Supergran* instead?" moaned the kids.

"Let's just see what's on next," I suggested with a sliver of hope. "It can't surely get any worse."

Mummy Patel already had her coat on to pop around to Aunty Belinda's (she wasn't my real aunty, just an eighties one) and my adopted dad had made a face as if to say he so wasn't sure, and to be honest neither was I, but I've always believed that patience is a virtue, and thankfully after a somewhat shaky start ours was to be rewarded tenfold. We'd got through the eye-gouging spectacle somehow, and now our little square peepers danced with zeal at the rest of that evening's televisual offerings. *Comic strip presents, The Paul Hogan Show, The Body Show, The People's Court.* All these graced our screens for the very first time that evening, each telly-titan nestled neatly in-between rib-tickling commercials written by clever London types, which at the time were almost as entertaining as the programmes themselves. Countdown aside, these shows were all absolute belters, packed full of suspense, exercise regimes and Antipodean humour, but there was still the jewel in the stations crown to come and although I was oblivious at the time, it was about to rock my world.

Brookside was a soap opera situated on a cul-de-sac on the outskirts of Liverpool and as an outsider looking in, I was mesmerised by the glum theme tune and drab surroundings from the opening titles. The second I witnessed a moustachioed Terry Sullivan vacuuming out the foot-wells of his gold Cortina in the driveway of number 7, I knew my life would be changed forever. The crispy pancakes and marrowfat peas that Mum (the adopted one) had made for tea remained untouched, my attention now wholly given over to tracksuits and tight perms as I soaked up this strange and wonderful Liverpudlian land of adventure. I peered, like a peeping Tom, into the living rooms and lives of the Grants and Corkhills who talked of marital affairs, shoplifting and mass unemployment. I had no inkling that so much drama could happen in such seemingly banal and ordinary lives and over the years, as the episodes progressed and their characters took on more meaning and dimension, I grew to love these flawed cast members like some kind of dysfunctional, extended family of my own.

Murder, buried bodies, kidnap, and the first ever lesbian kiss in the world (apparently) would all take place on that little suburban close in Merseyside. Watching each week religiously, I'd be taken on a rollercoaster ride of suspense and controversy as a grumpy Harry Cross chastised the local kids for stealing his garden gnomes or an innocent George Jackson was accused of warehouse robbery. I adored Brookside and thought these jubilant times would last forever, but callously, due to dipping viewing figures the soap drama would be brought before the dictator general of the station and executed before a live audience in 2003 when it was taken off the air for good. After twenty-one years of growing close to them like my own creep, I was dejected and heart broken. Even more so when I learnt it was to be replaced by a *dirty* version of after the watershed Hollyoaks. No longer would I share in the lives and trials of this stellar cast of characters as they faded from our screens, lost forever like tears in rain. In a way, it was like losing my family all over again, and not a week goes by that I don't wonder what Sinbad the window cleaner might be up to nowadays.

But back in 1982, as we watched history play-out in 4:3 ratio, that evening had flown by faster than any of us would have liked. At one stage, Mr Patel had risen from his armchair and flicked between the four channels in succession, just to confirm that what we were actually seeing wasn't a dream or parlour trick. Back then there was no such thing as TV remotes, so if you wanted to change channels you had to get off your backside and walk over to the box. Imagine that kids, having to move.

Ultimately, at 11:50pm, the station went off air for the night, bidding us a fond farewell and leaving us craving more. We returned to watching static like little Carole Anne's, trying our best to absorb what we'd just witnessed, and I suppose we could have stayed in that state of euphoria all night had my adoptive Mum not turned the telly off and ordered us all to bed. Without sounding petulant, being sent to bed at the age of a hundred and thirty-two years old took a little getting used, but whilst under their pan-tiled roof I opted to abide by their rules, though I didn't expect to get much sleep. Something ground breaking had happened to the people of the UK that day. We no longer had three channels. We had four.

Looking back now it all seems rather silly, but at the time it was a hugely important and momentous occasion. Today, TV goes on through the night, 24/7. We are bombarded with so many gazillion channels that we skip from one to the next without ever really knowing what to watch. Should we twist or stick? Stay or go? Netflix and chill? Lumps of metal spin around in outer space above our heads, beaming down thousands of tedious voices into ugly dishes that are bolted onto the sides of equally ugly houses, all of them vying for our eyeballs as they spew out a constant stream of bafflegab. There are shopping channels, sports channels, religious channels, and even the catch up channel has a catch up channel nowadays. In fact, I'm sure James Corden must have his own station too, judging by how often I see his buxom face as I channel hop in a desultory fashion.

And me? Well, I much preferred things how they were back then in simpler days. Four channels, just like four legs, are quite enough for anyone. And heaven knows why we needed channel five? If my cantankerous Scottish friend, John Logie Baird (1888-1946), who first invented the mechanical television set in 1926 (just two years after sliced-bread came along) was watching the box today, I think he'd have put his hands in his head, switched it off and gone to read a book instead. However, life is a twisted conundrum and it cannot be denied that the television has played a huge part in documenting the history of events in our lifetimes. I for one, will always remember fondly, that day we welcomed a new channel into our lives.

And Sinbad…if you're reading this, please get in touch and let me know how you've been.

"Well, I've enjoyed this little get together, Jonathan," says my dinner guest as we sit in the near dark restaurant that has recently been plunged into chaos. "It reminds me of a reptilian version of; Bill & Teds Excellent Adventure, one of my favourites. However, I think it's time to ask for the bill,"

I've never seen it, but I stare at him open beaked whilst motorcars, uprooted trees, and people fly past the window outside. Somewhere in the middle distance a window smashes, and I hear terrified screams from other diners as they cower from the biblical storm beneath tables.

"Are you crazy?" I say to him. "We haven't had dessert yet."

"But it's getting late," he pleads, looking at his watch for the fiftieth time that afternoon as he snatches at a passing fly. "My boss is a bit of a stickler, you know how it is."

"But I still have a few stories left to share with you," I point out with a hurt expression in my eyes. "Just a few more?"

He bites his lip pale lip and I notice for the first time just how gaunt my guest appears as he deliberates with a tap of his bony fingers on the tablecloth. "Well, I suppose I could sneak in a banana split," he chuckles.

As I turn my attention back to the window and peer through the rain, I'm sure, just for a second, that I see a familiar ancient ship swirl past in the grip of the burst Thames, its recognisable crew shouting obscenities from the waterlogged decks before a seagull flies into the restaurant window with a sickening splat.

"So, are you going to get on with this story then or what?"

"Sorry," I say, as I rub my deceiving eyes before I grab at a menu that flutters by in the wind. I notice they do a rather likeable looking crème brulee.

CHAPTER NINETEEN

"Everyone be cool!" shouts a well kempt woman brandishing a straight razor, and knuckles that dripped with diamonds. "This is a robbery!"

It's the 6th of March 1917. I remember the date well because it happens to be my birthday and despite the value of these special days tending to diminish as you grow arthritic and older, I was about to receive a huge surprise.

"If anybody moves I'll execute every last bleedin' one of ya!" shrieked another equally dapper lady who had appeared in a blink, at her side. I guessed then that it was going to be another one of those days.

In one of the oddest instances of fate, I'd ended up on sale in the pet's section of Harrods department store in London's Knightsbridge. An emporium for the affluent that at the time boasted a well-stocked menagerie housed on the fourth floor, just next door to soft furnishings. It was here, that stupidly rich people could browse and purchase any animal they so desired from its crowded animal shelves, which at the time included tiger cubs, elephants, Chinese alligators, and of course dozy Galapagos tortoises who'd wandered in off the street and had been put into the spring sale by mistake.

Or looking back now, perhaps it was a wanton cry for help?

For some time, I'd been considering becoming a pet. I'd always held onto the hope that one day I'd be part of a family again but I'd resisted the notion up until then, as it seemed like just another form of slavery at the hands of humans. But in all truth I wasn't getting any younger and a warm roof over my head with people that loved me, might be quite nice I remember thinking at the time. To be part of a surrogate family was worth a shot at I guessed, but I'd already been there for three weeks wearing my cutest face and nobody had purchased me despite several discounts. Like most things in Harrods, I imagine I'd been grossly overpriced.

That day I'd watched rooted to the spot, as suddenly a gang of around thirty well-heeled women flooded into the store like seasoned interlopers and began filling their bags and bloomers with expensive trinkets and jewellery, skilfully sweeping the shelves of their wares with shopping lists clutched in their larcenous hands. These respectable looking ladies who lived on the margins of society didn't seem like your usual career criminals to me, and I suppose that was the beauty of their clever scheme. They appeared just like regular upper class shoppers (wives of squires or daughters of aristocrats), and nobody would dare to suspect they could be involved in such a brazen and delinquent activity as theft. The sequined handbags and grand attire that these glamorous saboteurs wore made it simple for them to melt back into high society unnoticed, and this was the simple genius of their rouse. It was only when they opened their mouths and shaped their vowels, did you realise they weren't actually your genuine *Sloaney Ponies*.

"Wot ya fink you're staring at, Mister?" drawls one of the smash-and- grab artists, as I eyed the gang with curiosity from the safety of the reduced shelf.

"A criminal?" I suggested, before holding up my claws in surrender as a group of well-heeled women with pale powdered faces closed in on me like a pack of affluent she-wolves. I'd never seen so many expensive jewels, designer shoes and ornate flick knives coming towards me at once.

"You betta get in the bag, wrinkles," sneered the woman with the diamond digits who wore an Eton crop hairstyle and wasn't un-pretty. The knife she held looked sharp enough to shave with.

"A little ageist don't you think?" I'd said, before opting to pipe down when she'd pointed her glinting straight cut towards my unmentionables. The aroma of her Brilliantine lacquered hair was far more pleasant than her manner.

"You better listen good turtle, unless you want a throat full of these," she threatened with a crass generalisation and iron in her voice. She raised a perfectly plucked eyebrow as she cracked her knuckles and flashed the expensive rocks that festooned her clenched fist. "Now get in this bleedin' bag."

"I'm not a turtle. I am in fact…" I was bundled into a sack before I'd had the opportunity to explain my creed or even put up a fight, but of course, I'd been brought up never to raise my claw towards a woman. And this gang happened to be made up of just that. Women.

It occurred to me then, as I was slung into the boot of the getaway car before it screeched down Brompton Road, that this 'band of sisters', were in fact elephants. And in making this assumption, I am in no way being derogatory about their dress size you understand. I wouldn't have dared to after what I'd read about them in the national newspapers. The Forty Elephants Gang were a notorious all-girl group of prolific thieves who hailed from the Elephant & Castle area of London and had been operating in a life of crime since the 1700s. Centuries on, their historic circle was still going strong as new manicured hands replaced old in this Victorian crime dynasty. Not without their charms, they'd been dubbed 'bobbed hair bandits', and despite their debonair appearance they'd been making the most of a lack of CCTV in the London's West End for years.

Their modus operandi was simple yet effective. Their lady-gang would storm the big department stores on mass, plundering the stock and causing security guards huge headaches before fading back into society like social chameleons in the blink of an eye. A substantial bounty now hung over their well cropped heads, but so far they'd had the gumption to avoid the authorities with their clever racket. The Fleet Street media had described them as a band of six-foot tall Amazonian women, each hell bent on violence and villainy, but even then the salacious media was rife with fake news. Not one of them was over six foot and their accents were far from exotic.

"Please don't kill me. It's my birthday?" I'd squealed like a piglet in a hot bath, just as we reached our destination and they'd removed the itchy hessian sack from my head. I was still feeling car sick as my eyes adjusted to the light, but I could see I was being held in some kind of filthy disused warehouse, possibly housed in the East End judging by the smell of un-emptied dustbins that floated over from the slums (the smell floated I mean, not the dustbins). As my eyes became accustomed, I witnessed women of all ages and size emptying their bulging pockets and adding their ill-gotten gains to a row of never-ending shelves. Shelves stacked higher than Sputnik, which creaked with more consumer goods than you'd expect to find in an amazon warehouse. I doubted these ladies paid their taxes either.

"I beg you, please don't kill me. I'm an endangered species. You'll only end up with Greenpeace on your case."

"He's seen our faces. What we gonna do wiv him?" wheezed one of the common sounding older women in mild disapproval, her spine curved like a badly taken free-kick. She pulled out a string of pearls from her brassiere that were as big as butcher's sausages, before adding them to her growing collection pile with a glint and a grin. "Maybe we should kill him?"

"Einstein will pay the ransom. Please, just let me live." I'd begged shamefully, my voice fluttering between octaves as a blizzard of promises flew clumsily from my mouth. I was on the verge of hyperventilating, but thought it best not to trouble anybody for a brown paper bag.

"You really know Einstein?" another woman lisped, this one with chestnut curls and ruby coloured lipstick on her smudged teeth. "Albert Einstein?"

"Yes," I lied.

I knew Albert in passing of course, but at best we were loose acquaintances and I doubted he'd ever pay a ransom. He was notoriously frugal. Salvador Dali might have been able to help, but he had even shorter pockets. Often, at the height of his artistic fame we'd go out to dinner and he would pay the bill by doodling on a cheque, knowing all too well it would never be cashed by the savvy restaurateur because it was worth more as a piece of art by the pop-eyed master of surrealism than the price of a boiled crayfish and a few leafs of lettuce.

"Please. Just spare me," I begged. "I have so much to live for."

"Calm down, we ain't gonna bleedin' kill you," whispered a familiar voice as it crept out of the shadows. It was the lady with the expensive fingers who'd threatened to castrate me earlier, and as she came into the light she looked a little less scary without the long blade in her hand…but not much. "My name's Diamond Annie," she spoke as way of introduction, her stare filled with a dark intensity that flickered behind acorn brown eyes.

"I'm Jonathan." I said, because that is my name.

"Well, it's nice to meet your acquaintance, sir," she grinned with a simulated curtsy, the other ladies letting out a gentle giggle without looking up from their criminal activities.

As this queen of thieves deliberated what to do with me next, I observed her standing defiantly, almost Rubenesque like, with sparkling hands on her hips as she surveyed her industrious empire below. An empire built on hard work and sisterhood made possible by tenacious women who'd rose up from the slums and no longer accepted they had to be poor or inferior. These various wives, mothers, daughters and sisters had moulded themselves into breadwinners and their fists could match any man foolish enough to cross them. They no longer thought of themselves as the gentler, weaker sex, but as heroines of a new age. And if people were stupid enough to believe they weren't, then more the fool them. They'd use this chauvinist viewpoint as leverage to conquer the whole of the West End, leaving its shops out of pocket and its shelves as bare as newborn babies. This was girl power long before a cheeky Ginger Spice pinched Prince Charles' bottom, and the pride and delight in what Annie had built up was obvious on her vanquishing face as she turned towards me.

"So, me and the girls here were kinda wondering what kind of turtle you were?"

I felt the eyes of others upon me as I stumbled and stuttered. "I'm a tortoise actually," I corrected her with a nervous smile.

"Ok, smartarse. What kind of tortoise are you then?"

"One who's good at keeping his mouth shut," I offered.

Her frostiness thawed a little. "No. I mean what species?"

I peered over her shoulder to see that many of the women had now stopped their illegal work and were looking at me with quiet amusement. Nice they were taking an interest in nature I thought. "Well, I'm a Galapagos tortoise."

"Are you rare?" shouted out one of the more brassy girls with a grating shriek from halfway up a ladder. She couldn't have been more than sixteen or seventeen, and I later discover she was called Baby Face Maggie, which figured. "Rare, like a diamond chain, or sumfink?"

"I guess so." I shrugged, as I felt myself blush. "There aren't many of us left nowadays. A man called Charles Darwin…"

"We don't need your bleedin' life story," Diamond Annie interrupted. "It's just good to know you're an antique, that's all."

The women turned back to their criminalised cottage industry and continued stashing their swag. Though I didn't agree with their methods, I had to admire their work ethic.

"So is it really your birthday?" Annie had asked with a lopsided smile as she breathed on her knuckles and gave them a polish.

"Indeed it is. I'm a hundred and three today." I pointed to the concentric rings on my carapace, as if to prove my age.

"Wow, that's old."

"Thanks," I said.

She raised an eyebrow. "But a ripe age like that? That's something worth celebrating, right? Do you like champagne?"

"Who doesn't?" I'd stated, as she began untying my constrained claws with her cherry lacquered fingernails. The omens were good. I quickly sensed that I might live through my ordeal, and soon I began to think my perceptions about this all-girl group were a little misplaced. They were only doing what their rigid society had denied them for so long, and who was I to stand in the way of feminism. If you can't beat *them*, join *them*, has always been my grounded philosophy and before you judge, I don't need to be reminded of my moral failings. Although I was well aware I was now living life on the precipice of crime, it had to beat living life as a eunuch. Plus, you can get away with a lot more when you're old.

"Then let's get this *partaaaayy* started!" screamed Annie at the height of her voice as an elated cheer went up from the rest of the feminal assembly who began to bicker amongst themselves over which stolen dresses and pilfered perfumes to wear for the evenings celebration. Apart from a pair of sore wrists and a bruised ego that was already beginning to heal, the elephants had left me unscathed and now, on my 103rd birthday, I was to become an honorary member of the Southwark herd.

Without wanting to name drop (though I shall) I've hung with Hendrix at the Cumberland Hotel, pool-partied with Belushi in the Hollywood hills and even shared bubble-tea with Terry Nutkins in Sandwich harbour. Although these are trivialities in life, even in my decrepitude I've attended more shindigs and social gathering than there are plastic micro-beads in the sea. Unquestionably though, the impromptu soiree those girls threw for me that famous night in the warehouse (way before warehouse parties became popular, I might add) will go down as one of the best birthday celebrations I've ever experienced. Matched perhaps only, by Mahatma Gandhi popping out of an oversized chocolate cake and singing happy birthday to me decades later. I received more gifts that evening than the rest of my hundred and eighty-five birthdays combined, and though I was all too aware it was purloined contraband it's still the thought that counts.

As I binged on Moet champagne and quaffed vintage brandies almost as old as myself, I imagine I must have resembled a younger looking Hugh Hefner as I danced the Charleston with girl after girl on the swirling the factory floor, partying like an animal and knocking back peregrine shots well into the small hours. Those elephants certainly knew how to have a good time as they gambled, argued about things of absolutely no importance, and sang amongst themselves with impressive camaraderie. As the firewater continued to flow, a few of the girls dusted down old instruments, playing twin fiddles and blowing enthusiastically into squeaky harmonicas, but even then they struggled to make themselves heard above the arm wrestling, drinking games and debauchery. They even had the courtesy to give me the birthday bumps on the dance floor, which I thought was an exquisite display of compassion and acceptance.

It was that type of splendorous evening you never want to end, and as the sun began to rise early from its bed and began its job of warming a new day, I slumped down beside a florid-faced Diamond Annie, still feeling quite euphoric. With a yawn I watched the sunlight cut through the cigarette smoke whilst an overabundance of women lay wherever they'd dropped, as if gunned down in cold blood by the sandman after an eventful night on the sauce.

"I love you lot." I'd slurred to Annie with affection, the sentimentality of more than a few drinks plainly obvious.

"I think you're going bleedin' soft in your old age." she giggled.

"Tell me Annie," I asked with a hiccup. "What do you want from life?"

"I'll tell you what I want. What I really, really want," she'd divulged in a quite blithely spirit. " I want the rich to stop treading on the poor. I want women to have equal rights…and…well, I want another bleedin' drink."

Her choice of phrase reminded me of my dear and dead aunt Wilhelmina, so I nodded in agreement and poured us both another shot of lifted booze. You must remember this was a time when women had no right to vote, couldn't drink in the same pubs as men, and were even forbidden from eating Yorkie chocolate bars. I could see her point, and who could blame her for becoming fed up with how they were constantly perceived? I let out a caustic belch, way too drunk to even think about smothering it or apologising.

"And how about you? What do you want Jonathan?" Annie asked, as we reached the bottom of our glasses.

"Well, I do like the look of those Aga ovens," I'd replied.

"No, Jonathan," she said soberly, signalling towards her chest with a glitzy clenched fist. "What do you really want inside here? In your heart?"

" I guess I want to be part of a family again," I'd admitted, as I poured us another two-fingers and took a hefty drag on the unlit cigar that dangled loosely from my mouth.

"That's sweet," she'd said. "Maybe someday soon, you will,"

"I really hope so Annie," I answered with a biddable sigh. "I really hope so."

"These girls are my family now," she smiled with open arms, gesturing towards the piles of loudly snoring bones on the floor. "We're sisters who look after each other through the thick and thin, whatever comes our way."

"Could I be an elephant too perhaps?" I asked in a sleep-slurred voice, my eyes now growing heavy.

"We'll see." Annie had winked with a smile as bright as the diamonds that shone on her hand. "It's been really lovely meeting you Jonathan,"

"Thanks for my birthday party Annie," I'd mumbled, before my head slammed down hard on the table and rested, unconscious, amongst the empty bottles and popped champagne corks.

*

I awoke on my back in unfamiliar surroundings with one of the most crapulous of hangovers in my entire life. The smell of freshly cut garden grass and Sunday lunch entwined in the air, scenting my nostrils with a strange savoury spiciness that remind me I hadn't eaten in a while since. As I blinked against the sunlight and attempted to shake off my slumber, I could make out biped murmurings and four blurred figures floating over me like badly taken photographs.

"He's so cute," came the tiny voice of a young girl. "Can we call him Buttons? Or Flash?"

I could see the strangers swimming into focus more clearly now. A young brother and sister dressed in identical dungarees were flanked either side by their mother and father in a flowery dress and string vest. The father wasn't wearing the dress just to be clear, although if he had been, that would have been cool with me too. I was quite politically relaxed, even then.

"Where am I? What happened?" I asked, with a sand dry throat.

"You fell off the back of a lorry." said the vested man with a thick south London accent as he dug deep at something in his ear. Strange, I thought to myself. I couldn't for the life of me even remember riding in a lorry? Let alone falling off the back of one! However, I was relieved to find I appeared uninjured nonetheless. Just how much I'd had to drink the night before was anybody's guess, but I'd guess too much.

"So, who are you?" I croaked, rolling over on to my knees.

"We're the Shearing's. We're your new family." beamed my new adoptive mother, as the children began to pet my shell with miniscule little hands and gently stroke my wrinkled face which, let me assure you, is the best hangover cure in the world.

I later learned that the Forty Elephants Gang had sold me for thirty pounds to Mr Shearing, who was looking for a new pet for his children after their hamster had passed. I wasn't angry though, far from it in fact. I'd got my wish of a caring family, and if the Forty Elephant Gang could make a little something out of it too, then everyone was happy. Me especially.

The next few weeks were some of the most memorable of my life as I adapted to my new family and became accustomed to their noises, behaviours and smells. Lengthy, sun-filled afternoons were spent picnicking by the river or giving rides to the children around the garden, always being careful on disembarking so as not to start up another war. Evenings were spent snuggled up with the children under patchwork blankets and listening to the wireless as we told silly stories and tall tales. I'd fondly eavesdrop on bedtime arguments around tooth cleaning or untidy bedrooms, and would even help mum prepare their uniforms for school the next day, always popping a treat into their pocket for break-time. Once the kids were tucked up in bed, often I'd sit up late by the crackling fireside with Mr Shearing as he told me fascinating stories of his work as a fishmonger at Billingsgate market, and on occasion, he'd tell me of all the weird and wondrous creatures he'd seen plucked from the sea. The banality of everyday life was bliss and I'd hoped those heady days with the Shearing family, in their cosy Bermondsey two-up two-down would never end, but like everything in life (mine at least), the good times would not last.

One summers evening, as the sun began to lose its height and the hour grew late, the house was still sitting silent and empty. The children should have been home from school ages ago and I was beginning to become worried (and hungry), so I peered over the feather-board garden fence to ask next door if they knew of their whereabouts. I never usually talked to my neighbours as I'd really rather not get involved, but I was by now sick with concern. Surely they wouldn't have gone away without letting me know? I was family after all.

"Haven't you heard?" the neighbour had snorted with a disapproving look as he pruned back his delicious looking begonias with a curt; *snip-snip-snip*.

"Heard what?" I asked, the panic immediately flooding my green mind. Had they been involved in a terrible accident? *Snip-snip-snip*. Maybe Mr Shearing had suffered a heart attack whilst working on his fish stall? *Snip-snip-snip*. Perhaps little Billy had cut his thumb off in woodwork class? *Snip-snip-snip* "Just spit it out would you?" I snapped as I glared at the neighbour, my eyes swamped with fear.

"They've been arrested for receiving stolen goods, if you must know." he'd said in an uppity manner as he clipped the head off a blossom with symbolic intent. My heart sank at the prospect of no supper and the loss of yet another family I had grown to love and cherish. The stolen goods were indeed yours truly, and I quickly realised that I'd have to remove myself from the premises as incriminating evidence before the police came searching and I landed them in more hot water.

Into everyone's life a little rain must be expected to fall, but my own existence was the equivalent of Manchester. As I dug my way beneath the back garden fence with resigned claws and a weighty heart, I came to realise the harsh truth of crime. It never pays in the end. I made a promise right then, never to get involved in the criminal world again.

That promise wasn't to last long.

CHAPTER TWENTY

The introduction of prohibition in the United States in 1920 was designed to abolish the scourge of alcohol throughout the land and significantly lower the rate of student traffic cone theft. I imagine this was the absentminded intention anyway but not surprisingly, it wasn't a popular move on behalf of the federal government. All it succeeded in doing instead was ensuring that a number of gangland figures flaunting the streets of New York with their Italian shoes and waxy hair grew richer and even more powerful than ever.

One of which, was a mentally unstable man called Dutch Schultz.

His real name was Arthur Flegenheimer, but he'd decided to change it because he felt it was way too long for newspaper headlines. Here was someone who knew the true value of PR. Unfortunately he also knew the true value of hurting people with pistol whips, kitchen utensils and garage tools. He was the kind of character that my mum would have termed a 'nasty piece of work,' and what I would later term; the scariest man I have ever had the misfortune to meet in all my years. This is saying something when you consider I've hung around with Hitler, Manson and Charlie Sheen, no word of a lie.

With uneven and unenviable ears, and a face so ugly it was rumoured his dentist always made him lay facedown in the chair, this criminal man would strike consternation into anyone foolish enough to stand in his way. He always carried a gun tucked in his underpants and a wild look in his eyes, the kind that only those with a sick addiction to hurting people seem to possess. Most of polite society would unkindly refer to him as a raving lunatic, and though I'm always well mannered, I think they might have been putting it rather politely.

Dutch Schultz was no stranger to strife either. Having already served time for burglary in his teens at Blackwell's Island penitentiary, like most men of great civil disobedience he was bad news just waiting to break across the bottom of the ticker tape on television. With a thirst for liquor and a penchant for turning peoples faces into smashed lasagne, he'd command the illegal drinking dens of the Bronx employing good old-fashioned intimidation and racketeering. Trust me, with a work ethic like that and a trail of dead bodies littering your doorstep, it's only a matter of time before trouble comes knocking.

Turf wars had already broken out across the east coast as mobster gangs fought to maximise the distribution of illicit hooch and line their fecund pockets. This was a lucrative business shrouded in ambiguity and ran by a parade of mobster figureheads bearing glamorous names such as: 'Legs Diamond', 'Lucky Luciano,' and 'Bugsy Siegel', all of whom were compelled to compete for liquor sales amidst an all ready crowded black market. Howbeit, instead of cutting forecasts and beer prices like most sensibly minded business men might deduce, they'd take out a hit on their nearest rivals in order to hit their monthly targets. This was the pond in which Dutch Schultz wanted to become the biggest fish, and little did I know that I'd soon become the bait.

I'd always held a keen fascination with the monikers these hoodlum characters of gangland bestowed upon themselves in the 1920s and it would amuse me no end to hear of the latest bootleggers who'd arisen on the scene and assigned themselves a flashy name in order to state their presence. But despite my obvious attraction to the glamour, these American gangsters were dangerous people to get involved with and although it was true they did carry amusing names, they also carried an arsenal of evil looking weapons.

Neither were they the most pliant of people. The New York that Dickens had described had moved on some over the last sixty-years and as the city grew, so too did its dark underbelly as characters like; Pretty Boy Floyd, Bugs Moran and, of course Dutch Schultz, were free to roam the deadly streets like card carrying sociopaths. These bad eggs of the Bronx would lean heavily on anyone who stood in their path or refused to bend to their ways and whom you spoke with and trusted back then was of desperate importance. Not only for the length and success of your operation but also for the length of your life span.

Now, I'd never intended to become a mob accountant but this was a growth industry and I guess they liked me because I took my time, never skimmed off the top and always kept my mouth shut. Dutch might have been a belligerent whacko, but I have to admit he did have an un-floundering drive and ambition to succeed as he sought to move his booze operation way beyond the desultory base of Harlem. That's why he was keen to get me on board to help broaden out the franchise, I imagine. Gainfully employed to re-stock peoples liquor cabinets, deal with the numbers and take care of his financial ledgers. As a vessel of peace, I for one was horrified at the rising body count and methods employed by this vicious individual to expand his revenue, but he was a very difficult person to say no to. Those that did often didn't live to tell the tale. That is how I got involved with the notorious Dutch Schultz.

I wish I could claim to have led a fairy-tale existence, but I'm afraid I can't. My eyes can conceal the centuries, but this book you hold in your claws is a true a story as I can tell. When Dutch demanded I work for him that autumn, I'm ashamed to say the die was already cast. I'd simply nodded with silent discernment, invested in a camel hair fedora and began thinking up my own Mafioso alias to apportion myself. At the time, I was deliberating between Johnny 'Twinkle toes' Shelton, and Johnny 'Hard Shell'

Shelton, but neither stuck. I did develop quite a fearsome reputation for being good with numbers however, something I can only put down to my time spent with Charles Babbage. I realise now of course, that I was too swept up in the adventure and notoriety of the criminal over-class to understand that what I was getting involved in was wrong. I willingly took charge of the gangsters books, and what a story they told.

At the height of his empire, Dutch was bringing in $54,126 a week according to my number crunching. That's $780,000 in today's money (no chump change) and let me tell you, a score like that doesn't go unnoticed. Not only by rival gangs looking to move in on the wealth like pigs on a feeder, but also from the federal government who'd decided to go after him for income tax evasion, seeing as nothing else would stick. This meant that as his trusted accountant and financial advisor, the feds would also be coming for me too. I could be facing accessory charges, and not for the first time in my life I was a long way from the front door of my wheelhouse and in reminiscence I didn't handle it so well.

"I'm too pretty to go to jail, Dutch," I'd blubbered at the time, the prospect of incarceration weighing heavy upon my shoulders. "And a life sentence for me? Well we could be talking another hundred years, at least."

"I doubt wrinkly reptiles are a prison lags type," Dutch had croaked, with a voice that contained enough gravel to coat a driveway. I still had great skin back then, not the wrinkled green mess you see before you today, and I was worried for my welfare to say the least, petrified at most. And despite his inability to express emotion I think Dutch could at least detect my concern. "This thing will blow over soon, don't worry."

"But I am worried Dutch. Really worried," I stuttered, working myself into a lather as a whole web of potential future indecencies now raced through my mind.

"I've got it figured out," the career criminal had suggested, nodding sagely. "I'm going to make them an offer they can't refuse."

"Great. Well, ok then," I cried with relief, though in hindsight I should have perhaps have pressed him for more details on his plan. Then again, I've never heard of anyone who'd pressed Dutch Schultz for anything.

Rather than see the pair of us go to jail, Dutch told me to squirrel away $7 million dollars into a sealed steel box, which was hidden at the foot of the Catskills Mountain by his trusted, but forgetful bodyguard. Meanwhile, he sought to keep us both out of prison by using his contacts. At first I thought he'd do this by enlisting the best legal representation in the land and by mounting a robust and water- tight defence that ensured our liberty. Instead, because of his psychotic nature, he put out a hit on New York's special prosecutor Thomas E. Dewey. Already I was spending a small fortune on wrinkle-reduction creams and this reckless move was making me old way before my time. Dutch was a hard man, fossilised by years of violence and wrongdoing, but surely even he could understand the importance of a good skin regime. I decided to be super-brave and bring it up the next time we met (the hit, not the skin regime) at some place called the Hotsy Totsy club, over on Broadway and 54th as I recall.

"This isn't the movies Dutch," I'd coaxed gently, approaching his methodologies with a distinct lack of determination. "An assassination attempt? What on earth were you thinking?"

He shot me a testing look that I really wished he hadn't and it became as plain as a pikestaff that he was in a foul mood, his crazed temper stretched to its elastic limits. "Don't mess with the bull you little walking museum piece, or you'll get the horns," he threatened aggressively.

I looked around to see other patrons were eyeing his outburst warily, ready to head for the door at the first lick of trouble. "Calm down Dutch," I pleaded, trying to placate him. "You're acting crazy,"

His eyes darted around the room as if he were looking for someone, or perhaps, if someone was looking for him. "I fit out my enemies in concrete swimwear, Jonathan. I hang people up by their thumbs. What on earth would make you think I'm acting?" He began to pace, his face growing tight with irritation and I was quickly reminded of my place in the food chain. "Nobody gets in the way of Dutch Schultz."

I think I'd stoked his fevered temper and although I don't possess thumbs, I had no long-held desire to die a painful and gruesome death of stratospheric proportions. In fairness the man scared the bejeebers out of me, his swift changes of mood beginning to be of immediate concern to my welfare. I might be slow but I'm not stupid, so I did my best to offer him an olive branch and adopted my most casual tone. "I'm just a numbers guy, remember Dutch? Annual turnover, and dividend percentages is my thing, not murder. Couldn't you just have had a quiet word, told him to back off?"

"I'm the guy with the boom-stick," he'd exploded with a stentorian roar, his face now crimson with rage as he pulled a plated pistol from his undies and began waving it around. "And guys like that don't get a warning shot, you hear! The IRS tried to get me behind bars, and now it's affecting business. Why me? What have I ever done to them?"

He had done many things, including intimidation and attempted assassination, but I thought it inappropriate to bring them up right then. Judging by the detached stare that swamped his deluded gaze, the means of how he earned his money was obviously getting to him. As people ran away screaming, I tried again to calm him with a hint of caution.

"Why don't we just calm down, relax and take a long, deep…"

"Bath?" he said quizzically, with a hint of expectation.

"Gosh, no. I was about to say; long, deep, breath."

"Oh."

He began to redden again and I wasn't sure if it was through embarrassment or rage. If I was a more intelligent creature I probably would have left it there, but I didn't. "You really thought I was going to suggest we take a bubble bath together?"

"No, well of course not." he shrugged, all defensively.

"I'm flattered Dutch, but I'm not really into that kind of…"

"Say one more goddamn word Jonathan," he'd thundered, "and I swear, I'll shoot you in the beak!" He glared at me with a revolting grin that I'd prefer not to recollect, so I decided to stop talking and instead, withdrew into my shell with a forceful expulsion of air. This is often my Pavlovian reaction when someone decides to wave a loaded 70 series Colt 1911 around like a GI Joe/Chares Manson mash-up.

He was right of course. The tax interrogation was affecting business, but this brazen move took a special kind of carelessness and was bad for everyone. His mistake would come at a heavy cost and it seemed obvious to me that Dutch no longer had both oars in the water, if ever he had. He was dangerous, especially judging by this outlandish manoeuvre to whack Mr Dewey, and being dangerous, well, that was a dangerous thing to be in New York City at that time. As soon as the other mobster families had gotten wind of his wayward assassination plans against the tax inspector, they'd finished eating their baked dormice (a mafia delicacy believe it or not) and had decided that this time, he'd taken things too far.

Not one for toothless threats, they'd soon bandied together and enlisted the services of Murder, Inc. These were bad people, headed up by the ill-famed contract killers; Louis Buchalter and Gurrah Shapiro. There was no doubt they intended to put an abrupt end to the career of Dutch Schultz, because killing was their business, and right then, business was good. His contract was to be terminated with immediate effect and this time there would be no invitation with HR to carry out an exit interview.

"Perhaps I did go off at the deep end," mused Dutch a few days later, once his temper had subsided. He wasn't a man noted for his intelligence but even he knew he might have made a mistake. "Sorry if I went too far,"

"Not at all," I lied. Both of us were laying low in some filthy backwater roadhouse in a secluded corner of the city where the food was served cold and the whisky was served watered. We passed the time curtain twitching and playing Baccarat for matchsticks in the back room, Dutch, smuggling cards from his waistband when he thought I wasn't looking. We'd been on the run for barely a week, but already I was beginning to forget the better life I'd once led. One you could live without needing eyes in the back of your head, or a bullet.

"Funny thing is, I know I've got a temper and it looks bad," he'd admitted, scratching at the three-day growth on his carved face. "But maybe there's a way out of this? Any bright ideas, turtle?"

The psycho had some face on him. This situation was entirely his fault due to the fickle strops, and now he expected me to get us out of it? However, this was my pickle too, so I thought it over for a few seconds and then it hit me. It was time to call in a favour. "Yes, perhaps there is."

"What you got in mind, compadre?"

I didn't like this newly found chumminess but I went with it because it beat the flipside. "Well, I was thinking we could ask Arthur 'the Brain' Rothstein to act as a peacemaker and smooth things over," I replied, quiet sanguine. "He owes me a solid for fiddling his tax return last Tuesday."

"That is a great idea," grinned Dutch as he fiddled restlessly with his diamond pinky ring and relief temporarily filled my heart. "If, I hadn't gone and shot him dead last Wednesday, at the Park Central Hotel."

"You shot him?"

"Well, yeah. He shouldn't have been in the way,"

I took in my grim surroundings, took off my fedora and sobbed like a baby. "Then, indeed we're screwed," I cried. He had to concede I had a point.

The Bronx can be a lonely place when you're running out of friends and my enthusiasm for a life of crime had been extinguished quicker than a lit match in a hurricane. I longed for safe harbour and not to be stuck with a certifiable like Dutch Schultz any longer than was necessary. The cracks were definitely starting to show in our relationship by now too, as we nipped and squabbled at each other for no reason, like small dogs in an even smaller kennel. We couldn't trust anyone, only ourselves, and when the only person you can trust is an untrustworthy psychopath you don't trust, well, then you know you've got problems.

Over the next few days I felt eyes were following us everywhere, reminding me of those old oil paintings you tend only to find in haunted cartoon mansions. I'd walk the streets on trembling claws, jumping out of my ancient skin every time a car backfired or someone slammed the saloon door at the Hotsy Totsy with more force than was really necessary. We were on the underworlds hit list, I was off my food and both of us knew it was only a question of time before the murdery guys finally caught up with us. As we shuffled from gambling den to rooming house across the city, I imagine we resembled a pair of bone weary foxes being trailed by a ravenous pack of snarling dogs. Except these dogs walked on two legs, carried guns and ate a staggering amount of spaghetti. I was worried, and though unsaid, I could sense Dutch was getting twitchy too.

"Listen up," Dutch had grunted, as we parted ways by the Brooklyn waterfront that wet winters evening that turned out to be our last together. "I'm going away for a while. I suggest you lay low." I think by then, he'd had quite enough of me.

"That's a good idea," I'd agreed, trying to disguise my elation. "We'll be a lot harder to find if we split up. Going anywhere warm?"

'You could say that," he replied with finality, before his mouth buckled and his lips broke into a horrific smile. "Mind how you go, you were a good accountant."

"You too Dutch," I said with a fixed face, glad to finally be free of the insanely creepy criminal.

"I was a good accountant, too?" he snarled, his eyes scarier than a 1970s public information film. "What do you mean?"

"No, I meant…"

"Lighten up turtle," he'd said with a thick chuckle. "I'm pulling your tail." It was the first time I'd heard him laugh, and I never in my life want to hear it again.

"Good night, Dutch."

"See you around, Jonathan," he hollered, and I wasn't sure if it was a goodbye or a threat, but as soon as his car had driven away into the New York drizzle, I bolted inside my apartment before anyone could get a clean target on me.

I'd always known things weren't going to end well for Dutch Schultz. A few day later they caught up with him, shooting him just below the heart with a rust coated bullet at Newark's Palace Chophouse, a lovely little eaterie I still carry very fond memories of. It was an ambush at point blank range whilst he was on the toilet, so the odds were always stacked against him in that respect. Three of his men perished in the crossfire, (one of them being his new accountant, so another lucky escape for me) but

Dutch, stubborn to the end, had made it to the hospital alive by drinking cheap brandy to maintain his spirits and dampen the pain. The man had even more bounce-back than Jason Voorhees, and he survived for a further twenty-two hours in the infirmary after surgery, the rusty buckshot already having done its ill-boding job of destroying his blood stream and dismantling his already debatable sanity.

In the hospital, he'd summoned enough strength to send for me but when I arrived he was in a delirious state, falling in and out of consciousness as he battled to stay alive against the odds. At one point he opened his feverish eyes and asked me to come closer. "A boy has never wept," he wheezed, kindly covering my face in spittle. "Or dashed a thousand Kim."

"Eh?" I replied, searching his unseemly face for clues. Even the priest, brought in to perform the last rites had shrugged his shoulders. I was pretty sure Dutch wouldn't be heading to this guys side of the fence, anyhow.

"You can play jacks and girls do that with a soft ball and do tricks with it."

"Dutch, I'm afraid you've lost me," I said as I reached for a pen and paper to write down the gibberish he was saying. I could see he wasn't long for this world and the conquered look in his eyes told me he knew it too.

"Oh, oh dog biscuit," he sighed through his dying breaths. "And when he is happy he doesn't get snappy."

And with that the beer baron of the Bronx was dead.

His last words a stream of nonsense perhaps, as he recalled some distant memory from childhood? Or, just maybe a series of cryptic clues he'd imparted as to the whereabouts of that steel box containing $7 million dollars, hidden in the Catskills? I didn't hang around to find out. I could have used a drink right then, but quickly remembered that in a roundabout way, alcohol was the whole reason I was in this mess.

Shocked by the rising tide of violence all around me and fearing that the net was closing, my days in the mob came to an end as I entered my own version of witness protection, and went into hibernation.

CHAPTER TWENTY-ONE

I wasn't going to include this chapter in the book, but seeing as we'll soon be parting ways and time is of the essence, I'll be quick. After deliberating with my agent who was having serious authenticity doubts about some of the stories I've told in this compendium, I thought it only decent and proper that I should explain myself clearly. Just in case you're feeling disappointed or cheated that I've failed to recount your favourite historical disaster, invention, or character in my narrative so far.

Now, at this point, I already suspect you are reading this collection of entertaining memoirs and noticing rather large holes in my story and of course you'd be right. But let me assure there is no humbuggery at play on my part. Life can pass you by at speed, and I'll admit there is a lot I've forgotten over time, chosen to ignore, or simply missed. You won't find any account of the grisly murders of Jack The Ripper included within these pages for example, and nor will you read about the invention of Nylon in 1935 (disappointing I know) or even the trial of O.J Simpson in 1995. But I promise you, there's good reason for all of that. It's never been my intention to hoodwink you with apocryphal stories or to skirt over important historical events that have shaped the last few centuries, far from it in fact. If anything I've tried my best to report these incidents with clarity and correctness, but the truth is, despite my being around for such a ridiculous length of time, I have been asleep for perhaps half of it. No word of a lie.

Hibernation is a cross to bear for any reptile. It sneaks up and catches you unawares when you least expect it. Believe me, as a tortoise it's not wise to make any long-term future plans when you tend to nod off for six months of the year. I've lost count of how many momentous occasions, royal weddings and brainstorming meetings I've missed out on because of it. The American writer Ernest Hemmingway once remarked: "I love sleep. My life has the tendency to fall apart when I'm awake." I do see his point, but I have to say I strongly disagree. For me, sleep has the total opposite effect. It seems to ruins everything.

Every spring, I'll awake from hibernation half-asleep and still groggy, with a profound dread as to whose birthday I may have missed, which famous celebrity friend (or none celebrity) has passed away, and which war might have broken out in my absence. I'm often tempted to hit the snooze button when I discover my answering machine is filled to bursting with angst-ridden messages, mostly from lady acquaintances I'd promised to call back that summer but had failed to because of my affliction. Over the years (and without wanting to sound exultant) these dalliances have strayed from Marilyn Monroe and Audrey Hepburn, through to Twiggy and Princess Anne, each of them furious with me for standing them up on pre-arranged dates (usually the bottomless buffet at Magic China), or accusing me of ghosting them. Their grievances vary from: *'Why haven't you rang?'* and *'I thought we had something special'* all the way through to *'you've broken my heart'* and, of course, every guy's favourite: *'I thought you were different!'*

I am different, and that's wherein the problem lies. Sometimes I just forget winter is approaching before I drift into deep repose. In desperation, on awakening I've often sniffed the pillow for remnants of their scent, but by then its all but faded, much like my chances of ever winning them back. I think this could be one of the main reasons I comfort eat in my malaise, regardless of my low metabolic rate. Or why I've always fallen foul of proclivity (and Lion bars) and never settled down.

The great Ambrose Bierce once remarked that love is a brief insanity cured by marriage, but I guess I'll never be awake long enough to find that out. In all frankness I've had phone batteries last longer than some of my relationships. You'll also know by now (after my rant earlier in the Babbage chapter) that I'm no fan of technology, but at least nowadays I can still see how some of my lost loves are coping without me, thanks to search engines and social media. This isn't stalking, you understand. It's just that before the advent of Facebook, people had very little way of knowing what their exes were up to.

I'm sure at some point, most people have slept through a long haul flight or their alarm clocks. I've slept through the sinking of the Titanic in 1912, the 9/11 terrorist attacks of 2001, and the break up of the Beatles in 1970. No word of a lie, even the mass eruption of Krakatou in 1883 (loud enough to wake the dead, apparently) didn't stir me from my slumber. It's quite frustrating and even downright embarrassing at times too. I'm the largest living species of tortoise, but sometimes I've been made to feel so very small. In 1963 for example, I was perhaps the only guy walking around who still thought JFK was president for weeks after his untimely death. I appeared rather ill informed on that occasion, just as I did when trying to book a ticket to fly to the Republic of Rhodesia in 1979, only to find it no longer existed as a country.

Sleep can be disruptive and sucks worse than an aeroplane toilet in my opinion, so, as we continue our crawl through the timeline of history after this little stopgap (don't worry, you've almost made it through), I hope you'll forgive me for these unscheduled missing pieces in my own memory. I'm not perfect, I'm only reptilian, and despite my appetite for endless learning even I can't contend with the laws of nature.

CHAPTER TWENTY-TWO

I've been fortunate in my life to witness the spectacle of Edwards running the wings, Finney finding the net, and Dixie Dean fooling the best of defenders with his quick feet and impressive quiff, but for me it will always be a fat man from Derbyshire who remains at the top of my all time list of greatest players, my GOAT, as it were.

If music was my first love, then football was my marriage. Especially back when it was a real game, played by rugged men in knee length shorts with arms devoid of tattoos, rather than the neutered sport it has shamefully evolved into today. The once beautiful game has now grown quite plain and frumpy down the years, but at one time it had been an attractive and provocative spectacle to behold. Ninety blissful minutes of action filled drama with crunching tackles, reckless shoulder barges and the occasional head butt, made Saturday afternoon one to relish. I'll always recollect fondly, the pleasing tradition of hot Bovril permeating the bitter cold terraces that never failed to set my heart racing (despite my vegetarianism) as my eyes were fixed to the hallowed turf on which they kicked lumps out of one another. And just for the benefit of our American readers, I'm talking of course about the game played with feet not hands, hence the name football.

It's a game I often wished I'd been able to play myself, but despite my careful deliberateness and control on the ball, I lacked the required pace. Instead I was content just to watch from the wooden stands with the rest, as we cheered on our beloved athletes who wore cloth caps and smoked pipes as they booted back and forth a ball the weight of a piglet. Match day always brought with it a camaraderie amongst both young and old and I often longed to watch a game with my own father, imagining the both of us huddled high up in the stands whilst bonding over a flask of nettle tea in the cold sunlight, watching on as legs were broken and the goals flew in. Of course I knew this rite of passage would never come to pass, but at least amongst this sea of red and white I had at last found a family.

Football has always felt tribal to me, and a tribe is something I'd been sorely without for too long. This close-knit family of strangers, connected by the colours we pinned to our chests and geographical location, became my adopted creep, and even when outnumbered at away games we were rarely out sung. We stood together in solidarity like families do. We celebrated as one, we cried as one, and we screamed together like banshees when our team were losing, as was the case one Saturday afternoon in 1894.

"Who ate all the pies? Who ate all the pies? You fat goalie, you fat goalie…you ate all the pies.

I'd began this chant in frustration from the stands, as I whirled the wooden rattle above my head like a cowboy with a cattle rope in an attempt to revitalise the team who were already three nil down. Don't ask me why I'd decided to sing about pies in that moment, all I knew was it was catchy. So much so I couldn't resist repeating the verse again, just for prosperity.

"Who ate all the pies? Who ate all the pies? You fat goalie, you fat goalie…you ate all the pies.

It may have been the meaty tang in the air, or perhaps I just wanted to fit in with my northern counterparts, but whatever had prompted me to belt out the moreish verse that miserable afternoon, it would become forever stitched into the leather of football history. The song was like catnip to the larynx, and I sang it out aloud once more, accompanied by an accusing stab of my claw aimed squarely at the rotund lump that was keeping goal for United that day. In all honesty it was the worst performance I'd seen a footballer make until Chris Waddle's appearance on Top Of The Pops in the spring of 1987.

This 'lump' between the sticks had a name…Fatty Foulkes.

The well documented, pie-gobbler's actual name was William Henry Foulkes, but even the media at the time referred to our number one affectionately, as Fatty. I always considered this quite a brave stance on their part considering he stood as high as a raj on an elephant (over six-four), weighed around twenty-four stones and had palms like snow shovels. But like I said, football was a different ball game in the late 1800s. Can you really imagine Alan Lambourne or Martin Tyler possessing the pluck and backbone to do the same today?

Ironically, as much as I had lambasted the keeper with a volley of abuse for his nightmarish second half performance that day, this man mountain also happened to be my favourite player at the time. You can only imagine the songs I created for any players I took less of a shine too, and despite the shape nature had given him, Fatty moved well for a big man. The enormity of his hands came in quite useful as a shot stopper, or as a Derbyshire Colliery worker, of which he was both. He'd slotted comfortably into the first team on arrival, his colossal fists knocking away heavy leather balls like hammers, and his powerful kicks easily launched the ball the length of the fallow field so the forwards could get a head on it, sneaking in a lucky goal before the opposition even had time to put down their pint pots. The people of Yorkshire, famous for their batter pudding and little shaking dogs, were wary of outsiders at best, but they took Fatty to their hardened northern hearts as if he was one of their own and so too, did I. Though in fairness we were three nil down with only minutes to go, and as everyone knows, football fans can be fickle.

It was as I began another rendition of my infectious new ditty, that I noticed something quite remarkable. The crowd beside me who only minutes earlier had been silenced by the prospect of another home defeat, now decided to join in with my chant as we watched Fatty kick an opposing defender up the backside and receive a yellow for his troubles. At first, it was just a few hesitant murmurs from small pockets around the ground, but as the confidence in my song grew stronger and the simple lyrics were learnt, we became a band of chanting brothers, standing shoulder to shoulder as we belted out this moreish pie song with the vigour of a colliery choir. We lost the game that day but our voices had been heard.

"Who ate all the pies? Who ate all the pies? You fat goalie, you fat goalie…you ate all the pies.

Even the man himself was spotted mouthing the lyrics as the whistle blew. When asked about the song by a reporter after the match he quipped: "I don't care what they call me, as long as they don't call me late for lunch."

Much like Fatty, this quote carried a lot of weight, as it was rumoured he'd regularly sneak into the dressing room before kick off and snaffle the pre-match sandwiches before the rest of his team mates arrived. The game needs more characters like him today, and he was old school in both temperament and style.

Perhaps I'm looking back through sepia sunglasses, but I find the current incarnation of football to be a sanitized shadow of it's former self. A sport now dictated by VAR, faceless suits and ruthless agents who represent teenage millionaires that refuse to unplug their oversized headphones during team talks, wear too much body-bling, and are always harping on about the latest addition to their sleeve of tattoos, as if it has profound meaning. You wouldn't find Fatty collecting up sports cars like Panini stickers, or lording it up in high end nightclubs with the obligatory pop star girlfriend on his arm. Instead, more likely than not, you'd find him in the buff, chasing referees around the changing rooms at full time after a disallowed penalty, or manhandling the opposition and generally showing little regard for Football Association rules. But at least he brought some passion to the game with character to complement his size, as is described in this little snippet of commentary I recently came across;

"Allan charged Foulke in the goalmouth, and the big man, losing his temper, seized him by the leg and turned him upside down." – Liverpool Post 1889

And this one:

"It is a pity that Foulke cannot curb the habit of pulling down the crossbar, which on Saturday ended in his breaking it in two. On form, he is well in the running for international honours, but the Selection Committee are sure

But it wasn't just these fine saves and theatrics that Fatty would contribute to football. I remember fondly one rainy afternoon we were playing against Accrington Stanley, when their Lancastrian players began complaining that his red goalkeeping shirt was clashing with their own, and the referee was threatening to abandon the game. Due to his size, another jersey couldn't be found that fit him so instead, Fatty decided to play the remainder of the game wrapped in a white bed sheet I'd brought along to keep my claws toasty and warm whilst watching from the side line. We won the game 1-0 that day, and Fatty hadn't needed to make one single dive in the mud, hence keeping a clean sheet entered into the footballing vernacular. That's how I remember it anyway.

He did finally win a solitary cap for England, which is pretty mean considering Carlton Palmer won eighteen, but then when has life ever been fair? I'm sure he would have earned more if it wasn't for his marmite character, but then again at least he had some. Do you remember when Dan Walker used to present Football Focus? It seems to me he was piteously devoid of a soul, never mind a decent question to ask a midfielder.

When Fatty transferred to Chelsea for fifty English pounds in the twilight of his career, a huge gap was left between our goals that couldn't be filled, although we had to fill it because of F.A regulations and policy. We did sign another keeper but we had to find another chant, as the new chap was quite lithe. Who ate all the celery, just didn't have the same ring to it.

Although somewhat bastardized today (literally it seems) that song still fills me with pride, and the sentiment of solidarity remains. It has become the gravy that binds the tribe, the suet that connects supporters together through even the toughest of footballing times. 58,000 people went to bed that night all those years ago, humming my earworm into their pillows, and it still rings around the terraces every Saturday today if you listen out very, very carefully.

Sadly, unlike retired footballers of today that either step into management, punditry or advertise impotency pills, Fatty was flat broke once football had taken the best of him. In a time long before crowdfunding, he could often be seen roaming the streets of Sheffield wearing his FA cup winners' medal proudly around his neck, a sorry reminder of how football had moved on to a new era without him. He left behind him a legacy that few today can match, but you won't find a statue of him standing outside any football ground and I doubt it's because of the ample amount of bronze you'd need to sculpt it.

He spent the remainder of his life amongst the Wurlitzers, cheeseburger vans and kiss-me-quick hats, as he attempted to carve out a pauper's crust running a 'beat the goalie' sideshow on Blackpool pier as the constant rain rinsed away his stature. But despite his sorry circumstance, I couldn't resist knocking one or two passed my footballing hero whenever I paid him a visit. To my credit I did always buy the pies afterwards, though I was careful never to mention it was indeed I that had first coined the song.

Fatty died with his boots on in 1916 as a result of pneumonia, which tends to happen when you spend too much time on a northwest pier in winter wearing only a vest. I like to believe the big man is up there somewhere, saving penalties with one hand and eating pie with the other, whilst angels holding harps play his signature song. If only I'd gotten around to securing the royalties…

CHAPTER TWENTY-THREE

I used to think invisibility was a super power, but now I recognise its just another sign of the aging process. The older you grow, the less people seem to notice you're there and I fear the looks the mirror is giving me these days. Even health shakes and seaweed facials serve only to shave mere seconds of our appearance in the grand scheme of things and let's face it, I'm old now (although still well maintained). Most of my friends are lying as bones in the ground, those ones in heaven probably guessing I didn't make it up there, and I feel it won't be long before I myself am ushered off the stage and manhandled towards the exit. But I don't fear it.

I'm an ancient creature now, creaky and broken. I only need to consult my scowling reflection to confirm this tragic fact. I'm such an old crusty, I was walking around when the Napoleonic Wars were still raw in the mind and those in Europe had yet to see a real Hippopotamus. I've already reached the bleak milestone of a hundred and eighty-five, and likely overstayed my welcome by now anyhow. Glaucoma and arthritis remain the only company at my side as time catches up with me, the inevitable now but a mere formality. There is no hiding the evidence that my daily routine has become an indignity, or that the lines and planes on my charming face have become ruined with time. But this is the high price for a wristband to life's after party that you realise only too late, isn't that much fun anyway. I have to completely agree with Charles De Gaulle when he described old age as a "shipwreck".

And I rarely agree with a Frenchman.

But if it is indeed a shipwreck, then what happens to us once we find ourselves plunged into death's all-consuming ocean? Are we to be claimed by its unforgiving waves and submerged into the darkness of its eternal tide? Or do we wash up on some distant shore to be greeted by everlasting salvation and reunited with our long lost, loved ones? Essentially, I'm asking whether there's life after death but I'm figuring you worked that out already.

One man who certainly thought so was an old pal of mine, Sir Arthur Conan Doyle, who following the death of his son in the First World War became a devout believer in the cause of spiritualism. He may have been responsible for the creation of the arch rationalist Sherlock Holmes but that didn't prevent him gathering with others in darkened rooms whilst a clairvoyant summoned forth passing spirits. He'd desperately clung to the notion of speaking to his son again in the afterlife and spiritualism had gripped his imagination just as fiercely as he had gripped the imaginations of others with his forensic detective stories. I'd always admired the man, but on each occasion our paths would cross he continued to impress upon me his wives apparent ability to contact the dead. Much to my annoyance, finally I succumbed.

One evening in 1922 on the night of the Pentecost, he'd invited me over to his place to participate in a séance, where among the guests in attendance were Harry Houdini and Barry Cryer, (seriously, Barry had been lying about his age for years). I was at a loose end and had run out of excuses, so had crawled along to what I thought would be a fairly uneventful and stagnant social affair, but it proved to be anything but. Firstly, it was a delight to meet Houdini, who regardless of his status for his ability to escape any confinement was a complete gentleman. Barry, I'd first met when we were both entertaining the troops during the Boer War, delightful company as long as the sherry is kept out of reach.

In the rarefied settings of the Conan Doyle's front living room we'd spoke pleasantries before huddling together, bathed by hallowed candlelight, around a circular walnut table with reams of blank paper sitting upon it. The room- oak panelled with a large fireplace in the wall and fine Tabriz carpets- carried a smell of mustiness from the rows of leather-bound books that lined up like soldiers on the dusty shelves above, and as our fingertips rested lightly on the burnished surface of the table below them, Mrs Conan Doyle sat silently restive with eyelids firmly closed and fountain pen in hand. She was a proclaimed specialist in what was then known as automatic writing, an act which involved communicating with the afterlife and translating their sorry, departed ramblings into words on the page. It all sounded rather far-fetched to me and so far the evening had seemed pretty unconvincing.

After some light theatrics, she claimed to have made contact with a couple of misplaced spirits whilst in an apparent trance-like state, and had sloppily scribbled down some vague messages in inelegible penmanship from the other side, before snapping out of her reverie. It was nothing tremendous and I noted she had looked a little dark beneath the eyes, seemingly due to the exhaustive business of taking down secretarial notes for the dead. Disappointed not to have coaxed any better gossip from beyond, she'd covered a yawn and started to pack away her knick knacks and yogibogeybox for the evening. Houdini and his wife had risen from their seats and a downhearted Arthur collected the papers into a neat pile, summoning the scullery maid to fetch for our coats and canes as the night seemingly fizzled out to a whimper.

"Shame we never had a chance to hear from any of your contemporaries." I joked to Barry, my voice laced with sarcasm as I eased into my wingback chair. "I'd love to know how the Duke of Wellington is doing nowadays?"

"Get lost," he hissed, his face red from continuous sherry consumption.

"Gentleman, please," Sir Arthur had whispered, before the candles began to quiver and his wife stirred once more. Suddenly, I felt a coldness clinging in the air and I asked Sir Arthur if perhaps he'd left a window open in his study, but he didn't answer. Instead, his expectant eyes flitted back and forth between his wife and the pages sitting on the table in the splintery light. "Quickly. Link hands once more," he'd spoke with urgency. "We need to summon more energy."

I looked towards his wife who was now staring with dark piercing eyes across the table as she began to emit a low unnerving hum that vibrated from somewhere deep within. Without warning, she threw back her dark curls and began to groan and thrash violently in her chair as though in a tug-of-war between an invisible good and evil. I felt something within me loosen, and as she continued to convulse we each looked at one another to decipher whether this was more of Jean's amateur dramatics, or whether we should call for an ambulance.

"To understand the living, first we have to commune with the dead," she'd mumbled in a distant and detached voice as she clutched the pearl beads that hung around her neck and gasped the mildewed air as if it were her last. My head began to feel dizzy and my bowels watery.

"What do you mean Jean?" asked Houdini, already halfway inside his coat.

"When do the snacks arrive?" asked Barry, his sweaty palm now locked tight in mine, as once again Sir Arthur declined to answer. With a ritual snarl quite out of character, Jean held the pen tight in her fist and began staring intently at an unsettled Houdini from across the table. He groped for his chair and decided to sit back down.

"Everything Ok Jean?" the escapologist had queried with a contemplative bite of his lip. In all honesty, the renowned escape artist looked kind of rattled, but it was obvious he didn't intend on going anywhere in that moment as Jean glowered at him with vacant dark pools that were once her amicable eyes.

"Your mother's in here Harry," Jean croaked, with an unflattering grin and a guttural growl. "Would you like to leave a message? I'll see that she gets it."

Before Houdini could garner a response, Jean's eyes had narrowed to nothing, and trembling like a weed she began performing a series of strange incantations through threatening lips. Gripping the pen, her contorted hand began to write in childlike, slanted capitals on the page as sheet after sheet became covered in chaotic ink, Sir Arthur struggling to keep up with fresh paper for his potentially possessed wife to write upon. As my leathery knees began to quake beneath the table, I began to realise that although this type of stagecraft offended my sense of rationality, perhaps I'd underestimated the enormity of this dark art we were witnessing.

"I don't like this jamboree one bit," groaned Barry, echoing my own thoughts as we witnessed Jean's mouth twisting in the shadows as she talked in ancient tongues. "It's giving me the heebie-geebies,"

"Then why come?" I whispered as the table gently began to wobble.

"The sherry I guess," said Barry, as his grip tightened again in my claw.

As Jean continued her conduit duties for the dead, the diamond paned parlour window suddenly blew open with a clatter and a cold wind rushed through the room, rattling ornaments on tables and throwing books to their deaths from high shelves. I couldn't quite believe my eyes, and mine were the most honest I'd met. Sir Arthur ran to close it with a shriek before the papers could blow away and the messages from the hereafter were lost to the outside world.

"What the hell is going on?" cried Barry, as he took care of his own priorities and reached for his sherry glass.

"Please. Don't panic." Sir Arthur said, in sheer panic.

"Is it really my mother?" Houdini demanded to know, as Jean's spooky eyes remained locked upon his, the words continuing to flow from the pen with even more urgency as they tore deep into the paper lain out before her.

"Oh my god! What on earth is that?" I suddenly proclaimed, as I sensed something ungodly present itself as if from the very bowels of hell, or at least the bowels of somewhere.

"Sorry," said Barry with a smirk, having just let off the most horrendous of smells. I don't think he was sorry at all.

"Gentlemen, please," Sir Arthur repeated absently, looking anxiously at his wife. "Jean darling, are you ok?"

The thing that was no longer Jean growled huskily, hunched in the chair like a screaming pope from a Francis Bacon oil painting. "I'm not Jean!"

"Then where is Jean?" Sir Arthur had asked. "Where is my wife?"

"In here, with us," the shape spat.

As Jean (or whoever it was) finally completed her scrawling, we all watched on in troubled disbelief as her chair rocked back and forth with a rattle, before she flung both hands into her mess of hair and rested upon the table with heaves of exhaustion. I was relieved not to have observed her head rotating at 360 degrees like a wood owl, but I felt unsettled nonetheless. The room fell silent in the swimming gloom of the sitting room, as each of us looked at one another open mouthed, Sir Arthur piling the sheets together like a teachers pet (I used to be one too) as he waited for his wife to come round from her unearthly trance.

"Well, that was quite something," said Houdini breaking the silence, and I could hear the workings of his clever mind begin to whir as it searched for a sane solution to what we'd just seen.

"I need a drink," commented Barry, helping himself to the decanter on the side table with shaking hands. "I'm not usually one who goes in for all this mumbo jumbo. Too much for my nerves,"

"It's called psychography," corrected Bess, Houdini's wife. She was a dinky woman, no doubt a bonus when having to contort yourself into cramped Selbit saw-boxes whilst your husband cuts you in half on stage, but right then I imagine she'd rather have been sawed into a hundred pieces than explain this whirlpool of paranormal to the veteran comedian, who didn't seem at all interested in anything but drink.

"Parawhatwhat?" Barry cried.

Sir Arthur shot him a cold stare before his eyes fell upon Houdini who was looking particularly on edge as he shifted restlessly in his chair. He and his wife had been attempting to make contact with his dear deceased mother for years, but as vaudevillians they were well aware of the cheap tricks employed by fake clairvoyants to dupe the public. In fact they had taken great delight in exposing several of these charlatans in the past. None more so than Margery Crandon, a Boston medium who performed half naked and claimed to be able to emit ectoplasm from her more intimate parts. No word of a lie. The Houdini's themselves had previously drawn upon their own theatrical skills to stage bogus séance's in order to earn money, so they were well versed in the fakery and tricks that inhabited the lucrative world of spiritualism. It would be interesting to see what they would make of this impromptu live performance of Jeans 'gift'.

Jean took a sip of water as she started to come round and gather her senses. "It was indeed your mother, Harry," she gasped, as Sir Arthur passed over the sheets of paper he was holding to the great escapologist.

"Well I'll be blowed," Barry said as he helped himself to another glass of sherry. "Didn't know your mother was called Harry."

"No you don't understand." Jean replied.

"Ignore him." I sighed.

"This is extraordinary," Houdini announced, as he and his wife poured through the pages in front of them with eyes alight. "Utterly extraordinary."

Sir Arthur grasped his wife's hand in a show of glowing pride. "I thought you might be impressed," he'd said to his friend.

"Oh, I'm impressed alright." Houdini replied briskly, a hint of anger now seeping into his voice. "Impressed that this is all in English."

"Is there a problem?" Jean had whispered faintly, still a little groggy from her ghostly translation duties.

Houdini pinched the bridge of his nose as if he could sense a headache coming on. "Well, not unless you consider the fact that my mother was Hungarian and couldn't speak a single word of English."

Arthur and Jean had exchanged glances, unsure of what to say as Harry and Bess got to their feet in a quite unapologetic manner. "I believe it's time to leave," Houdini had spluttered, trying to keep a lid on his temper as best he could. "The secret of showmanship consists not of what you really do, but what the mystery-loving public thinks you do."

He no doubt feared the bond of friendship they shared with Sir Arthur wasn't enough to prevent him and his wife from attempting to dupe them, but Conan-Doyle tried to brush off any awkwardness and reassured them as they left with their coats. "I'm sure there is some explanation. Are we still on for tennis doubles next Tuesday?"

"We shall see," Houdini had said with an unforgiving glare before grabbing his storm lamp and his wife, swiftly vanishing through the door with haste.

The friendship between the two men was never to recover. The relationship, however strained, broke down completely over the course of the next few years as Houdini continued to denounce mediums that Sir Arthur believed were genuine. As the door slammed shut behind them, Jean cried into her husband's arms and I was left to reflect upon the sour note the evening had ended upon. Who knows, maybe there is a language school in the after life where Mother Houdini has been spending some of eternity learning English? Or maybe once you die, you're handed some kind of translating system to speak through that converts every tongue into English? I really can't say, although now in the autumn of my years, I'll know pretty soon enough, I'm sure.

I'm convinced Sir Arthur hadn't intentionally set out to deceive his old friend that evening, but what I did know was he was a decent old soul if not a little gullible. I'd once posed for a picture with some cut out fairies from a magazine to pass the time, and had showed the image to some friends who'd howled with laughter. We then thought it would be an idea to get Elsie, their oldest daughter, and her cousin Frances to pose in various settings with them. These were even better, and both the girls looked equally as angelic as the paper nymphs they sat besides.

"I know who'll fall for this." I'd told them at the time as I clutched the pictures and stuffed them in an envelope addressed to Conan-Doyle with a giggle.

But I digress, something I have a tendency to do quite often nowadays, and this future discretion was of scant consolation to Sir Arthur as he hugged his wife after having watched Houdini disappear in his quickest escape routine yet. I thought it best to make my own exit at this point too, but as I prepared to climb down from my chair there was a sudden disturbance in the room.

The table began to rock back and forth on its ornate feet, followed seconds later, by a terrible bestial groan. The Conan-Doyle's and I stared at one another in disbelief, right before Sir Arthur scrambled out of the room to grab his camera. Had an errant spirit from the other side become trapped in this realm and wanted to make it's phantasmal presence felt?

Still the groaning continued, as a vacant chair toppled over before our very eyes with some invisible force and a primeval instinct caused my tail to retract. I was frantically dialling up my courage but so far it was ignoring my calls as I felt a hollow, familiar fear encompass my bones. Was this an angry presence from the spirit world, whose ghoulish cries for help had gone unheard? A poltergeist perhaps, not even aware that it's existence upon this plane had come to an end?

As Sir Arthur rushed back into the sitting room with his camera poised, we discovered it was in fact none of those things. Merely Barry Cryer, who'd slid off his chair in a drunken blitz and had wound up underneath the table, bashing his head in the process.

"You lot look like you've seen a ghost," he'd slurred, as he clambered to his feet before staggering off in the direction of the upstairs loo.

"Is it possible to get an exorcist?" I asked, as Sir Arthur fetched my cane and I bade them both good night. As I stepped into the cool night air I had to snigger at my naivety, deciding that would be the last time I would dabble in any unearthly mumbo jumbo.

I can barely bring the spoon to my beak as I attempt to eat my dessert. The wind howls through the restaurant now, as I hear more glass smash and the relentless rain pours in through the roof. I sit across from my guest, and it's as though we are the last men standing in a western (except we're sitting).

"It's time to go," he shouts against the wind, as the tablecloth whips up into his face and the wine bottles crash to the floor.

"But we haven't had coffee yet," I shout back as the storm water begins to touch my claws and suddenly I feel a familiar presence. I look up from my waterlogged crème brulee to see my mum looking down at me with shining pride, her face just as radiant as it was all those years ago. She wipes remnants of pudding from my face with her maternal claw.

"Mum?" I say with a tear welling in my eye.

She smiles and places her claw on my shell as I feel its warmth resonate through my bones. It had certainly been a strange evening, and I quickly realise my dinner quest has spiked my soup, because I'm hallucinating. Unless it's hibernation sickness? No, I'm definitely hallucinating.

It wouldn't be the first time such a thing has happened.

CHAPTER TWENTY-FOUR

It wasn't until I was in my late nineties, mid-life I guess, that I started taking drugs. I haven't really talked about it much since rehab, but I feel it's something I must be candid about if this book is to be a true representation of my life, because aside from the hard drinking, smoking, fast cars, fried foods and an edacious obsession for scratch-cards, I'd always led a relatively clean life up until then.

But once in a while, life can give you a thumb in the eye or throws a curve ball your way, sometimes fast ones that aren't always so easy to catch, throwback, dodge, or whatever else you're meant do with curve balls. Through a downturn of luck and circumstance in the morass of the 1950s, I'd become hooked on moreish pills, synthetics and party powder. Some might even suggest my sick addiction was a sign of naivety and weakness, whilst others with a more charitable view would understand that it all began when I'd fallen in with the wrong crowd. One made up of appalling low lives with no moral fibre or conscience, trained to feed off of misfortune and addiction like vampiric leeches, and often referred to today as the United States Central Intelligence Agency.

It fills me with disgust to admit that in the thrust of the 1950s, whilst under the ambiguous supervision of the CIA, I was to become the sorry subject of animal testing. In the company of these unpleasant spymasters housed in a furtive laboratory in the bowels of God knows where, I would have to endure the indignity of being jabbed with javelin length needles and force-fed serums under the wafer-like guise of scientific research. For a time those mephitic chemicals swirling around my system became my only substitute for life, having a lasting impact on both my mental wellbeing and my toilet habits. Ultimately, it would strip my decorum to its very ossein and I wasn't the only one who would suffer at the hands of their abuse and misuse. In some respects, despite feeling half-dead these days, I'm lucky to be alive.

Non-consenting guinea pigs, beagles, white mice, monkeys and rabbits were all housed in this drugstore for the degenerate too, each depraved of their dignity as unwilling participants in this cruel regimen of animal research. We would sit for days in silence, caged like ghoulish convicts as we waited with a sardonic mix of fear and wanting for the toxins to be pushed into our veins or the acid dripped into our corneas at the whim of man. As I've mentioned on numerous occasions (possibly too many), humans can be cruel creatures, and in those toxic times you could forget all about the war on drugs, because the drugs of war proved to be a far more lucrative business. The malingering CIA had focused on one area of synthetics in particular that they believed showed great potential in the scientific field of mind control and psychological torture. It's name; Lysergic Acid Diethylamide.

Perhaps better known nowadays as LSD or acid, this drug was hailed a game changer when once it raised its ugly head from the test tube of tyranny. Although it may sound far-fetched, for years the government had been dabbling with the possibility of creating human soldiers who could fight future wars whilst under the influence of mind control, using radio waves to increase aggression and stimulants to make them more compliant. That's why, long before acid became a recreational pastime with west coast hippies, or wide-eyed teenagers littering English fields in the mid 1990s, this mind-altering drug had been earmarked as a conceivable weapon for the US army to use against their enemy counterparts in the naivety of the 1950s. No word of a lie.

Project *MKUltra,* was the codename given to this malignant program of experiments and though most of the files regarding this illegal indoctrinating exercise were destroyed by the agency in a botched cover up during the 1970s, its existence was irrevocably real. If you have any doubts of my account, I still have the paranoia and flashbacks to prove it. It's without an ounce of pride then, that I declare I've had my moment in the sky. On the 5th November 1954, at precisely 9:36am, I became the first tortoise to drop acid.

That morning, the guinea pigs fell silent, the mice ran for cover and the pink-eyed rabbits shivered in fear as the windowless lab door opened with a depressive air and in walked lead chemist and spymaster; Sidney Gottlieb (1918-1999). As he entered his monstrous domain, a cumbersome gait cast an eerie shadow on the buttermilk walls and I retracted further into my shell with gloomy apprehension.

The face that looked intently into mine was not human, or at least didn't look it. There was something of the night about his gaunt features, and to me he had the unfortunate resemblance of a Nazi war criminal with a gradual suntan. A look not particularly helped by starched blonde hair, swept and parted, to reveal an angular face that looked back at the world through rounded glasses and an annoyingly neutral gaze. Most strikingly, he carried a Blackthorn walking stick and limped on his left side due to a deformed clubbed foot since birth. This only added to his villainy and regularly marked the freshly mopped floor with shoe rubber, a janitor's worst nightmare. This glorified drug-pusher without a handgun was trailed by an entourage of nondescript acolytes in white surgical coats, who slathered praise on his perverse work at every opportunity. I believe they were called scientists.

Sidney Gottlieb was responsible for coordinating the whole *MKUltra* operation, and although I loathed the man with a hatred that burned brighter than a thousand suns, he had my full attention as he opened his mouth to speak. Not in the German vernacular as you might expect from his appearance, but with a drawling Bronx accent that matched the sluggish pace of his mangled foot. "And *hoooow* are we all this morning, my pets?"

I knew the others were unable to pipe up for the animal kingdom from behind the filthy cages that confined them, so felt it my duty to reply. "We aren't your pets. We're your prisoners, so I am led to believe," I declared with revolt.

"Now, now. No need for that." He spoke with a gross indifference, making it plainly obvious to me he had no interest in our hardihood or wellbeing. We were mere test animals to him and his stooges, hostages kept under lock and key until called upon by science to participate in their next round of 'government backed' experiments. I rolled my eyes as he pootled over to where I was housed, the venal man clearing his throat as he leered at me through the grilled steel that confined me, his grin stretched wide enough to expose a gap between his front teeth, a trait I usually find endearing, but not so much in this case. "It's such a glorious day outside, wouldn't you agree?"

"I wouldn't know. There aren't any windows," I replied.

He rubs his hands enthusiastically. "Well it is, trust me,"

"I'd rather not trust a cretinous…cretin," I burst out. Agonizingly I couldn't think of another word in that moment, although I can think of plenty now. Isn't that always the case?

He shrugged his thin shoulders, as if wriggling himself free of a guilt-lined culpability coat. "Does that make me a bad person?"

"In most peoples books, yeah."

I caught a devilish glint in his bespectacled eye. "Not my circus, not my monkeys," he drawled with another shirk. "And besides, I'm not interested in books. Instead, we're going to try you with something new today, Jonathan."

"Marvellous," I'd replied sarcastically. "Is it going to be bad, or really bad?"

He duped delight and shot me a half grin as he leaned in closer and lowered his voice to a whisper. "Well…that's the whole point of testing drugs on animals I guess. You have to relay to us the severity of the effects."

"Oh dear God on earth," I'd groaned outwardly. Regardless of my being agnostic, I had to complain to someone. "It's not a laxative again is it?"

He tittered as I shifted my heft up against the wall and bared my gums with as much aggression as I could muster, preparing my claws for the inevitable intrusion about to be sprung upon my private life. They'd been trying me out with a lot of new things lately, suppositories included, and despite my appetence for narcotics and their unwavering hold over my addiction, I was growing weary of this animal exploitation. I missed those simple life choices that freedom offers and the very thought of crisp lettuce was too much to endure.

 "Really Jonathan, there's no need to worry," sighed Gottlieb, with a sickly squint and little conviction. "This latest test campaign, I'm sure is harmless,"

"How reassuring," I scoffed. I knew the man didn't have a hit of compassion in his soul and perhaps worst still, there had been rumours going around the facility that a high-ranking biological warfare specialist had already been unsuspectingly dosed up with this 'new' stuff. Just a week later whilst away on business, he'd thrown himself out of his closed hotel window wearing only his underpants. As a fully-fledged member of the conspiracy club, I felt now might be the time to bring it up.

"This wouldn't be the same antigen you gave to Frank Olsen before they sponged him off the sidewalk, would it?" I asked with an impenetrable glare, and for the first time that morning the scientist stopped smiling. Instead, he looked down at his twisted foot awkwardly as I waited for his response. Now, experience over the course of my life has shown that when you've got no other option but to wait for someone to reply, sighing heavily always helps. Finally, he answers.

"That was just a blip," he explains with a cornered expression, looking to his fellow scientists like a child with his hand caught in the honesty box. He then takes the vaunting decision to share his boastings. "Myself and my colleagues have been testing out our experimental drugs in hospitals, universities, coffee shops and other facilities like this for years now. And with very few psychotic episodes, I might add."

I was taken aback by this confession of his half-baked ideas. The morality of their secretive project seemed to have sunken to new depths, and already they were lower than a snakes belly in a wagon rut. "Sorry…you mean to say you've already been testing out serums on the public in cafes, hospitals and universities?"

"And prisons," he added, proudly. "We just pop it in their coffee in the morning and see if we can't coax out any hidden confessions, garner responses to hypnotic access codes, or at the very least, wipe their minds so we can control them. It's a simple exercise really."

I was astounded, as you might imagine. "But shouldn't these people be told your lacing them with mind altering drugs? Don't you need consent or something?"

"This isn't a school trip Jonathan," he'd shrugged, with all the compassion of a serial killer. "Why should they need to know?"

"Because it sounds unethical and illegal, for a start."

"You misunderstand me Jonathan, we couldn't possibly tell them," he explained as a smile took over his entire face. "*MKultra*, is top secret program of research into behavioral modification. If we told them, well now it would no longer be a secret would it?"

"But, what you are doing to is plain wrong,"

"There are pros and cons to any scientific research Jonathan," he preached with open arms. "Like fighting disease and helping humanity to live longer, for example."

"And the pros?" I asked.

I could see he was done with the listening to my high-horse orations. The loaded syringe he proceeded to stick into my leathery backend whilst I was distracted informed me of this, and as I let out an undignified scream of surprise, the monkeys next door went into hysterics as they banged on their cages with their humanlike, hairy fists.

"That wasn't so bad now was it, so why so woebegone?" he smirked.

I huff sarcastically, rubbing my sore bottom. " Sorry, my face sometimes does that. It depends whose company I'm in."

"That's rather hurtful Jonathan," he sulks. "Apologise please,"

I offer him my sincerest smile. " I'm really sorry for all the mean, awful, and completely accurate things I've said. So, now what?"

"Welcome to wonderland, Alice," he says rather cryptically, as he scrapes a chair across the floor with more noise than necessary and slots himself into it, tapping his silver pen against his teeth. "Now we wait, and we observe,"

In all the time I'd been under house arrest I have no memory of him, or anybody else, having expressed any feelings of guilt or contrition for the unfettered misery caused to animals in the name of twisted science. It seemed to me they didn't give a hoot about the depressing karmic implications of their work, but by then I should have been used to the distressing ways of humans.

As the substances began getting to work on my inner parts, the symptoms hadn't seemed all that bad at first and I was determined not to let them shake my equilibrium. Apart from clenching my jaw a little more than usual and the beginnings of a slight flush, whatever drugs he'd pushed into my system didn't seem to be having much effect. They certainly weren't up to the potency of his usual stash in any case, and the mad scientists began whispering amongst themselves, seemingly underwhelmed as they continued to stare at me from behind their clipboards.

"Perhaps we should take a little stroll," Gottlieb had suggested after twenty or so minutes of not a lot happening.

"Are you sure about this Sidney?" one of his minions whispered nervously, taking a step back from my cage. I'm not a meat eater, and at my speed I would never be able to chase my food anyway, but I recognised this particular white coat as one whom I'd nipped on the calf earlier in the week. I've since been told that this is common behaviour when administered enough spice to knock out The Happy Mondays and their road crew.

"Where's he going to go? He's a tortoise," Gottlieb reasoned, suitably pleased as he unlatched my cage and stepped aside. As the door to my prison swung open, he gestured for me to follow him as he led the way down a brightly lit and white tiled corridor, dragging his stymied appendage behind him like a pied piper of pharmaceuticals. Myself, and his entourage of duplicitous lab-rats duly followed in his swervy footsteps like a macabre travelling circus. The monkeys began to scream again.

Flanked by this posse of beards, I began to feel a little claustrophobic as they cloaked me like a pod of orcas stalking a sickly whale calf. Perhaps it was my imagination, but someone seemed to have turned the lights up in the place and my four little legs began to feel very odd indeed. It was a remarkable feeling, as if they no longer corresponded with my body and had gained independence from my brain having decided to defect after many years of me looking after them. If this was mind control then someone needed to explain that idea to my feet I began to ponder, as I let out a chuckle.

Up ahead, Gottlieb glanced at his watch before deliberately dropping his pen to the floor with an exaggerated flourish. "Oh dear, clumsy me. Pick that up please, Jonathan."

I shielded my eyes from the headache inducing strip lighting above. "I'm not touching it. It's been in your mouth." I'd pointed out, his virulent mind control methods useless against me.

"Then tell me whom you work for," he'd demanded, waving his walking stick in front of my face as though he belonged to the Jedi order. " The Russians, I shouldn't wonder?" He was getting on my nerves by now, but this wasn't the only reason I was becoming more unsettled.

"Oh, do stop with all the bafflegab," I'd said to the chemist, as suddenly his cheeks turn a delicious shade of green and his head remodelled itself into a rounded lettuce with ears, before my eyes. The scientist glared at me with his emerald face made of leaves, his eyes growing ever more delicious looking as my stomach groaned with desire. This was certainly unexpected, and as my sense of reality continued to erode, all I wanted to do was eat him. I let go of the wheel and my mind span out of control.

When the other scientists faces began to transform into an array of multi-coloured fruit and vegetables with human features, I knew something was amiss. Well you would, wouldn't you? When you find yourself taking an afternoon stroll with the Munch Bunch, you've likely got mental issues. Of course, with experience I've since learnt that I was in the beginnings of a 'bad trip', brought on most certainly, by the copious amounts of LSD injected into my bottom by heedless medicine men. They must have miscalculated my dosage, because paranoia began to settle into my conscience as if it were a favourite armchair, my skin starting to itch incessantly like a taboo disease.

Slowly but very surely, my mind began to unravel as I continued to be tracked by this meaningless collision of fruit & vegetables who scribbling on clipboards and teased my appetite with their ripeness. I'm acutely aware, as I commit this to the page, just how abstract all this sounds in the cold light of day, but hang around awhile because things are about to get a lot more messed up. Just say no, kids.

As I was shepherded through a network of corridors towards the staff canteen, it was now no longer just my legs that felt detached from my own self. Each menial task (like walking, talking, breathing, that kind of thing) soon became a mammoth challenge as my face leaked sweat and my world pulsed a fluorescent mad.

"Everything Ok Jonathan?" Gottlieb had asked with profound desperation, a hungry greenfly buzzing around his appetising head. "Any adverse effects I should know of?"

"Hahahahahahahahahahahahahaha." was my simple reply.

I stumbled in pursuit of the chef's pantry at this point, an insatiable appetite suddenly gripping me. I was famished after being surrounded by this walking banquet of delights and I ransacked the storage cupboard with savour. As I searched for food amongst the vegetables and dried pulses, I was distracted by an unopened box of fine grain rice sitting on the shelf and gave it closer inspection through delirious eyes.

"Help yourself," coaxed Gottlieb, like a snake in the gardens of Eden, except he looked more like a leafy green, of course.

"Mearrrghhhh," I'd garbled with the patience of an angry drunk, eyeing the box again with a look resembling suspicion. I knew it was inconceivable, but I was pretty sure the jovial black man who adorned the frontage of the packet, (Uncle Ben, I believe) had just tipped me a wink. In fact I could have sworn he had. Palpable fear grew in my chest and crawled up into my throat as I rubbed the moisture from my eyes for clarity. Then, not a split second later he went and did it again, only this time a smile lit up his trademarked face. I gaped at the smartly dressed man wearing his dapper bow tie, and as he began to sing in a baritone chocolaty-rich voice, I joined in his chorus by screaming several octaves higher.

"Snap out of it, Jonathan," Gottlieb shouted, his leafy hands shaking my shoulders as if trying to coax ketchup from a new bottle. The other discourteous creatures had to hold me back at this point as I tried to bite his scrumptious looking arms. "Get him offa me!" he screamed, and I began to scream too, for quite some time. As the lab technicians pushed me back through the double doors with haste, the strains of Uncle Ben still rang fresh in my ears and the vanilla ice cream walls began to melt.

All their sick assay had achieved was to send a reptile half screwball in the mind and entice a tune out of an elderly black man who lived on the front of a food packet. That sentence sounds quite absurd when reading it out aloud, but the hallucinations I experienced that day were so vivid and so ghastly, that even today I can only buy supermarket own brand rice. If the government had hoped their experiment was going to reveal some crucial warfare advantage, they were to be sorely disappointed.

I was thrown back into my cage without ceremony later that morning, my green lips babbling nonsense about lettuce people and long grain rice, until mercifully, my mind could take no more as it shut down and drifted into a gargantuan sleep. Finally, the trip was over, and a very lousy one it had been too. I haven't touched drugs since that day, as you might well imagine. Or much rice either for that matter.

Not long after my psychotic episode, I was deemed unreliable as a subject and surplus to their evil requirements. I knew what kind of people they were, and having the heart of gold that bottom-feeders tend to possess, I was tied up in a sack, driven to the countryside in an unmarked laundry van, and tossed into the Mississippi river like an unwanted puppy. Of course, they had no idea I could swim a little, or that I'd once been good friends with Harry Houdini. After a few days of withdrawal and excruciating cold turkey I went straight to the cops, then straight into rehab.

I told them everything I knew. The illegal experiments, the curious death of Frank Olsen, the spiking of innocent members of society with secretive drugs. Although surprised by my whistleblowing antics, the authorities decided my story sounded too preposterous not to be true (as I'm sure you are too) and after some digging around discovered the truth about the CIA's dark movements. An inquest by *The Church Committee* was hastily set up in light of my revealing accusations into thousands of human experimentations, and as the story picked up pace with the press, the public began to demand answers from their senators as to why on earth the government were secretly testing out potentially lethal stimulants on their own citizens, without a care and without a consent form. I thought it a fair question to ask.

Under growing pressure, a series of investigations were hurriedly carried out and broadcast live on prime-time television, with viewing figures going through the roof. It was soon discovered that the CIA had conducted improper behaviour, and that Intelligence agencies had undermined the constitutional rights of its US citizens (and most members of The Grateful Dead so I believe) by exposing them to mind altering narcotics without their knowledge. No word of a lie, check the papers if you don't believe me.

I found this interesting quote from Senator Ted Kennedy whilst looking back through my notes, regarding the abhorrent behaviour of the CIA in retrospect, and you can understand why people might well be angry:

"The Deputy Director of the CIA revealed that over thirty universities and institutions were involved in an "extensive testing and experimentation"

program which included covert drug tests on unwitting citizens "at all social levels, high and low, native Americans and foreign." Several of these tests involved the administration of LSD to "unwitting subjects in social situations."

Belatedly, this led to Frank Olsen's family getting an out of court settlement of $750,000 and an apology from President Gerald Ford and CIA director William Colby, along with new legislation being drawn up stating there should no longer be experimentation with drugs on human subjects, except with the informed consent. This law was designed to protect future civilians from unauthorised testing by the government without their knowledge, though sadly there was no mention of animals anywhere in the small print. Why am I not surprised?

The *MKUltra* operation was shelved not long after, due to the discovery that the use of LSD wasn't much help in the fog of war, unless you were planning on screaming the enemy into submissions rather than using traditional guns and tanks. The operation was sequentially abandoned and most records destroyed, but a clerical error meant that seven boxes of evidence (1738 documents in total) survived, helping to expose the abuses of the project that became an embarrassing footnote in the history of a decadent and corrupted CIA. I just hope they are more transparent today.

Sidney Gottlieb would spend the remainder of his years running a commune and teaching folk dancing in Culpeper, West

Virginia, whilst fighting a continuous mountain of law suits for the irreparable damage his experiments had caused. In truth I never saw a penny, however, I imagine folk dancing with a clubfoot is no easy feat. Pun intended.

I know to my own cost that drugs don't work. But disgracefully, animal testing still continues today, especially in the cosmetics industries. I can't think why anyone would want to hurt a defenceless creature and it needs to be stopped, whether by boycott or demonstration. Over a hundred million animals are burned, crippled, poisoned and left to die a painful death every year in laboratories all around the world.

The testing on animals was banned in the EU in 2003, but is still prevalent in countries like China and the US, with many of these atrocities on captive animals carried out in the name of beauty. Personally, I think it's an ugly business and it needs to stop, which is why I agreed to pose naked in an advertising campaign for PETA in the late nineties.

Before you recoil in disgust, it was either me or McCartney.

CHAPTER TWENTY-FIVE

Margaret Thatcher. Idi Amin. Freddie Flintoff. These are all people who I haven't seen eye to eye with down the years, and though I disliked them all intensely, I believe you have to live with someone to determine whether you despise them or not. I've heard it said that if you've never had a weird flatmate then you're the weird flatmate, but the man I'm about to tell you about really takes the biscuit. No really, the degenerate would snaffle all my bourbons and pink wafers when I had the misfortune of sharing a flat with him in the late eighteenth century. He was a glutton in personal habits and high up on the oddity scale. His name was Samuel Morse.

"Tap. Tap. Tap. Tap. Tap. Tap."

This was the bothersome noise I would have to endure constantly, day upon day, for almost twelve months when I lived with a man who'd recently invented a covert code named quite modestly, after himself. Nowadays I call it my 'tap' year in the States, but I still find it painful to reminisce. Morse code was a torturous method of communication that used a series of encoded dots and dashes that corresponded with letters from the alphabet. It was designed not just to annoy reptiles, but to allow the transfer of important messages quickly over long distances, all of them tapped out via electrical pulses on yet another of my flatmates ludicrous inventions called the single wire telegraph. I hope you're still with me?

"Tap. Tap. Tap. Tap. Tap. Tap."

He'd invented this code in unfortunate circumstances after his wife had fallen gravely ill and he hadn't received news of her predicament until weeks later when the postman had arrived with a letter. By this time, she'd already been buried in the soil and the cheese cubes speared on cocktail sticks consumed at the wake, before he'd received the doleful news of her death. Consumed with grief for his deceased wife, Samuel Morse had set about coming up with a solution he claimed would revolutionise the way we'd correspond with one another across vast continents in quick time, and it would allow important news to be circulated around the globe at lightning speed. This was all very commendable, unless your green head happens to be sleeping a paper-thin wall away from the evil machine designed to send it.

"Tap. Tap. Tap. Tap. Tap. Tap."

I felt for the man's loss, but the heavy bags below my eyes were growing thicker and my patience thin. All I'd wished for was a considerate flatmate and some sleep, but this was becoming impossible because of the continual tapping out of these fist-gnawingly annoying messages every night. I began developing wrinkles way before my time and despite the eternal pleas for him to pipe down he ignored my requests with a waspish intolerance. It's fair to assume there was a micro-climate of tension growing at this point.

Morse was in his early sixties by then, though the circles around his blood flecked eyes made him look ten years older than he was and his fingers had turned crooked with rheumatism from constant use of his baleful machine. He smelt vaguely of occult bookstores and was a man of very few words, which I found quite extraordinary seeing as he never actually shut up. If I wanted to speak to him on the rare occasion he left his room, or politely remind him that it was his turn to do the dishes, he would thrust a reference sheet full of his dots and dashes into my claw and have me try and decipher his response, whilst he tapped repeatedly on whatever was close to misshapen hand. It was like having to live with a cast member from the physical theatre group *Stomp* as he banged his way around the kitchen with a teaspoon in only his underpants.

"Have you moved my biscuits?" I'd ask.

"Tap. Tap. Tap." Would come the coded response.

"Did you eat them? I specifically put my name on them,"

"Tap. Tap. Tap. Tap. Tap."

"Just keep your mitts off my goddamn stuff Morse," I'd shout on many occasion, as I slammed shut the door to my bedroom, which seconds later was filled with pillow-muted sobbing. I strongly suspect he did plunder my bourbons, but he never owned up and neither did he do the dishes, which was fantastically irksome. Nobody likes washing up (except for my mum), and I agree it's a complete waste of life, but it's no exaggeration to say Morse was quick becoming the flatmate from hell with his lazy approach to housework and loquacious spoon smacking.

Even the next-door neighbours thumping through the wall did little to temper his constant din. I imagine he thought they were trying to communicate using his own infuriating Morse code. Can you return our garden shears? Did the postman drop off a package to you my mistake? Could we borrow a cup of sugar perhaps? Perhaps not, but I began to dread bedtime as I lay on my mattress with my head buried in my shell, enduring a torture usually reserved for Japanese prisoners of war. I'd often join in with the neighbours and bang on the wall with my night slipper, pleading for him to give it a rest, but my cries were in vain. To say I was exhausted is perhaps not putting enough emphasis on the meaning of exhausted, but as Desmond Tutu famously said: "*If you want peace, you don't talk with your friends. You talk to your enemies.*" With that in mind I called a house meeting.

"Look Sam. I don't mind you talking with your friends." I'd reasoned, as I watched him drink directly from the milk bottle in the fridge. "But could we maybe give it a rest after 10pm?" He'd tapped something out on the chestnut mahogany sideboard and using the reference sheet he gave me, after fifteen minutes of intense concentration I'd eventually deciphered his response. The answer was a resounding, Amy Winehouse-esque; *no, no, no.*

I once shared a flat with Keith Moon in the 1960s, and despite his stubborn refusal to use the front door and the annoying habit of leaving King Kong fingers in the toilet bowl without flushing, he was a dream compared to this psycho with whom I had to share the milk with. Something had to be done about his noisy contraption because winter was around the corner and I'd need lots of peace and quiet to hibernate. I was growing paranoid too. Through lack of sleep, I'd convinced myself that Morse had devised his secret little code as a way of talking behind people's backs without them knowing. He seemed the type, like footballers that cover their mouths when they don't want the cameras to pick up a tactical order from the bench or a racist slur. I became certain he was slagging me off to whomever he was chatting (or tapping) to as he sat bent over his machine into the early hours, munching on my biscuits for sustenance.

I'm not ignorant to the fact his telegraph machine would go on to assist people in maritime distress and help unfortunates stuck up mountains with only a torch for company, but seriously, I hadn't slept in weeks. As you know by now I am of very placid character, but I'd reached the end of my shackle and I'm not proud to admit I rather lost my temper. One evening, whilst Morse was taking a rare bath, I snuck into his bed quarters and I saw the architect of my misery sitting upon his battered writing desk along with an empty packet of custard creams. My custard creams.

The red mist descended as I took an ornamental fire poker to the telegraph machine in a fit of pure rage. Never before or since have I been so angry at an inanimate object, but by the time I was finished distributing my wrath, the guts of technology were scattered across the scarred wooden floor like the metal entrails of a murder victim. I returned to my room and packed my bags, openly ignoring the howls of raw pain I heard as Morse entered his room and saw the grisly crime scene lain out before him. Sometimes in life, you come across people you just don't gel with and that's just part of nature I guess. Samuel Morse was one of those people in my opinion. He threatened to have me arrested for criminal damage, but when I said I'd counter sued for biscuit thievery he soon backed down.

You might assume that I felt regret for destroying a lifetime's work and for making a grown man cry like an infant, but I didn't in the slightest. It may sound cold blooded (because I am) but the only ones I have sympathy for are the unfortunate souls who moved into my old room, and the Goldstein's next door at number sixty-two. If I were ever to be stuck up a mountain with four broken feet, hypothermia, and only James Corden for company, I still wouldn't use his stupid code to provoke a rescue. I bumped into Morse again months later whilst at the theatre one evening and I had only one thing to say to him and I'll leave you translate that for yourself: ..- .--. / -.-- --- ..- .-. ...

CHAPTER TWENTY-SIX

Almost 150 years ago today, on March 10th 1876, I was sitting in my parlour and putting the last delicate touches to my model aeroplane when suddenly, I became rudely distracted by the shrill ring of the telephone. The fragile wooden wing had broken clean off in my claw in the kerfuffle (a real pain in the hoop) and I cursed the machine for ruining the perfect present I was going to gift Orville Wright for his 5th birthday. Filled with annoyance I picked up the receiver and answered in the foulest of moods.

Here's a transcript of how that conversation went:

ME: Yes. Hello.

CALLER: Mr Watson, come here. I want to see you.

ME: Sorry. I think you must have a wrong number.

CALLER: (louder) Mr Watson, come here. I want to see you.

ME: Is this a crank call? Who is this?

CALLER: Mr Alexander Graham Bell. Who's that?

ME: Jonathan Jennifer Shelton, if we're insisting on full names.

CALLER: (*tittering, you get used to it*) Isn't that a girl's name?

ME: It's unisex actually.

CALLER: So you're not my assistant, Mr Watson?

ME: No I'm not. Do I look like an assistant?

CALLER: I've no idea. This is a telephone so I can't see you.

ME: Look, as I've said, you must have a wrong number.

CALLER: Oh, how very queer.

ME: What do you want anyway? Have you seen the time?

CALLER: Calm down good man. No need to be argumentative.

ME: I'm not being argumentative.

CALLER: Perhaps you are a little.

ME: Yeah, but I'm not.

CALLER: Mr Watson, is that you having a little joke with me? I have the press here and everything.

ME: I've told you already. My name isn't Watson. It's Jonathan.

CALLER: I see. Well Jonathan, have you been injured in an accident recently that wasn't your fault?

ME: Look! Whatever you're trying to sell, I'm not interested.

CALLER: It's a no win, no fee!

ME: It's a no, thanks.

CALLER: Well, how about payment protections insurance then?

ME: How did you get this number anyway? I'm ex-directory. I'd suggest you hang up immediately.

CALLER: Well you hang up first.

ME: Nope. You hang up first.

CALLER:…I'm still here…still here…Helloooo….

I hung up the phone and tried my best to repair the damage the telephone call had done to my model aeroplane, but it was irreversibly ruined and I'd have to start again. As it turned, the first ever telephone call made by its inventor, Alexander Graham

Bell, happened to be a wrong number. Ironically, he didn't have a telephone in his own home as he'd invented it by mistake and saw it as a distraction from his work. As I threw the spoilt wooden plane in the waste bin, I understood his point.

CHAPTER TWENTY-SEVEN

In 1936, I did another stretch behind bars. One of the many downsides (and believe me there are many) of having such a long lifespan is that you usually outlive those who acquired you as a companion and if nobody else can step up and take care of you then you inevitably end up on the streets, or if you're really unlucky, in the hands of the authorities. This was the situation I found myself in when I was incarcerated in Hobart zoo, a faraway penal colony on the island of Tasmania, many harvest moons ago. The place was a dilapidated tourist attraction in a forgotten part of the world where gawping visitors were few, cockroaches grew to the size of spaniels, and the rust was left to feast uninterrupted on the iron cages that held us, but lets not dwell on the positives.

Now, believe me when I say that it's every wild animal's worst nightmare to wind up in captivity; to have your freedoms taken from you for the sole purpose of entertaining the human race and helping to sell stuffed toys in the gift shop. Before being banged up, I'd been enjoying the high-life as a guest of residency with the Tasmanian Premier; Sir Neil Elliot Lewis, before he'd succumbed to a brief illness and had left me high and dry with my tail in the wind. Now I was forced to watch my nodular back in this hellhole of a prison system, picking oakum all day and drowning in self-pity as I read the graffiti scratched into my cell by past residents who'd once woken up surrounded by those same suffocating four walls.

Unlike most zoos you might decide to visit nowadays, the monosyllabic keepers at Hobart (or *'screws'* as we termed them) were an austere and unpleasant bunch that couldn't care less for our welfare, and you always made sure to avoid the pygmy hippos at any cost, especially in the showers. Due to my vintage I was deemed a low risk category inmate and was given the servile job of wing librarian, although most of the animals doing bird could barely remember their own names, let alone read. It was whilst on my daily rounds as I walked the dystopian corridors of B-wing, filled with the shrieks, growls and howls of its noisy residents, that I first came across a charming lifer pacing his cell in silence, whose name I'll never forget. He was called Benedict. No wait, he was called Benjamin.

At the time he'd been placed on the notorious B-wing, a section of the zoo that was reserved for the more dangerous inmates. The kind that bite, peck or sting, and need to be kept separated from the rest of the animal kingdom. Zoos are designed to wear you down, to strip you of your natural habitat and tame you into submission, and because of his wild instincts Benjamin had wound up amongst the Hyenas and other low life slime at the less upmarket end of the wing. However, from the first moment I met him I saw no malice in his obsidian eyes. In fact he seemed pretty harmless to me.

Despite his reputation for being unpredictable he kept himself to himself (a wise thing to do in Hobart) but as we became more acquainted and began to trust one another, I grew to like him a lot. Sometimes just having someone to spin a few yarns with in that stone hotel made the toil of prison life that bit easier to deal with, so when he got transferred over to E-wing for good behaviour later that spring, I was glad of the company. Plus, I've always been a sucker for a hard-luck story.

He was a handsome marsupial with a huge mouth, yellowish fur, canine features, and striking stripes that ran the whole length of his hindquarters. It was these distinguishing markings that led to his native kind being delightfully nicknamed the Tasmanian tiger, but of course he wasn't an actual tiger. If he was, I doubt we'd ever have gotten on so well. He was in fact an animal called a Thylacine. If you've never heard of one before then I'm not at all surprised, because they don't exist.

Before you assume I'd been at the prison moonshine or was hallucinating again, just hear me out. The Thylacine doesn't exist because bipeds had decided it had to be that way. These majestic creatures that once roamed the outback in numbers were regarded as a pest to farmer's livestock, so mankind did what is often the case when faced with a threat to their wallets. They took up their shotguns, fired up the trucks and went *nuclear*, hunting the unfortunate animals into total extinction around eighty years ago. The last recorded Thylacine to roam the wild was shot in 1930 by a deficient farm rancher thicker than a submarine door, called Wilf Batty from Mawbanna. This left my friend Benjamin as the very last surviving member of his kind.

His future plans of settling down to start a marsupial family of his own once he got out had now been extinguished by human hands, and as we struck up a kinship together over the days and weeks that followed, I'd often note the sadness in his dark watery eyes as he prowled the exercise yard with a haunting howl at the demise of his bloodline. I knew all too well what it was like to lose family in such tragic circumstances, but the idea of knowing you are the very last of your lineage? Well, that must be quiet overbearing for anybody. Who can really blame him for snapping at the keepers on occasion and winding up in solitary again for his efforts? As our friendship blossomed inside the walls of that miserable dungeon of confinement, I knew we'd have to find a way out of that place if not for welfare, then for our sanity. I didn't want to run the risk of discovering what would happen to us if we didn't, especially considering the unwanted looks I'd began receiving because of my gym-honed body. I started thinking up an escape plan with haste.

As a rule animals can't talk (I'm the exception obviously) but already I was hatching a means of escape and the agreeable yelps that Benjamin made once I'd relayed my prudent plan to him after lights out told me he was most definitely in. I consider myself a master of escape (even Houdini has complemented me on my routine) so I was confident, with a dash of luck, I could outwit the zoo's lacklustre security systems and even bribe the corrupt guards if needs be. My blueprint for freedom was simple, and without any possibility of parole, over the coming days I went about fine-tuning the arrangements to ensure it was flawless and watertight.

You'll probably be all too aware of my *modus operandi* in these situations, so it will come as no surprise that my escape involved the artistry of digging. Already, I'd worked through the nights carving out a hollow tunnel beneath my cell, and by removing some of the books from my push trolley, I intended to smuggle Benjamin past the guards on my evening deliveries. The idea was that once we'd made it to the outer perimeter, my marsupial friend would be able bite through the rattletrap wire fence with his sharp teeth and together we'd negotiate the searchlights and make our run for freedom. Well, that was the slender plan anyway.

"Leave it to me," I'd said. "We'll both be out of here in no time,"

Back in those days I could bench lift around 6lbs on a good day, and the next morning I was doing just that as I worked out amongst sweaty, semi-naked animals in the grey squalor that passed for the exercise yard at Hobart. If everything went to plan, in a day or two all this would become a distant memory, but at right that moment I had bigger fish to fry, as I noticed the pygmy hippos eyeing me up again as I flexed my muscles in the blazing sun. One of this West African gang, who I thought particularly fat for a river pig, batted his long eyelashes at me from across the yard, and as I waved towards one of the guards for urgent help, he blatantly neglected his duties, turning a blind eye and his back.

The pygmy with the thick waist must have been a decoy, because before I knew it they were on me, four slippery hippos trying to drag me into the laundry room with their stubby pink hooves wrapped around my midriff. I've always been a lover not a fighter, but in this case I was adamant the former wasn't going to become reality. If I was to become prey I wasn't going down without a fight, so with a hot flush of adrenaline filling my ears *'Blub dub, blub dub, blub dub'* I balled my claws and reared up on hind legs, a ritual performed by tortoises for centuries to ward off predators or to attract a mate. However I must stress it's important you get this the right way around.

Since the emu's had been released back in to captivity, this mob had taken up the mantle of prison bullies and they would bribe the guards and terrorize the other 'fraggles' just for kicks. Some said they were worse than the honey badgers when it came to tormenting the inmates with their violent tendencies, and in fact, even the honey badgers said they were worse than the honey badgers. As they landed a few glancing blows to my shell, in the struggle I managed to wriggle free an arm, dispatching a smooth left-hook into the doughnut flesh of one of my assailant's who'd swiftly doubled up in pain with a snort. "That one's for Mandela," I huffed, beginning to enjoy myself although in no way would I condone this level of violence.

As I threw back my head and heard the satisfying crunch of pygmy snout as another dropped to his knees, the old moves I'd picked up in those days of the Richmond Bread Riot (1863) soon returned with muscle memory. I think my assailants were surprised at my speed, but not as surprised as I. Spinning around without even a hiss of warning, I delivered a flurry of uppercuts (I've always been a south-claw) that connected well, little piggy noses exploding everywhere like beans inside a microwave. I had the upper claw, no doubt about it, and they were definitely on the ropes, but as I began to look for a route of escape my eyes must have given away this intention and the overweight hippo with the eyelashes appeared from nowhere, launching himself at me with everything he had as we fell to the floor in a fleshy heap.

I was pinned to the ground by his mass, and despite my best efforts I couldn't move as he sat upon my plastron as it threatened to cave. Not being able to move was a setback, but not being able to breathe was becoming a more immediate problem. I gasped for air as the boss-pygmy bore down on me with all his weight and my vision became blurred, the *'blub dub, blub dub, blub dub'* of adrenaline in my ears beginning to ebb. Was this the way it all ended, sprawled dead beneath a hippo's mottled backend? I looked into his whiskery face that was patterned with battle scars, perhaps the last face I was ever going to see, when suddenly his ladylike eyes widened and the weight on my chest speedily vanished, along with his ugly features.

Benjamin had him up against the fence, baring his teeth with a low growl as the petrified hippo squealed and dropped a few nuggets from the place that seconds ago had been sitting on my chest. My good friend had come to my rescue, and though I'm sure I could have handled it myself, I was glad of the help. "Easy boy," I said to a snarling Benjamin. "Easy."

The rest of my aggressors now lay at odd angles on the floor surrounded by their own teeth, and with another growl and a threatening snap of Benjamin's considerable jaws, the remaining rotund hippo had scarpered away with an apologetic whimper and a sour stench.

"We leave at first dawn," I affirmed to my stripy tailed friend, the bodies that lay around us in hot-blooded revenge making me all the more determined to make sure my plan wasn't going to fail.

That evening in the clattering noise of the mess hall, I passed Benjamin an old paperback novel contained within it a map of the prison boundaries and the guard's nightly rota that I'd managed to swipe from the governor's office and was crucial for our escape. I'd also included some contraband in the form of a doggy treat, just as a thank-you for saving my skin, although as I've said previously, I'm sure I could have handled it. He'd yelped with delight at the prospect of liberation and something decent to eat, because there's only so much prison food a marsupial, or indeed an epicurean reptile can stomach in a place like that, although it was the ideal residence if you planned to lose some weight. Whilst Benjamin snaffled the biscuit I went through the plan with a whisper one more time, making sure to keep out of earshot of the prowling guards who walked with a jangle and would have wanted paying handsomely to keep their mouths shut if they'd learned of our intentions.

"So, you're clear what we have to do?" I'd smiled with a conspiratorial wink once I'd gone through everything thoroughly and Benjamin had nodded his angular head in understanding, both of us gazing out towards the freedom that lay beyond the razor wire and prison walls. The distant skies had begun to darken with brooding black clouds, and as one of the lags on kitchen duty removed our empty plastic plates with a grunt, the depressing chime of the watchtower bell rang out its bilious cry across the courtyard.

The lethargic guards began their nightly task of rounding up the animals for lights out as afternoon began its grapple with evening in a wrestling match perfected over millennia. We crossed the yard together in the fading light of a lugubrious red wine sun, ready to return to our cells one final time before a new life beckoned outside of those joyless walls. I'd turned to Benjamin with hopeful abandon in that moment as he looked at me with optimism burning bright in his eyes. "So, I'll see you on the other side, ok?" I'd whispered, as I bid my friend goodnight. "And don't worry, everything will be fine." Unfortunately it was to be anything but.

That night the weather was wild and rotten and I found it hard to sleep as my thoughts churned uncontrollably within. As the sky grumbled its discontent and the air grew thick, it was as though the devil himself had relocated to the small island state of Tasmania that lay vulnerable to the elements in the Tasman Sea. The wind had whipped up from nowhere, fluently ripping the limbs from exposed trees and blowing roof tiles off the bell tower that loomed over the prison yard like a gothic monolith. The unrelenting gusts rattled through the bars of my concrete cage and the rain soon followed, hard enough to cut the skin as it hammered like timpani drums on the door of my cell as if it were a screw demanding to be let in. This type of weather always brought with it memories of my time at sea, and as the lashing continued and the ancient walls leaked chilly air, I prayed for its passing and huddled down in the wisps of straw to escape my sleepless purgatory.

Next door I could hear Benjamin's persistent howling, something dogs often do in stormy weather due to their nervous disposition and acute sense of hearing. I could feel the fear in his call and shouted out into the darkness to reassure him, though I suppose it impossible for him to have heard me over nature's unstable din. As the elements continued to batter the prison, as if trying to scrub it clean from sin, eventually his howls subsided as they quickly turned into sorry whimpers before melting away into silence. There was no chance of making a break for it in weather like this and we'd surely have to delay our escape until the storm had passed. I was exhausted, and a restless sleep finally washed over me like a calming balm, the wind and rain outside becoming an unlikely lullaby. That night I dreamt of crisp, pickle-green lettuce leaves and the stretching open fields of heather-blue that we were soon to share together as unfettered jailbirds.

Unfortunately, Benjamin wouldn't live to see the morning.

He was found stone dead in his enclosure on the 7th of September 1936. Not at the hands of another lag or by suicide, but by ineptitude. Due to neglect by the birdbrained guards, he'd been accidentally locked out of his quarters and forgotten about during the downpour, and without adequate shelter he had died a slow and wretched death from exposure, fates final jest. The only comfort I could take from his passing was in knowing he'd finally got his wish to get out of the place, even if it was to be in a plastic body bag. The last known Thylacine on earth was gone forever, his empty cell and a chewed rubber toy all that remained of this resplendent creature.

I shall leave my narration there for a second, because without meaning to preach or make you feel bad for being born a man, woman or non-binary (yes I move with the times), I must point out there seems to be a sinister theme emerging here. In the last few years alone we've said goodbye to: *The Western Black Rhino (2011). Pyrenean Ibex (2000), Baiji Dolphin (2007),Caribbean Monk Seal (2008),Javan Tiger (1998). Zanzibar Leopard (1997), and the red colobus monkey (2000).*

Your kill rate is quite astonishing, and if that brute Darwin did indeed get his facts right on evolution, then that makes the colobus monkey virtually family right? You do know we can't bring these keystone species back? That once they're gone, they're gone? I certainly don't enjoy announcing a long list of animals, now sadly passed, like the memorial tribute at the Oscars, and nor do I want to nag. All I'm saying is, if you don't wake up and sort your act out soon, there won't be much left for the grandkids to see.

Mourning the loss of a dear friend, I'd decided that even without Benjamin by my side, it was high time to make my exit from Hobart. With their lax attitude towards animal husbandry, it would only be a matter of time before they left me out in the elements to perish too, plus I was pretty sure the hippos were planning something in revenge. Quickly, I went to task building a replica Jonathan made from pillowcases that I'd stuffed with pages from old books, and I left the decoy sleeping sound in my bed as I made my departure. It wouldn't win any craft awards for sure, but it was good enough to fool those imbeciles as they went around doing their half-hearted nightly checks, weather permitting.

Under cover of darkness I'd slipped through the tunnel made for two, vaulted over three fences, ducked the razor wire, and made my hasty escape. Well…I say hasty. The whole operation took me around seven hours to complete because I am a tortoise, but eventually, as I'd crawled to the highway and hitched a lift to freedom, I had one final score to settle.

I arrived at my destination before dawn, just as the sun was pulling up and punching in for another days work. With determination burning like magma inside my courageous belly, it didn't take me long to find the overgrown dirt track that peeled off towards the ramshackle farmhouse surrounded by un-harvested fruit trees and wheat fields. A rusty truck sat parked like a guilty accomplice in the yard, and I approached it on tippy claws so as not to alert the snoozing cockerels in their coop. With covert stealth, I sharpened my claws on the rocks and slashed the tyres on the vehicle as the life hissed out of them like asthmatic snakes. Not quite done, I slipped behind the wheel of the dilapidated pickup, lifted my tail carefully and with a little push of effort, deposited a dirty protest upon the drivers seat with a satisfied grin. Whoever criticises this memoir for being based mainly on heavy drinking and excrement, may have a point. Once done with my deed, I felt filled with gusto and abandon, because after all, revenge is a dish best served at body temperature.

I leaned on the horn of the truck a few times before crawling for cover in the scratchy undergrowth as seconds later, the cockerels came to life like car alarms and the lights flickered on in the farmhouse. From my spying place I could see a hirsute, bloated figure slowly emerge from the door in only his underpants and slippers, a loaded twelve-boar clutched tight to the rib cage as he wiped the sleep from his eyes. When Wilf Batty from Mawbanna saw the damage I'd done to his tyres, the murderous farmer dropped his shotgun with a shriek and kicked the dust in anger with a slippered foot. When he'd discovered the little present I'd left for him on the upholstered interior, his ferocious cursing could be heard right across the hills and into the next village. It was the least I could do for a departed friend.

Unfortunately you'll never get to meet Benjamin or his family which is a real shame as they really were the most interesting of marsupials. Despite rumours that they still exist somewhere out there in the wilds of Tasmania, I'm afraid it's game over for their kind. The nearest any of us will ever get to seeing these once magnificent creatures is a sixty-two second black and white clip of Benjamin walking around his enclosure and scratching his bits on YouTube. It really is a sad world we live in at times.

The room feels different somehow. The lights are back on and the storm seems to have passed through. Tables and chairs are reset for the evening trade and the sun shines, almost too brightly, through the fenestra windows. Soft music reaches my ears from a four piece in the corner, and if I'm not mistaken it sounds like an orchestral version of Shalamar's greatest hits. It's good. I'm good.

Even the nettlesome flies have gone.

I look around the room and am suddenly taken aback to see a sea of familiar faces sitting at tables and clinking glassware, as the hum of gentle conversation and merriment fills the cavernous dining room. I see Wilbur and Orville Wright, united once more, as they busy themselves making folded paper planes from menus, whilst across the table Orson Welles is showing Diamond Annie one of his new tricks, his big fat face beaming. I give them a dreamlike wave.

I honestly have no idea what is going on, but I'm beginning not to care anymore.

*I turn to my attention to another table with a smile, and see
Rosa Parks is spoon-feeding a chuckling Howard Carter dessert
from a spoon. Besides them, Fatty Faulkes has his head buried
deep inside a meat pie, his medal still hung proudly around his
neck as he snaffles the crust with appreciation.*

*Whatever it was that my guest has laced the soup with, it
must be good stuff. Way better than anything the CIA can get
their hands on in any case.*

*I turn my attention to see Nikola Tesla and Thomas Edison,
both deep in conversation at another table, whilst Abraham
Lincoln sits between them as referee in his tall stovepipe and
wrestling tights. The room is filled with love. Filled with people
I have shared the path with on my life's journey. Filled with
celebration. I'm quite glad we didn't go to Magic China now.*

*A polite smatter of applause rings out around the walls and
quickly grows in volume. I'm assuming it's for me as I blush,
and clear a lump in my ancient throat. I'm about to stand and
take a take a humble bow, when I notice the whistling and
cheering is in fact for James Dean who is standing upon a chair
and removing his teeth. That could have been embarrassing,
but it was nice to see him all the same.*

Laika and Benjamin are now curled up at my feet, their soft fur tickling my claws, and I don't care if I'm hallucinating anymore. It feels good. No word of a lie.

I look down at my unfinished dessert to find it's no longer there. Instead it's been swiped by a rotund Charles Babbage who I can see stuffing his face underneath an adjacent table, the greedy so-and so.

Death has risen from his chair with creaking knees and is by my side now, here no doubt, to collect the final bill. "Do you take chip and pin?" I ask him with a smile.

"Don't worry Jonathan," he says as he lowers his dark glasses and slips me a wink. "The bill has been taken care of by your friend over there."

I follow his eye line, to see Charles Dickens in conversation with Dutch Schultz and Sir Arthur. The famous author (Dickens) glances up at me with a warm smile, combs his hair and raises a glass. I raise mine in mirthful reply and I'm happy he's finally stood his round at last orders. Although to be fair, he'd cut it pretty fine.

"Are you ready to leave now Jonathan?" my dinner guest asks, lifting his cowl so his face is filled with shadows as he takes my claw in his bony grip and my eyelids grow heavy.

"Yes, I'm ready," I respond, as I feel myself preparing to hibernate one final time. I'm so tired. So very, very tired. It's been fun, one hell of a ride you might even say, but now my tank is running on empty, and as I look up at the welcoming stars that shine in the galactic highway beyond, my engine splutters on fumes towards the gloriously blinding light.

EPILOGUE

I can feel the searing heat on my back, and for a second I think there's been a clerical error, and that I've been sent to the wrong place by mistake. But, as I blink open my eyes and hear the gentle sound of waves and sweet birdsong filling the salt air, I realise I'm not in hell and that death isn't as bad as I'd expected after all these years.

The black powder sand beneath my claws feels like an old familiar friend and I lumber towards the sound of breakfast bickering, a smile wider than the annals of time spread out across my face. My story has been told, and has now reached its ultimate conclusion, although if it's successful my agent will be screwed for a sequel, seeing as I'm dead it seems.

"What took you so long?" says mum with a grin, as I take my rightful seat at the table with the rest and I look out over the clear blue ocean with a final smile as the sun begins to fade. It's nice not to see any sharks, ships or humans, but more than that, it's nice to finally be home.